NICE TRY

ALSO BY SHANE MALONEY:

THE BRUSH-OFF
STIFF

ARCADE PUBLISHING • NEW YORK

NICE TRY

A MURRAY WHELAN MYSTERY

SHANE MALONEY

FIRST NORTH AMERICAN EDITION 2000

Originally published in Australia by Text Publishing

This is a work of fiction. Names, characters, places, and incidents are
either the product of the author's imagination or used fictitiously.

Library of Congress Cataloging-in-Publication Data

Maloney, Shane, 1953–
   Nice try / Shane Maloney. —1st North American ed.
    p. cm.
  ISBN 1-55970-513-2
   1. Whelan, Murray (Fictitious character)—Fiction.   2. Government
investigators—Australia—Fiction.   3. Melbourne (Vic.)—Fiction.
I. Title.
PR9619.3.M2645 N53 2000
823—dc21   99-59581

Published in the United States by Arcade Publishing, Inc., New York
Distributed by Time Warner Trade Publishing

Visit our Web site at www.arcadepub.com

10 9 8 7 6 5 4 3 2 1

Designed by API

BP

PRINTED IN THE UNITED STATES OF AMERICA

To Gary Foley
Dare to struggle, dare to win

In Memoriam
Kevin and Aileen

"Athleticism can occasion in man the most noble of passions and also the most vile."

—Baron Pierre de Coubertin, Founder of the Modern Olympics

"Yibbida, Yibbida!"

—Rex Hunt, Australian sports philosopher

A Note About Australian Football

Characterized by long, high kicking and spectacular aerial contests, Australian football is a fast-moving contact sport played by teams of eighteen on an oval arena three times the size of a gridiron field. Indigenous and unique, it is the traditional religion in the southern part of the country, engendering fierce tribal loyalties and regularly attracting crowds in excess of 100,000 spectators. It should not under any circumstances be confused with rugby, an imported code similar to American football that retains an obscure attraction for many people in the northern states.

NICE TRY

Melbourne, 1956

They confronted him at the Royal Exhibition Building, just before the first lift of the final round. It was safer there, away from all the prying eyes at the Athletes Village, and he did not suspect anything until it was too late.

He was a very strong man, not as big as some of his teammates in the higher weight divisions, but formidable enough to be a medal contender. When he bolted for the door, it took four burly trainers to subdue him and force the gag into his mouth so his cries for help could not be heard by the Australian officials in the warm-up area. Even then, he continued to put up a struggle and the first hypodermic needle snapped off in the muscles of his arm.

That's when the deputy chef-de-mission struck him with the heavy steel lifting bar. The bone snapped immediately. After that, for all his strength, he offered less resistance and the doctor was able to administer the drug.

The Australian volunteer driver had no reason to suspect that the heavy bags of equipment they were loading into the Bedford van contained anything other than the usual sporting gear. He was, however, disappointed to be told that he should immediately drive them to Appleton Dock. It was only fifteen minutes away through the early summer sunshine but the trip meant that he would miss the final of the tournament. As the Bedford pulled into Nicholson Street, the Duke of Edinburgh was already arriving to present the medals, the Olympic standard fluttering on the hood of his black Bentley.

The weightlifter did not regain consciousness until he was on board the ship. By then, further resistance was futile.

Despite the speed and secrecy of the operation, the Australian Security Intelligence Organization was soon aware that something untoward was happening. Officers manning the observation post in the cargo shed across the turning basin became suspicious when they noticed that the official supervising the unloading of the van was far too senior for such a task. The fact that Russians were seen carrying aboard heavy equipment belonging to the Polish team was also considered unusual enough to warrant a telephone call to headquarters.

By late evening, lights were burning in the large Victorian mansion in Queens Road and the Director himself was being briefed. A deeply conservative man, steeped in military culture, Colonel Spry had a face which did not display his thoughts. His subordinates could easily imagine, however, the depths of the dilemma that now confronted him.

The Games of the XVI Olympiad of the Modern Era, the Friendly Games, were rapidly descending into farce, a circus which threatened both Australia's reputation as a sporting nation and the future of the Olympic ideal.

A week earlier, one of the Russians had eluded her escort at the Melbourne zoo and fled through the animal enclosures. A brawl had erupted at the Russia–Hungary water polo final and blood had been spilled in the water. Soviet competitors had been openly jeered at the fencing. President Brundage of the International Olympic Committee, an American and no friend of the communists, had already protested to the organizing committee at this lack of sportsmanship. The CIA was busy in the background, attempting to provoke incidents. Emigré groups had invaded the Athletes Village and torn down flags.

It was an informant from one such group who alerted ASIO to the sudden withdrawal of the Polish medal contender only moments before his final lift in the medal round of the weightlifting. Officially he had strained *a ligament but, according to the contact, the lifter was planning to defect from the podium during the medal-presentation ceremony.*

Two years earlier, Colonel Spry had not hesitated in ordering his officers to assist Commonwealth Police snatch Mrs. Petrov from the hands of Soviet agents who were hustling her aboard a plane on the tarmac at Darwin airport. But this time, the interests of the nation were different. The Gruzia *was moored under the terms of the Olympic truce. To search it would be a violation of that truce. If nothing was found, the communists would gain a great international propaganda victory. ASIO would be embarrassed and Australia's honor tarnished before the world.*

Only one course of action was possible, decided the Director. Three days later, a battery of twenty-five-pounder guns fired the final salute and the Friendly Games concluded in triumph as the athletes danced their way through the Closing Ceremony.

1

Melbourne, 1990

SHE WAS GIVING ME THE EYE. No doubt about it.

Every time I glanced her way, I caught her looking at me. Her gaze would dart somewhere else, but she was definitely checking me out. She was twenty-two, maybe twenty-three, with a body that looked like it was molded from fiberglass to a design by Benvenuto Cellini. Smooth. Firm. Flawless.

Too flawless for me, surely, a man teetering on the cusp of his late thirties. A man whose waist measurement was almost as high as his IQ. Not that I automatically assumed it was impossible for a woman like her to be interested in someone like me. But you get to a certain point, you know what's reasonable and what's not. Christ, she was practically a teenager.

She tossed back her blonde ponytail, parted her thighs and thrust her hips forward. "Come on," she urged. "Do it. Do it."

I couldn't. I just didn't have the energy. Wiping the perspiration from my eyes with the hem of my T-shirt, I lowered my vision to the electronic display panel of my exercise bike and urged my faltering muscles on. For more than half an hour I'd been at it. First the warm-up, then the super circuit. Three sets of leg extensions. The front lateral press and the rowing simulator. The mini-trampoline, the squat rack and the Stairmaster. Thirty-seven minutes of self-imposed agony.

Beyond the window of the aerobics studio, the gorgeous creature had turned away. She was on her knees on the carpet now, extending first one leg then the other, her flanks as fine as a gazelle's. She was inexhaustible, her energy boundless, her body unravaged by time and cigarettes and a sedentary occupation. "Keep it up, keep it up," she cried. Her every move was immediately replicated by the twenty women in her class, flexing their Lycra-sheathed limbs to the syncopated thud of the sound system. Madonna.

God, I hated Madonna. I tried to think of something else, to force my mind off that taut blue leotard. That pert, peachy derriere. Those surreptitious glances. To find some thought I could use to focus my energy on the last, muscle-quivering kilometer up the computer-generated incline. Concentrating my attention on the liquid-crystal terrain-simulator on the console between the handlebars, I screwed up my determination, bore down and pedaled into the final sinew-searing five minutes of my daily work-out. Every fiber of my mortal being screamed at me to stop.

With a sharp electronic beep, the stationary bicycle announced that I'd arrived at my destination. Ten kilometers at Mark 8, a total kilojoule burn of 250. The calorific equivalent of two cherry tomatoes and a haircut. Responding as surely as Pavlov's dogs salivating at the sound of a bell, my legs went limp. With one last surge of willpower, I forced them to continue for the final minutes of my warm-down.

I was warming down but the gym was hotting up. At the bike beside me, a furiously pedaling endomorph looked up from his copy of the *Financial Review*. "No pain, no gain," he muttered. Probably rehearsing his statement to the shareholders.

The City Club was located in the Hyatt Hotel, but few of its clientele were hotel guests. Most, like me, worked in the surrounding office buildings. Many, judging by their furtive eyes and abrasive manner, were members of the finance community. The women tended to be younger and better togged out. The average male was a laterally expanding desk-jockey teetering on the brink of middle age. My kind of guy.

My fellow City Club members, I reflected. Desperate old farts and despicable yuppies. So what did that make me, an AWOL apparatchik, sneaking away from the office to work on his personal downsizing plan? Not for the first time, I reminded myself that I'd chosen the place solely on the basis of its location, a three-minute walk from Parliament House. That, and the incentive provided by its astronomical cost.

It was, I had told myself a month earlier, crunch time. Either face up to my need for constant maintenance or surrender entirely to my inner beanbag. So it had been on with the training shoes and out with the credit card.

At $1500 a year plus joining fee, the City Club was more than I could really afford. On the other hand, I was getting a lot for my money. You name it, the City Club had it. An atrium-roofed swimming pool in checkerboard tiles. Microchip-regulated warm-up bicycles. A front lateral press and a modular triceps extension machine. Rowing simulators, each with an in-built computer-generated opponent. Weight machines, both Universal and Nautilus. A boutique offering a comprehensive range of swimsuits, pedal-pushers and Musashi high-protein snacks. Shiatsu massage. Boxercise. Wet and dry saunas. Slide, step and low-impact aerobics. Complimentary cotton swabs in the changing rooms. An attentive staff of chipper young men and perky young women, each with the calves of a Sherpa and the smile of a toothpaste testimonial.

Including, it seemed, the nymph with the wandering eye. My mysterious admirer. I'd first noticed her earlier that week when she started taking the midday aerobics session, replacing a rather fey young man with a taste for Vangelis and a cute little backside that was entirely wasted on his all-female class.

Aside from the body of a goddess, clearly a prerequisite for the job, she had an open, frankly inquisitive face and wore her mandatory smile with a slightly ironic twist that didn't quite match the earnest, professional cheerfulness of her workmates. With a perennial tilt to her head and large, wide-open eyes, she appeared to regard the world with amused scepticism, as though nothing could ever quite manage to surprise her.

Just the expression she used when she looked me over. A cool, appraising look which, while I found it flattering, seemed oddly perverse when directed at a man with trembling knees, a low-slung chassis and the motto "I'm With Stupid" printed across the front of his sweat-soaked T-shirt. Perhaps she needed glasses.

The aerobics class was finishing. Twelve-thirty. My cue to start making tracks for my lunch appointment. I climbed down off the bike and waited for my head to stop spinning. Four weeks I'd been a member of the City Club and so far most of the weight loss had been in the region of my bank balance. On the other hand, where else did I get ogled by bodacious young babes? One bodacious babe, anyway.

Now she was staring at me. As I slung my complimentary towel around my neck and staggered toward the locker room, she advanced across the floor, cocking her head and peering dubiously into my face.

"Hey!" she declared, pointing knowingly. Women from the aerobics class looked our way. Shit, I thought. She hadn't really been looking at me. She'd been catching me looking at her. I was about to be banged-up for perving. Denounced as a sexual harasser. "Your name's Whelan, isn't it?" Her rising inflection was a clear accusation.

"Murray Whelan," I admitted cautiously.

"Thought it was." She clapped her hands in self-congratulation. "Am I good or what?"

I stared at her blankly, not at all sure where this was going.

"You don't remember me, do you?" she said, crestfallen. And what a crest. I made a point of not looking at it. "Holly. Holly Deloite."

"Of course I remember." I racked my brains. As offsider to a politician, I meet a lot of people. More than I could ever hope to remember and quite a few I'd prefer to forget. But this Holly Deloite definitely wasn't in that category. If I'd ever pressed her flesh, I was sure I would've recalled.

"Hadfield High School, tenth grade work-experience program," she prompted. "I've probably changed a bit since then."

Had she ever.

She was taking me back almost seven years. Back to when I was electorate officer for Charlene Wills, Member of the Legislative Council for the Province of Melbourne Upper. Running a shopfront office in a working-class electorate on the northern edge of the suburban sprawl. Keeping the constituents happy, massaging the grassroots of the political process, soliciting campaign donations, that sort of thing.

Every year we'd take a work-experience placement from each of the local high schools. Give bored and slightly bewildered fifteen-year-olds a taste of real life. Teach them to stuff envelopes and make coffee, let them answer the phone if they were exceptionally capable.

Holly Deloite had been a mumbler, if I remembered right. Mouth full of braces, a tubby bubby, pimples. Well stacked for her age and shy about it. Head always down, hiding her face behind her hair. But keen to please. It was all coming back to me. "The photocopier girl!"

She blushed and her hand flew up to her mouth. "You bastard," she grinned. "You still remember that."

I liked the bastard. It was a big improvement on Mr. Whelan. "How could I forget?"

Truth be known, I hadn't given the matter a second thought since the day it happened. The day she'd misread my handwriting. Made five hundred copies by two o'clock instead of two copies by five o'clock.

"Got the zeros mixed up with the noughts," she laughed. "But you were real nice about it. Even bought me lunch at that Chinese restaurant."

The Dow Sing. Along with the rest of the office staff, courtesy of the petty cash account. Our standard farewell gesture for work-experience students. Nothing untoward. But clearly I'd made quite an impression on the young Miss Deloite. So, too, had the intervening years. All trace of the dumpy, bashful teenager had vanished.

"You had that little kid, didn't you?" she said, now in the full throes of reminiscence. "What was his name again?"

Work experience occasionally included the development of child-care skills in the visiting students. With my wife Wendy seconded to the Office of the Status of Women in Canberra, I had assumed the prime parenting role. Which inevitably meant that our son put in a fair bit of time at the office. Keeping a four-year-old amused had been about Holly's intellectual speed, far less demanding than the technological challenges of the photocopier. There were little brothers somewhere in her background, I seemed to recall.

"Red," I said. "He lives in Sydney with his mother. We're divorced. I'm on my own now."

"Aww." She tilted her head even further to the side and pursed her lips into a sympathetic little frown.

Yes, it was a pity. Red, at least. Not the divorce. Wendy could look after herself. She was Director of Equal Opportunity for Telecom now, tapping away at the glass ceiling on behalf of the sisterhood. And herself. Remarried and doing well, thank you very much.

At this declaration of my marital status, our conversation lurched into an awkward silence. Unnecessarily so. My assertion that I was footloose and fancy-free was not intended as a pick-up line. Young Holly Deloite was a delight, all right, but she was still too young. Even if she was interested, what would we talk about afterward? Not to mention the potential damage to my reputation. An older woman with a younger man, that was an historic advance. Vice versa, and the belles of censoriousness began to peal.

Still, it was nice to be fondly remembered, especially by a ravishing young thing. And her frank manner reflected well on the employment policies of the City Club. Nothing worse than subservient help, in my opinion. You never know what they're really thinking. "You like it here?" she said. "Good, isn't it? Great place to work."

"Yeah," I enthused, looking around at the heaving flesh and clanging metal. "Just started this week, have you?"

"Nah," she shook her ponytail. "Been here ages, nearly a year.

Just come back from six weeks in Queensland, but. The Hyatt Coolum Beach Resort. The chain has this sort of exchange thing with their instructors. Like I specialize in slide, okay? So I was doing that up there, training their staff, and they sent their low-impact guy down here."

Mr. Bottom, the vanished Vangelis fan. Visiting Fellow in Bump and Grind at the University of Soft Knocks.

"Sounds great," I said. Holly had clearly found her vocation, gun aerobics coach. Have leotard will travel. I was pleased for her but it wasn't an area I felt qualified to discuss. We were running out of subject matter.

"Still with Mrs. Wills?" she said, casting about for a safe topic. "Out at the office."

"Charlene died a fair while ago," I said. "It's Angelo Agnelli now." The Honorable Member for Melbourne Upper. Minister for Water Supply and the Arts. My current employer.

Nearly six years Angelo and I had been together, ever since he inherited me from Charlene. Ours was a shotgun marriage of political convenience and, frankly, the relationship was wearing a bit thin. It was one of Angelo's remarks which had prompted me to join the City Club. "Lucky I'm not Minister for Agriculture," he told me. "Or they'd start calling you Beefy Whelan." This from a man with three chins whose only exercise was running off at the mouth and jumping to conclusions.

Never heard of him, said Holly's face. A politician. Inhabitant of a distant galaxy. Holly's was the world of the here and now. Politics just wasn't in the frame. Life was elsewhere. Anywhere, really. Everywhere. She was young.

"Anyway," she said. "Just thought I'd say hello. Really great to see you again, all of that. Anything you need, I'm here ten 'til eight every day." She flashed me the corporate rictus. "Maybe you'd like to join a class."

"Maybe." I nodded amiably. "I'll think about it." Like hell. Nothing more pathetic, in my book, than the sight of a man doing aerobics. Prancing about to infantile music in a room full of mirrors, making a complete dick of himself. If I really wanted to look like an idiot, I'd start riding a bike to work.

Holly Deloite's wandering eye was beginning to wander elsewhere, over toward the front counter where an unattended member was waiting impatiently for his complimentary fluffy towel. Nice girl, Holly. Beautiful body. Mind like a muesli bar. We parted, then, with a nod and a smile, she to customer service, me to the locker room.

In the buff, all men are equal. But, even bare-bummed, class finds a way of expressing itself. No tattoos here, no amputees, no horny hands or industrial injuries. Only the best-bred, corn-fed flesh in the locker room of the City Club. Vivaldi humming quietly in the background. Fresh flowers on the washstand, limitless conditioning mousse in the showers. Silk ties and tailored jackets. Wooden coat hangers in ash-paneled lockers. An atmosphere redolent of Eau Sauvage and insider trading.

As I stepped under the shower, the sudden shock of cold water reminded me of the dickheads I'd been dealing with that morning.

Union officials, they called themselves. Back in my day at the Trades Hall, they would've been lucky to get a job with the Amusement Employees Federation, Circus Division. Clowns whose idea of negotiation was to start with a threat and work their way up to personal abuse. Typical Miscellaneous Workers Union bullshit. The Missos were never what you might call Mensa material.

For months I'd been playing umpire in their interminable wrangling with the bureaucrats at the Department of Water Supply. Trying to convince them that the government was in no position to meet their demand for an across-the-board productivity bonus for the entire maintenance division.

A productivity bonus, for Chrissake, as if the water was suddenly getting wetter as a result of their improved work practices. All they had to do was to keep the stuff running downhill, after all. And now these absurd threats of industrial action. "Such as what?" I wanted to know. "Putting LSD in the reservoirs? Making the toilets flush in reverse?"

The dipstick drongos didn't seem to realize that it was 1990, that we were in the middle of a recession. Their obscure attempts at intimidation were the last straw. I'd finally lost it, given the miserable pricks a piece of my mind. Not my finest moment, professionally speaking. The meeting had ended in acrimonious disarray.

There has to be a better way to make a living, I thought as I toweled myself dry.

An elderly patrician with a washboard stomach and a mat of gray on his chest combed his temples at the mirror with all the gravity of a Roman senator. Paunchy plutocrats, towels at their midriffs, emerged dewy from the sauna. A consortium of brash young go-getters commandeered the benches, swapping their Florsheim brogues for Nike trainers, self-assured as Olympians.

The Olympics, I thought, pulling on my jocks. My big chance.

Brian Morrison had been insistent but tantalizingly vague when he rang and suggested we catch up. An old mate, Brian had wangled himself a berth with the Melbourne Olympic Bid, Incorporated, the organization running the city's candidacy to host the 1996 Olympic Games. "Let's have a bite," he said. "I might have a job for a man of your experience."

I wasn't really in the job market. But I was curious. To exactly what aspect of my experience, I wondered, was he referring?

Surely not my current situation as Senior Adviser to the Minister for Water Supply, formulating policy options on the privatization of the Mordialloc Main Drain, negotiating staffing levels with maddies from the Missos and making sure that Angelo didn't fall out of the boat while inspecting the catchment facilities.

Nor, I thought, had Brian been referring to my brief sojourn at the Arts Ministry, my employer's other area of current responsibility, where I'd briefly grappled with transgressive postmodern cultural practice. Perhaps he meant my time at Ethnic Affairs, Angelo's previous portfolio.

Yes, I thought, that was it. Athens was Melbourne's main competitor for the prize of the Centenary Games, after all. And five years at Ethnic Affairs, arm-wrestling the largest Greek community this side of the Peloponnesian peninsula, had taught me a thing or two about the Hellenic psyche. Helping to outwit the Athenians, I assumed, was what he had in mind for me.

As I knotted my tie, my face stared back at me from the mirror. Assessing my presentability, comparing it with that of my fellow City Club members. No doubt about it, almost a decade in the antechamber of political power had done wonders for my wardrobe. What would the blokes back at the Municipal Employees Union have said about my Hugo Boss suit, I wondered? Or the electors of Melbourne Upper? Holly Deloite was not the only one who had changed.

Smoothing my shirt front and buffing my shoes on the complimentary shoe-buffing machine, I strapped on my watch. Twelve-forty-five. Well exercised, well presented and on time. An ornament to the Australian Labor Party.

Holly was at reception, sprucing up the motivational books and videos in their revolving display rack. Buns of Steel. Abs of Alabaster. Pecs of Polycarbon. "Lookin' good," she said. Just the sort of thing they said at the City Club, but that didn't stop me drawing encouragement from it.

"What's it like?" I nodded at the book in her hand. *The Seven Keys to Eternal Youth*.

Holly studied the object like she wasn't quite sure what it was. "Um," she said. "He's supposed to be really deep. You know. Philosophically." On the back cover was a photograph of the author, a man in a turban with heavy black-rimmed spectacles and a full beard.

"Is he?" The guy looked like a myopic yak.

"He did this one, too." From the rack she handed me *Mastering the Forces That Shape Personal Identity*.

"Interesting title," I said. Refreshing in its brevity.

I scanned a page at random. *"Man is an air animal,"* it said. *"Shed your clothes whenever possible. Take off your shoes, loosen your collar. Sleep in the nude."*

"Perhaps we could workshop this together," I suggested.

But Holly wasn't listening. She was staring over my shoulder to where a customer was coming through the glass doors from the elevators. He wasn't one of the regulars, not one I'd seen before. He advanced toward us with the swaggering gait of a man acutely conscious of his physique. And with good reason. He was built like a small truck. Something compact but substantial. A Hilux two-tonner, for example, or a Ford Transit with aluminum dropside tray and dual rear wheels.

"Uh oh," said Holly. "Here's trouble."

He was a very solid piece of work. Medium height, oval face, a neck like a hatbox. Arms like legs. Legs like I don't know what. They were enclosed in voluminous pants made out of what appeared to be parachute silk. His torso bulged beneath a loose sweat-top that must have been a size XXXXL.

He was somewhere in his mid-twenties, although his dark hair had already begun to thin at the forehead. The rest of it was slicked back over his skull and pulled tight into a rat's arse of a ponytail. The loose drape of his clothing seemed to accentuate rather than conceal the solid bulge of his body and he carried himself with the bow-legged strut of a man who has watched a few too many Sylvester Stallone movies. He'd probably been reasonably good-looking, in an over-masculine sort of way, before the acne got to work on his cheekbones.

He smiled, showing a wide gap between his front teeth. "Hey, babe," he said.

I took it that he was not addressing me. Holly's smile snapped shut like a venetian blind and her chin shot up about ten centimeters. "Excuse me a moment," she murmured, moving out from behind the counter to block Arnold Schwartzenschnitzel's advance.

"Thought I told you to stay away." She spoke in an undertone, her irritation unmistakable.

"Holly, babe." His voice was jaunty, undeterred. "Don't be like that."

Holly folded her arms across her chest and glued her feet to the floor. "Listen, Steve." She spoke through gritted teeth. "It's all over between us. Can't you get that through that thick head of yours?"

"Aw, be nice," Steve cooed, rolling his shoulders, a couple of performance artists trying to get out of a satin sack. His arms hung so far out from his sides he looked like he was doing an impression of the Sydney Harbor Bridge.

Holly tossed an apprehensive glance over her shoulder and dropped her voice to a steely hiss. "You'll get me sacked if you don't stop coming around like this. And I want my stuff back."

By this stage, I'd realized that I wasn't witnessing a bad moment in customer relations but a disagreement of a more personal nature, probably romantic in origin. Returning the hairy guru to his place in the wire display rack, I began to edge away, heading for the exit.

"Don't be like that," Mr. Muscle said again. He was trying hard to sound casual but there was a note in his voice that I wasn't sure I liked. Holly didn't like it either, especially when he reached across to stroke the side of her neck. "I roolly miss you, babe."

Her arm shot up and brushed his away. "I'm warning you, Steve."

As I angled around them, Holly suddenly grabbed my elbow and thrust me forward. "This is my lawyer," she declared. "Stop harassing me or he'll have you in court, dead set."

Too astonished to contradict her, I cleared my throat, squared my jaw and tried to look jurisprudential. A damsel in distress and all that. The Hulk gave me the slow once-over, not much impressed with what he saw.

"What choo wanna lawyer for?" Now his feelings were hurt. "They just rip you off."

I concurred with the general sentiment but resented the specific insinuation. Behind me, I heard a click like the latch falling on a closing gate. Garth, the club's deep-tissue masseur, was emerging from the pool deck with an armful of folded towels. The clicking noise was the sound of his tongue rebounding off the roof of his mouth. He steamed toward us.

"Holly," he commanded tersely. "Put these in the stock room for me, please."

Shooting me a quick look of thanks, Holly grabbed the towels and evaporated.

Garth wasn't quite as hefty as this Steve character, but he had a good half-head on him. And a very butch manner, considering. He inserted himself between me and Steve, arms akimbo. "Come in here again," he said, "I'll call security. This is your last warning. On your bike, Tinkerbell."

If looks could kill, Garth was a goner. Tinkerbell's lip curled back and his nostrils flared. But he managed to restrain himself. "Hey, man," he sneered. "Call this a gym? This ain't a gym. It's a pussy factory." He pirouetted on ballerina feet, tiny in comparison with the inverted triangle of his torso, and stalked contemptuously out the door.

"Sorry about that, sir," said Garth. "Not our kind of person at all." On the other side of the glass doors, a balled fist was pounding the lift button, hammering it into the wall.

"No trouble," I reassured the masseur, glancing first toward the stock room then at my watch. "No trouble whatsoever."

Of course, Steve hadn't killed anyone at that stage. Not yet, anyway.

2

LEAVING THE HYATT by way of the food court, I lit a cigarette and strolled up Collins Street, allowing myself to be swept along by the Friday lunchtime crowd. At little tables on the footpath, women in haute couture sat sipping coffee and toying with overwrought pastries. The boutiques of the carriage trade were doing a brisk business in steamer trunks and silk handkerchiefs embossed with little interlocked initials. Yellow and green trams click-clacked past at a dignified pace. It was a long way from Paris, but it possessed a certain well-heeled charm.

The weather didn't hurt, either. Spring arrives in Melbourne as a relief, an end to dismal winter, a harbinger of a summer that might or might not eventuate. Autumn, however, is its own reward. It stands alone, dependable, often glorious, sometimes sublime. The sky is blue and the air invigorating, the canopies of the trees turn to russet and the bounty of the season is upon us. Time to start making provision for the chill days ahead. And chill they would no doubt be, if the polls were to be believed.

It was late April 1990 and the Labor government in whose ranks I served was on the skids. Bankrupted by financial mismanagement and special pleading. Riven by factional shenanigans and two-bob power plays. Skimmed by fast operators and administered by slow ones. Cactus. A political *Titanic* adrift in a Sargasso of lost opportunity. Our credibility was so seriously shot we'd be lucky to survive the two years until the next election. Nothing short of a miracle could save us.

Dream the Dream, read the banners fluttering from every light stanchion. Bring the Olympics to Melbourne. Above the words was a stylized flame, the logo of the Melbourne Olympic Bid, Inc.

Everywhere you turned, there it was. Emblazoned on the sides of trams, plastered to bumpers, stuck on the doors of stores, dangling from power poles. We wanted this, and we wanted it bad. If the support of the populace counted for anything with the International Olympic Committee, Melbourne had to be odds-on favorite.

At the top of Collins Street stood the Old Treasury Building. Thick with baroque curlicues and neo-classical flourishes, the ornate edifice stared down at the city with all the imperious condescension of one of Queen Victoria's colonial secretaries. It had been built to store the rivers of bullion flowing from the goldfields of Ballarat and Bendigo. But that was more than a century ago. The mines were long exhausted and the wealth long spent. Our hopes were currently invested in new and more magical sources of wealth. Rich foreigners would come from the sky and shower us with gifts. As if in anticipation of their imminent arrival, Brian Morrison stood at the building's front door, staring up into the heavens.

A tall, curly-headed man of my own age, Morrison wore a tailored charcoal-gray suit that must have set him back a good eight hundred dollars. What with his executive tie and his air of self-satisfied affability, he was the very picture of the corporate man. There was certainly nothing about his current appearance to hint at the fact that in his younger days he'd once been the Socialist Left candidate for Mayor of Collingwood, that most mythically militant bastion of the working class.

Once upon a time, Brian had been a lowly ministerial adviser like me. Offsider to the Minister for Planning, responsible for seeing that nobody crept up on his boss in the dark and blind-sided him with a leaked memo or a preselection threat. Before that, back in the dark ages before Labor was in power, he and I sat on the odd committee together. More recently, he had been party campaign director during the last state election, a role roughly analogous to that of Mandrake the Magician.

Now he was an up-and-comer in the corporate sector, Director of Government, Corporate and Community Relations for the Olympic bid. DOG for the MOB, as he put it when he rang and suggested we have lunch. As I ascended the wide terrace of steps toward him, he cackled with pleasure and thrust his forefinger into the air, inviting me to turn my attention skyward.

A born conspirator, Brian was never happier than when he was cooking something up, putting something over. I followed the angle of his finger. Far above, a tiny plane was looping-the-loop, etching great white circles in the otherwise unbroken expanse of blue. "The Olympic Rings," he declared, in case I was unfamiliar with the design. "A welcoming gesture for Don Pablo Cardena, the IOC's representative from Costa Rica. Cost me twenty grand but worth every penny. Don Pablo's very influential with the Latins. Plus it'll make a great front page."

The pictorial editors would need to move fast. Even as the last of the four-thousand-dollar rings was inscribed in the air, the first was melting away, reduced to a few faint wisps of pallid vapor. We stood for a moment, reverently watching Brian's budget disperse into the stratosphere. Then he grabbed my elbow and propelled me through the front door. "Take a gander at this," he commanded.

For most of the preceding century, the Old Treasury Building had housed the Department of Administrative Services in conditions reminiscent of a scene out of *Great Expectations*. But now the public servants had been relocated, the facade scrubbed, the linoleum carpeted, the desks French-polished and the walls painted in heritage colors. An electronic display on the reception desk spelled out the countdown until the IOC made its decision. *142 days*, it flashed, *Welcome Don Pablo Welcome Welcome Welcome.*

Brian nodded briskly to the receptionist and led me along a short corridor lined with earth-toned dot paintings. "Clifford Possum," he murmured. "Turkey Tolson."

We arrived at an ornate set of double doors, their heavy brass handles buffed to a high sheen. Brian pressed a button on the wall and the portals swung silently open to reveal a darkened chamber lined with black curtains. We stepped inside and the doors closed behind us. A beam of light descended from the ceiling, illuminating a plinth upon which sat what appeared to be a ball of compressed shrapnel.

"The Baron Pierre de Coubertin, founder of the modern Olympics," whispered Brian. "Artist's impression."

He put a finger to his lips, the lights dimmed and we were plunged into pitch darkness. Sounds began, faint at first, rising in volume. Bushland noises — the cackle of a kookaburra, water tinkling over stones, leaves rustling in the breeze. Then, gradually, came the low thrum of a didgeridoo and the rhythmic click of clap-sticks. A voice joined in, an adenoidal Aboriginal chant. *"Manuyangka nyiyarlangurlu, jarntungku marda, yankirrirli . . ."*

Gradually, the one voice became many, a babel of tongues. French and German, Spanish and Chinese, accumulated into the clamor of a massive crowd. Whistles blew and commentators whipped themselves into a frenzy. The hubbub built to a deafening crescendo. Then, with one final triumphant honk of the didgeridoo, the din ceased and the curtains parted.

A large well-lit room opened before us, its walls covered with glossy images of sporting venues. Glass-fronted cabinets displayed sporting memorabilia. Historic hockey sticks, famous fencing foils. Great moments in sport. Gold medals and team pendants. *Celtius, Fortius, Altius* read a scroll stretched between the beaks of two stuffed fairy penguins.

"The bottom line," said Brian, indicating a series of architectural models. The Athletes Village, old docklands at the edge of the city transformed into cluster housing with water views. A media center rising fifty stories above the railway switching yards. New swimming and diving pools, a baseball diamond, cycling velodrome and soccer field. "Sixty thousand jobs, minimum. A total revamp of our public infrastructure. Revenues of four billion dollars, mostly from American television. That's the beauty of this thing. The fucking Yanks will pay for it."

It was indeed an inspiring possibility. "Yeah, but what are our chances?" The question on everyone's lips.

Brian fluttered the palm of his downturned hand. "We're in the lap of the gods. At the end of the day, mate, it's about kissing arse. And these IOC types are experts at having their arses kissed. At any given time, there are six cities bidding for the Summer Olympics and six for the Winter, each spending upward of twenty million US dollars. That's nearly $250 million being spent to schmooze ninety people."

"So it's a bidding war?"

He shook his head. "It's more subtle than that. Half these guys are princes and dukes. You can't just buy their votes. Not all of them, anyway. You've got to play them individually." He hunched over and wrung his hands like Uriah Heep. "Demonstrate your commitment to the sacred ideals of Olympism. Speak of the brotherhood of man and the importance of the athlete. Then wine and dine the bastards to within an inch of their lives. Above all, convince them that you won't fuck it up."

"What about the competition?" I prompted. "Athens?"

"Definitely the big risk. Still the sentimental favorite, despite the smog, the chaos and the security problems. Frankly, we're praying that terrorists blow up an airliner on the runway at Athens airport between now and the vote."

This, I hoped, was not the job he had in mind for me. "Toronto?" I asked. "Manchester? Belgrade? What about Atlanta? Big money, media-friendly time-zones, the ghost of Martin Luther King."

"Forget Atlanta," he snorted. "Everybody hates the Yanks. Personally, I reckon we've got this thing in the bag. Long as nothing happens to dump us in the shit."

"Such as?"

"Come upstairs," he said.

We went up an imposing staircase to a broad hallway on the first floor. A conclave of suited men spilled from one of the rooms. Big chiefs, conversing importantly among themselves. I recognized one of them as Hugh Knowles, chairman of the MOB and chief executive of Mincom Resources, one of the country's biggest mining companies. Brian all but genuflected as Knowles passed.

"Thought we might have lunch here," Brian said, shouldering open a door. "If that's okay with you."

The door opened into a small conference room overlooking the Treasury Gardens, a vista of autumnal red and gold. A gilt-framed landscape hung above the marble fireplace and beneath the window was an antique walnut sideboard covered with platters of food. Helping himself to the smoked salmon was a gnarled leprechaun in a tweed jacket and rimless bifocals.

"You two know each other, I think," said Brian.

Indeed we did. Denis Dogherty was one of my colleagues, senior aide to the Minister for Sport, Recreation, Racing and the Olympics. He looked up from his plate and scrutinized me in an oblique, testing way with the sort of face that could once be found in the front bar of any hotel in Australia, usually topped with a pork-pie hat and tilted in the direction of the racing results. He gave a long, low whistle.

"Very respectable threads, Murray," he said. "Was the magistrate impressed?"

"How original," I replied. "You old spiv." Denis was somewhere in his mid-sixties. He was wearing a burgundy pin-corduroy shirt with a button-down collar, a mustard-colored tie and a pair of tan permanent-press trousers. His hair, a gingery thatch, was brushed forward in the manner of a Roman emperor or an aging Beatle.

"Go ahead and eat," urged Brian Morrison. "I'll be back in a minute." He disappeared, shutting the door behind him.

Denis Dogherty and I were old friends. I'd first met him more than fifteen years earlier, back when I started work at the Trades Hall and possession of a university degree was regarded as proof positive of homosexual tendencies by many of the older union officials. But not by Denis. A job delegate for the Stevedores Federation, a man who'd spent his formative years digging wharfies out of grain spills and fighting the ship owners over slave labor on flag-of-convenience rust buckets, he had a high regard for the value of learning.

"Always remember who your enemies are," he told me. "And never forget your friends."

The last time I'd seen him was at the quarterly briefing sessions the Premier conducted for the staff of his ministers. Bible class, Denis called it, a bunch of political fixers being lectured on the need for scrupulous standards of probity and professionalism by a man so far above the ruck that his feet never touched the ground.

"All the dough we've given this Olympic mob," he said, thrusting a plate into my hand. "Might as well get in for your chop."

For the previous few weeks, lunch had been an alfalfa sandwich and a glass of mineral water, all part of the concerted attack on my love handles. Maintaining discipline, I forked a couple of slices of smoked salmon and an artichoke heart onto my plate, averting my eyes from the platter of petits-fours and chocolate-dipped florentines. Denis uncorked a bottle of white wine and poured me a glass. It was a fragrant drop, redolent of wildflowers and the fruits of office.

"Off your tucker?" Thin as a rail, Denis was one of those people who never put on weight. "I'm not surprised. Running messages for that dog Agnelli'd be enough to ruin anyone's appetite."

Our masters were factional allies, so I was unperturbed by Denis's disparaging remarks. "I'm in training," I said. "Thought I might see if I can get a run with the Royboys this season."

"Fitzroy?" Denis arrested his fork in mid-air. "Thought you were a South man."

His memory was amazing. It must have been a good dozen years since we'd slipped out of the Trade Union Training Authority seminar on Confronting the Issues of Industry Restructuring to listen to the South Melbourne–Fitzroy match in the public bar of the Dover Hotel. Both of us barracking for the Bloodstained Angels. For Denis, to change football teams was tantamount to class treason. Even when the money men threw a net over his beloved South Melbourne, dragged them north of the border and rebaptized them as the Sydney Swans, Denis did not desert them.

That's what I liked about Denis. There was a commendable permanence to his allegiances. For Denis, fidelity was a primary virtue. He might have lacked the formal qualifications that were so highly valued by the lawyers, sociology lecturers and assorted technocrats who inhabited the higher reaches of our administration, but Denis

Dogherty had the certainty of conviction it takes to hold a political party together. And a good thing, too. Whenever the Labor Party finds itself in power, loyalty tends to be the one thing in shortest supply.

"Fair go," I said. "Fitzroy is the closest thing left in town to the Bloods. They have the same martyred qualities." Eating irons in hand, we plonked ourselves down at the round six-seater dining table and thrashed out the ethics of my decision to change football teams. Since I lived in Fitzroy, Denis was reluctantly prepared to cut me some slack on the issue.

As the subject moved to premiership prospects and injury lists, I began to wonder what scheme was being hatched here. When Brian Morrison suggested we get together for a nibble and a natter, he made no mention of Denis Dogherty. Yet Denis's presence was clearly no accident. So what was going on? The Ministry of Sport etc. was the point of overlap between the government bureaucracy and the MOB. Chances were that anything too sensitive or complicated for MOB to handle would get handballed to the minister's office where Denis would deal with it. Or find someone who could. Such as me, I wondered?

"How's Woeful?" I said.

"The Right Honorable Minister for Sport, Recreation, Racing and the Olympics?" Denis looked past me. "Ask him yourself."

Coming through the door, followed by Brian Morrison, was a tall, D-shaped, bald-headed fellow about the same age as Denis. His long, oval face wore a hangdog expression and his broad shoulders drooped as though carrying the weight of the world. As well they might, for it was Douglas "Woeful" McKenzie's responsibility to see that the government's $15 million investment in securing the Olympics, and its own future, was not wasted.

"G'day, Murray," he sighed wearily. "Not talking about me behind my back, I hope."

I knew Woeful only slightly, a nodding acquaintance from fundraising barbecues and factional powwows. An ex-wharfie like Denis, he was that rarest of anachronisms, a blue-collar worker in the Cabinet of a Labor government. Beyond that fact, about the only other thing I knew for sure about Woeful McKenzie was that, despite appearances, it was not his lugubrious demeanor which accounted for his nickname.

Back in the early fifties, according to legend, young Doug McKenzie was a pretty fair footballer. Not a star by any means, but a league-standard fullback who clocked up a couple of reasonably successful seasons with South Melbourne before buggering his hamstring. Built like the proverbial, he played a solid defense, plugging up the goal-mouth with his lumbering body and long arms. But, like many a fullback, he was an erratic kick. As often as not, when he sank the slipper, the result was an absolute shocker. Either a wobbly punt off the side of his boot or a turf-skidding worm-burner of a drop-kick.

"Woeful McKenzie strikes again," declared a radio commentator one afternoon, coining a tag so apt that Woeful had been Woeful ever since, even to many who knew nothing of his athletic prowess.

Woeful and Denis had always been thick as thieves. Port Melbourne lads, born with seagull shit on their shoulders, they had grown up together in the shadow of the biscuit factory, dived recklessly off the end of Station Pier and eventually slung their hooks in the same work crews. But Denis was no footballer, not even a nippy little rover. The spirit was willing but the flesh never quite made the team. Instead, he settled for the job of trainer. Water bottle in hand, he lurked at the boundary line, waiting for the right moment to dash onto the ground and pass a word of tactical advice to his burly mate.

Despite the disparaging moniker, Woeful's reputation as a sportsman had done him no harm in the years after he quit the football oval and the cargo sheds and began his slow but steady ascent through the industrial and parliamentary ranks of the party. And wherever he went Denis went with him. First into the Stevedores as his branch organizer, then as his electorate officer, finally as his ministerial adviser. Whatever the title or the game, however, their roles remained essentially what they had been on the footy field. Woeful played a dogged defense while Denis monitored the moves and proposed the play.

The Laurel and Hardy of the labor movement, somebody had once called them. Physical and temperamental opposites, the two old operators had been rusted together for the best part of forty years.

"Good afternoon, Minister," I said, properly respectful.

McKenzie was no great stickler for protocol but there was no point in taking uninvited liberties. If this was a job interview, it had just gone major league. The Minister for Sport, Recreation, Racing and the Olympics hadn't just dropped by on the chance of an open-face sandwich and a petit-four.

With an audible sigh, Woeful lowered his ample frame into a chair. He wore a dark brown suit with a club tie, a presentation number by the look of it. Garden City Bowls Club. When he sat down, his neck sank so far between his shoulders that he looked for all the world like a thumb with a face painted on it. Brian dealt him a hand of cutlery and a plate of sandwiches and sat down.

"Meeting go okay?" said Denis.

"This bloody Evaluation Commission," grunted Woeful, knocking back a solid slug of chardonnay. "Hugh Knowles never shut up about it."

Evidently, listening to Hugh Knowles had a stimulating effect on Woeful's appetite. While the big man laid into his lunch, Denis brought me up to speed.

"Big week next week, Murray. Three IOC high flyers winging into town to run the tape measure over us. Facilities, security, hospitality, you name it. Without the nod from this lot, we're down the gurgler in no uncertain terms. The MOB here have been running round like blue-arse flies, making straight the way. Anything upsets these blokes, it's bye-bye Olympics."

"Crunch time," added Brian Morrison, in case the point had escaped me. "Get the picture?"

Woeful washed down the last of his sandwich and dabbed his lips daintily with a paper napkin. Then he pushed his plate away and turned his full attention to me.

"So, Murray," he said. "Brian here tells me you know a bloke named Ambrose Buchanan."

3

THE CHANGE OF TACK was so sudden I wasn't sure I'd heard right.

"Ambrose Buchanan?" I said. "The Aboriginal activist?"

"Yeah. The blackfeller."

"Koori," said Denis. "They're called Koories now."

"Jesus Christ, Denis," said the big man. "I know that. They've been Koories for donkey's years. Well, have you, Murray?"

My appetite had gone right out the window. Denis and Brian, too, had stopped chewing and were observing me closely. "We've met," I admitted warily. "But it was a fair while ago."

Back in less morally equivocal times, back when doing good and doing well were less likely to be confused.

"Go on," urged Brian. "Tell them."

"You tell them," I said pointedly.

Ignoring my sarcasm, Brian unbuttoned his jacket, put his elbows on the table and eagerly launched into the story. Hand gestures, facial expressions, the works. Could have got a job on "Play School."

"This is back in the late seventies, right. Ten, twelve years ago. I'm running this federal housing project. Murray here is Charlene Wills's electorate officer in Melbourne Upper, just been kicked out of the Labor Resource Center."

I let that one go by. My decision to leave the Resource Center was entirely voluntary, albeit accompanied by sighs of relief all round. And Brian wasn't in charge of the housing program, he was acting assistant administrator on temporary secondment.

"Anyway," Brian continued. "The project involves replacing run-down public housing stock and relocating the tenants. Some of which are not exactly keen to cooperate. Think it's a trick to evict them. There's this one old duck in particular, really digs her heels in. Merle Plunkett. An old Aboriginal woman, originally from up Mooroopna way. She's had a pretty rough time over the years at the hands of what she calls The Welfare and we just can't persuade her that there's a nice new place waiting for her."

Merle had raised six grandchildren in that two-bedroom Housing Commission box of hers, and filled it with her memories. But the plumbing was rooted, the damp was rising and the entire block was slated for immediate demolition. Her new flat was right beside a community health center, close to public transport and the rent was lower. Still she wouldn't budge.

"Tried everything we could think of," continued Brian. "Including having a representative of her local member of parliament call around, speak to her in person."

Merle was one of Charlene's few Aboriginal constituents. One of the few locals not indigenous to the greater Mediterranean. "Brian was clutching at straws," I told Denis and Woeful. "There was no reason to think that I would have any influence at all."

"Anyway," persisted Brian, building up a head of narrative steam. "There's me and Murray, sitting at Merle's kitchen table, attempting to persuade her that we're not trying to pull the wool over her eyes, when her son Reggie barges in. Now Reggie is one cranky Koori and he reckons he's sick to death of white bureaucrats hassling his dear old mum. To emphasize the point, he produces a rifle, sticks it in Murray's face and declares that unless we agree to let Merle stay where she is in perpetuity he'll redecorate the place with gubba brains."

Denis opened his mouth. Before he could say anything,

Woeful stopped him with a look. He knew what a gubba was. The two of them were like an old married couple.

"The gun wasn't loaded," I said heavily.

We'd agreed at the time that it was best for all concerned if certain aspects of the story remained untold. And I, for one, had stuck to that commitment. But Brian was plainly unconcerned about ancient promises.

"I immediately offered to convey Reggie's demands to the appropriate authorities," he said. In other words, the chicken-shit coward took off so fast I thought it was a vanishing trick.

Not that I blamed him. Reggie Plunkett was indeed a very angry man, forty going on sixty, one of the walking wounded. A man who'd had it rough all his life. Rough red by the smell of him. And when he cocked that rabbit gun and pressed the muzzle against my forehead, his hands were shaking so badly with booze and rage that I was halfway through the Act of Contrition before I remembered I was an atheist.

"Reggie would never have really shot me," I insisted.

Denis had picked up on my reluctant tone. "Black with one sugar, Brian," he said, tilting his chin toward the sideboard. "White with two for his nibs. Murray?"

Brian took the hint and busied himself with the coffee pot.

"Nobody's asking you to do the dirty here, Murray," said Denis. "We're just trying to get a handle on this Buchanan bloke, that's all."

I didn't know where this little show-and-tell was going, but now that we'd come this far I figured I might as well go on. Better the truth than Brian's drama-school documentary. Woeful gave me a nod of encouragement.

"Reggie's problem was how to back down," I said. "Which became a major problem once the police arrived."

Summoned by Brian, the silly prick, the cops had the place surrounded within twenty minutes. An entire SWAT team, peeing themselves with excitement at the prospect of what they called a hostage-type siege-situation. When they shouted through a bullhorn for Reggie to come out with his hands up, he yelled back that he'd meet ten of them in hell first.

Which was a pity really, because Merle had just about convinced him to take the gun out of my face and start to think about getting himself sober. "You've really gone and done it now, Reggie," his mum said, fetching him a wallop around the ear-hole with a hand the size of a frying pan. At that point, I thought I was one dead whitefeller.

"Fortunately, I had the presence of mind to ring the Aboriginal Legal Service," said Brian, unable to help himself. "Who sent a mediator. Ambrose Buchanan."

Buchanan was originally from Wilcannia or Walgett, one of those shit-awful racist dumps in the backblocks of New South Wales. He'd been radicalized as a teenager when the Freedom Riders arrived in the mid-sixties, busloads of activists inspired by the American civil rights movement. He joined up and hit the road, helping desegregate municipal swimming pools. By the time he walked through the police lines and into Merle Plunkett's kitchen, he had a national reputation as a firebrand agitator.

"And Reggie knew who he was?" said Woeful.

I nodded. "He was pretty impressed, I think. But mainly he was sick to his guts at the thought of going back inside. He'd already spent half his life in prisons of one kind or another. But Ambrose gave him his money's worth. Started off by dressing me down, saying how high-handed we'd been." We being Brian. "Said we should've worked through a Koori community organization and that Reggie would be quite within his rights to shoot me where I sat. Then he suggested that I apologize to Merle."

Which I was not reluctant to do, given that Reggie was still holding the rifle. And because it didn't seem unreasonable, all things considered.

"The gun," urged Brian, irrepressibly. "Tell them about the gun."

"Ambrose eventually convinced Reggie to put it on the table between us. Then he stuck his head out the front door and put the coppers on hold while Merle made us a big pot of tea. Then we spent an hour trying to figure out what to do next."

"Which was to make me look like an idiot," said Brian cheerfully.

I didn't bother to contradict him. "The firearm was the problem," I said. "So Ambrose unloaded it and got Reggie to chop the stock into matchwood with his mum's kitchen cleaver. I shoved the bolt and the bullets down my underpants and the two of us, me and Ambrose, went out and explained to the posse that it was all a misunderstanding. Told them that Brian had misread the situation, that the gun was just a harmless old barrel and that I didn't want to press charges."

"They buy it?" said Denis.

"Put it this way," I told them. "Last I heard of Reggie Plunkett, he was running a very successful twelve-step alcohol rehabilitation program up in Rockhampton."

"How about Merle?"

I left that one to Brian. "Died of a diabetes-related illness," he said. "Three months after she moved into her new flat."

Denis exchanged a meaningful look with Woeful. "Seen much of Ambrose Buchanan since then?"

"Only in the press," I said. "Mind telling me why all the interest? I thought you wanted to talk to me about Greeks."

"Greeks?" Brian was mystified.

"Show him the tape you showed us," said Woeful.

"What Greeks?" Brian leaned back in his chair and opened the walnut sideboard. Inside was a television set and a VCR. "German documentary. Just gone to air in Europe. Seen by fifty million people. The PR firm that handles our European lobbying sent it to us. They don't think it's done much for our prospects."

A long shot of Uluru filled the screen, superimposed with the words *Roter Kontinent — Schwarzer Kampf.* Brian held down the fast-forward button. Images skittered past. Rock art, desert landscapes, talking heads, old monochrome images. Black men chained to trees, mission-station children, Bobbi Sykes in an Angela Davis afro, police dismantling the Tent Embassy outside the old Parliament House in Canberra, Gough Whitlam pouring dirt into Vincent Lingiari's hand, street marches, black babies with flies in their eyes. Brian removed his finger and the tape slowed to normal. Ambrose Buchanan appeared.

The footage was recent and he looked remarkably unchanged by the decade that had passed since he stood in old Merle's kitchen, Reggie Plunkett sobbing in his arms, while I stared down between my feet, speechless with relief, thinking how badly the floor needed wiping. Busting for a piss after all that tea.

He still had the same cocky body-language, the same fine-boned, nut-brown face with its hint that some long-gone Afghan had watered his camels at the gene pool of the western plains. The beard was a new addition, if you could call it a beard. Overgrown designer stubble, flecked with silver. But Ambrose Buchanan was no tribal elder, not yet. He still wore faded blue denims, emblem of our shared generation. I hoped I'd weathered the years as well as he had.

He was standing at a microphone on the tray of a flat-bed truck. Behind him, on a row of plastic chairs, sat a dozen old Aborigines, men and women, as ancient and impassive as the landscape. As Ambrose spoke, he gripped the microphone stand with one hand and punctuated each phrase with an upward sweep of his other, as though gently but forcefully freeing an injured bird.

Brian's finger found the volume control and suddenly we could hear what was being said. Buchanan's voice was reedy with excitement, but the measured cadence of his phrases rose and fell like an irresistible tide.

"They say that our demands are unreasonable. They say that we should be content with all we've been given. They say that everything that can be done is being done. They say that we must put the past behind us. They say that before the law we are all one nation. That is what they say."

Buchanan paused here and lowered his head, as if pondering an impenetrable mystery, as if burdened by a sorrow too deep to communicate. As if inviting us to join him in a moment of silent contemplation. Then, emerging almost reluctantly from his reverie, he drew himself up to his full height and once again gripped the microphone stand. "And what do we say, eh?"

The camera panned across the flags and banners of a huge demonstration, a sea of red, black and yellow, hemmed in by the hard blank facades of city office buildings. "And what do we say to them?"

The question hung for a moment, then a great chant welled up from the crowd. "Land rights now! Land rights now!" Buchanan's open palm became a closed fist that punched out the beat. "Land rights now! Land rights now!"

Brian hit the stop button and the screen turned to snow. "Brisbane," he said. "Two years ago. Quite impressive, don't you think?"

Impressive? It was bloody fantastic. Buchanan was a natural orator, one of the best I'd ever seen. Which isn't saying much, admittedly, for ours is not a culture characterized by public eloquence. Woeful and Denis had turned in their seats, waiting for my reaction.

"Very impressive," I agreed, cautiously. I was beginning to suspect where all this was leading.

"Ambrose's been in Brussels for the past six months," said Brian. "Arguing some case before the International Court of Human Rights. He arrived here in Melbourne a few days ago. Says he wants to talk to us, got a proposition."

"Hmm," I said. "And?"

"Demarcation dispute," said Denis, humor crinkling the edges of his foxy little eyes.

Brian explained. "We've already been through the community consultation process with the local Koories. The full corroboree. Even went up the bush. Echuca, Robinvale, Mooroopna, Eunamit. Explained how there'll be plenty for everyone if we win. Politely requested their assistance."

"And not just because of the black vote on the IOC," said Denis, a man whose heart had always been in the right place. On race issues, the Stevedores' credentials were unimpeachable.

"We were advised to employ a Koori liaison officer," continued Brian. "Which we did. Bloke by the name of Charlie Talbot."

The surname struck a distant clap-stick. The Talbots, I recalled, were one of the more prominent families in local Aboriginal matters. Back at Ethnic Affairs, according to hearsay, half the Koori bureaucrats in Victoria were Talbots. Koories, of course, are not ethnics. Laotians are ethnics. Eritreans are ethnics. If we had any Eskimos, they'd be ethnics. But Aborigines aren't ethnics.

"So what's the problem?" I said.

Woeful leaned back, let his belt out a notch and crossed his hands over his belly. "Charlie's in Nairobi right now," he sighed, shaking his head. "On his way to Lusaka for a meeting of the Organization of African Sport. Hugh Knowles and the rest of the board thought we should have at least one black member on our delegation. God knows what the Africans will make of Charlie Talbot. With the light behind him, he's whiter than I am."

"Not that the minister's saying you can't have a fair-complexioned Aborigine," said Denis, tipping me a sly wink. "You're not saying that, are you Woeful?"

"Murray knows what I mean," said Woeful irritably. "This isn't a fucking Rotary meeting, Den." He started patting his pockets. Denis tossed him a roll of antacids. He caught it without looking, peeled one off and ground it loudly between his molars.

"The point being," Brian said, moving right along. "Ambrose and the Talbots don't get on. He reckons they're coconuts."

Denis cupped a hand around his mouth and leaned across the table. "Brown on the outside, white on the inside."

"Piss off," grumbled Woeful. The days of vaudeville, it seemed, were not entirely dead.

"Ambrose Buchanan said that?" I was surprised. Washing black linen in public didn't sound like Ambrose's style.

"Shit no!" said Brian. "Charlie Talbot told me. Anyway, the point is, Buchanan's in town and Charlie isn't. And we all know that Buchanan won't be satisfied with a company car and an overseas trip.

He'll want something big, something unrealistic, something outside the scope of the MOB to satisfy."

"What about the Department of Aboriginal Affairs?" I asked. "Isn't this their jurisdiction?"

"Leaks like a wickerwork basket," said Brian. "If the Talbots suspect that we're cutting a side deal with Ambrose, they'll get their nulla-nullas in a knot. Accuse us of reneging on the agreed consultation process, maybe even pull the plug. Then we'll really be in the shit, indigenous support-wise. So, until we've got a better idea of what Ambrose has in mind, we need to tread carefully, go at the whole thing sideways." He made a sinuous, inserting gesture. "Know what I mean?"

At that point, I had an overwhelming urge to make a break for the door.

Before I had the chance, Woeful leaned forward in his seat and put his hands flat on the table. Big shovels of things that once humped sacks of sugar out of the holds of cargo tubs at Swanston Dock and punched footballs thirty meters into the crowd at the Lakeside Oval. He levered himself upward and fixed me in his melancholy gaze. "I don't have to tell you how important this bid is to the future of the government, Murray," he said. "And I know we can rely on you."

Denis already had his hand on the door knob. "C'mon, Your Excellency," he said. "Let's leave these young blokes to sort out the details. See you later, Murray."

As the door closed behind them, Brian Morrison slid the plate of chocolate biscuits across the table toward me.

"No way known," I said. "No fucking way, pal."

36 • **Shane Maloney**

4

BRIAN MORRISON STOOD at the window, backside on the sill, heels angled into the carpet, hands thrust deep into his pockets. Behind him, reflecting the coppery foliage of the parkland, rose the glass wall of a brand-new office tower. A banner hung from its roof, ten stories high. *To Let*, it read. Brian cast his eyes downward and took a long draught from the cup of bitter disappointment.

"Thought you'd be in this like a shot, Murray," he sighed. "A chance to get yourself out of Water, put your talents to better use. Get in on the ground floor of the hottest project in town. Do your bit for the party's reelection prospects."

I was looking at the painting above the mantelpiece, a landscape of the old school. One of those bush scenes politicians love to borrow from the National Gallery to hang in the office, impress the constituents. The vision splendid of the sunlit plain extended, the murmur of the river on its bars, the distant smudge of innumerable grazing merinos. Australia Felix.

"Listen to yourself, mate," I said. "Next you'll be appealing to my sense of patriotism. If you're going to softsoap me, at least work up a decent lather."

"Okay," he said. "How much do you want?"

"You offering me a job?"

"Fair go," he pleaded. "This should only take you a couple of days. Woeful can talk to Agnelli, arrange a temporary secondment to Sport."

"You appear to be mistaking me for Mother Teresa," I said.

"Okay, okay. I suppose I can wangle you a consultancy fee on top of your salary. Say five grand."

"Five thousand dollars?" I whistled. "That the going rate for putting down a native uprising?"

"Jesus, Murray," said Brian. "Don't tell me you're having an attack of conscience."

That crack was a low blow, an assault on my integrity. No worse allegation can be leveled against a paid functionary of the Australian Labor Party than the insinuation of morality. My position was entirely pragmatic. Five grand was a tidy sum for a few days' work, but it was scant compensation for what was being asked. Aboriginal politics were just too complex, intractable and thankless. A morass of good intentions gone wrong. The domain of missionaries, mystics and mercenaries. None of which categories included me. For Brian to suggest otherwise was an insult to my commonsense and an attempt to prey on my better nature.

Nor had I forgotten what happened last time I agreed to do Brian a favor. I nodded toward the blank television screen. "You already know what Ambrose wants — land rights and an end to two centuries of injustice. You reckon your budget will run to that?"

The Director of Government, Corporate and Community Relations hung his jacket on the back of his chair and rolled up his shirt sleeves like maybe he was about to beat some sense into me. He poured two fresh cups of coffee and plonked one on the table in front of me. "I'm begging you, mate. If Ambrose succeeds in making race an issue in this bid, I can kiss my brilliant new career goodbye."

"Don't go hysterical on me," I said. "Or I'll be forced to slap you."

Morrison jerked his thumb in the direction of a hypothetical top floor. "Hugh Knowles is really spooked by this. And, believe me, anybody who underestimates the viciousness of the Australian business class just isn't getting out of the house enough."

"I can see you've really bonded with the corporate sector," I said. The coffee had been standing for too long and had turned bitter. Just to cut the taste, I had a biscuit. A cigarette would have been better but I didn't dare.

"Less than twenty years ago, Mincom was burning blacks out of their homes to make way for its bauxite mines. Federal legislation and the land councils put an end to all that but the mining industry will still only deal with indigenous people if the courts force it to. There's a lot of corporate ego involved in this bid and these guys are terrified by the idea that a media-wise Abo might hold them to ransom. Ambrose knows that and he'll play it to the hilt."

I shrugged. "More power to him."

"I agree. I absolutely agree," said Brian. "Except this isn't about the mining industry or corporate ego. It's about creating sixty thousand jobs in this city. It's about saving the government that you and I sweated our tits off to get elected. Losing Melbourne's Olympic bid isn't going to eliminate trachoma in the Northern Territory. But if the blame can be slated back to the blacks believe me it will be. And that's not going to do much for race relations."

"And you think Ambrose Buchanan can do that, single-handed?"

Brian topped up our coffees. "For Ambrose Buchanan, the Olympic bid is part of a bigger agenda. He knows that the real political constituency for Aboriginal rights in this country is the white population of the southeastern cities. If it was up to the voters of Queensland and Western Australia, the pastoralists and miners would still be free to chain blackfellers to trees. Ambrose's self-appointed role is to keep the issue of racism to the forefront down here in the south. He's unencumbered by any official position in the Aboriginal bureaucracy, he's well networked internationally and he's got a good local power base."

"It's all a bit big-picture for me, mate," I said. "You want a branch stacked or a ballot rigged, I'm your man."

"Exactly," said Brian. "You have the sensitivity to deal with the issues. On top of which, you and Ambrose have a history. He'll trust you. I'm only asking you to find out whether he's prepared to deal, that's all."

"You're offering me five thousand dollars just to find out if Ambrose Buchanan can be persuaded that black interests won't be served by an attack on the Olympic bid?"

"More or less."

"It's not my area of expertise. I'd stuff it up. Honestly."

"Crap," he said, vehemently. "You've just spent five years working with the Greeks. After that, how much of a problem can a solitary Aborigine be?"

He had a point. But I wasn't about to concede it. Not until he played his trump card. "That son of yours . . ." He snapped his fingers to jog his memory, back in pantomime mode.

"Red," I reminded him. Brian's eldest was about Red's age, I seemed to recall. Matilda, Mabel, something like that. Red decked her at her third birthday party. Brian's wife Sandra was something in public advocacy at the time, back when Wendy was executive officer of the Women's Information Exchange. They still kept in touch.

"That's right," said Brian, confirming my son's identity for me. "Wendy was saying to Sandra the other day on the phone that Red was one of our junior runners in the *Dream the Dream* Torch Relay."

The torch relay was a public relations stunt being run by the MOB. Two thousand children carrying an anodized aluminum baton down the east coast of the continent, a demonstration of the commitment of the youth of Australia to the ideals of Olympism. Participants got a free Coca-Cola T-shirt and a McDonald's voucher. Every kid in the country wanted a piece of the action.

"Two hundred meters along Parramatta Road last Sunday afternoon," I said. "The banners in the used-car yards lent the occasion a particularly festive air."

Or so I imagined. Unfortunately, I hadn't been there to see it. After Red made the cut at Little Athletics, I booked a plane ticket to Sydney to witness the big event. But Agnelli insisted I stay in town in case the union dispute went critical. It didn't, of course, and I missed my first opportunity in four months to see the kid. He was, Wendy made a point of telling me, "bitterly disappointed" by his father's failure to show.

"What's Red got to do with this?"

Brian adopted a guise of innocence. "The thing is, a bit of an opportunity has arisen. We're looking for a kid to present the torch to the visiting IOC members at the gala dinner next Thursday night. Hugh Knowles's grandson was lined up for the job — nothing warms the heart of the IOC more than a bit of nepotism — but young Nicholas has come down with the Hong Kong flu. We're thinking of selecting one of the interstate runners at random and flying him — or her — into town especially for the occasion. Good media angle and so on. Anyway, I might just be able to organize it so your boy Red gets the gig."

Pleading, flattery, persuasion. Now bribery. You had to hand it to Brian Morrison, he didn't rest until he'd found the right button to push. "Is this the lowest you've ever sunk?" I asked.

"Shit no," he beamed. "Back when I was with the Minister for Transport, I started a rumor that a particularly troublesome secretary of the Railway Workers Union was a closet pixie. Took off like wildfire, it did. He lost the next election by forty-three votes." He puffed out his cheeks and stared up at the ceiling. "You'll probably want to discuss it with Wendy," he said. "Sandra reckons she'll be thrilled at the idea."

Bribery buttressed by blackmail. He caught the rush of green to my gills and moved in for the kill. "Tell you what," he said. "Sleep on it over the weekend. Talk it over with the ex. Let me know what you decide. Monday at the latest." He put his flame-embossed business card on the empty plate in front of me. Somebody appeared to have eaten all the chocolate biscuits.

Brian was on his feet again, staring out the window. "Beautiful weather," he exhaled. "This town's really at its best at this time of the year. Don't you agree?"

5

WHEN I CAME OUT of the Old Treasury, Sir Charles Gordon was standing across the road with a swagger stick under his arm and his gaze fixed on the far horizon, oblivious to the traffic swirling around his feet. He'd been standing there since 1938. *He would not desert those dependent on him* was chiseled into the plinth at his feet. A pigeon was shitting on his head.

Like Gordon awaiting his doom at Khartoum, I was in no great hurry. Agnelli was in Canberra for the annual meeting of Ministers Responsible for Public Infrastructure. There was nothing for me at Water that couldn't wait. My next appointment was still half an hour away. My cigarettes were already in my hand. Twelve left of a pack broached fresh that morning.

"Nine," I said, out loud. Keep count advised the brochure issued by Quit. Counting contributes to a sense of control.

With a control born of constant practice, I slipped the filter between my lips, made a small flame in the cup of my hand, lowered my head and inhaled. A violent inrush of smoke penetrated to the core of my metabolism. The tension which had been building since my arrival at the Old Treasury broke like the wall of a dam and a calming energy permeated my entire being. I exhaled slowly, tilting my head back and expelling a column of evanescent vapor into the lucid afternoon air. Then I inhaled again, less urgently this time, letting the calm spread within me. God Jesus, I needed help.

Beyond Sir Charles sat Parliament House, the nominal seat of power. Just down the hill were the office towers of the nation's biggest corporations. The companies whose directors had conceived the Olympic bid and raised the money to fund it. Ten million dollars, so far. A grubstake which the government had readily doubled. Small beer, considering the potential payoff. A marketing bonanza for the corporate sector, reelection for the Labor Party. Someone had to win, so why not us?

Idle speculation. Returning Messieurs Benson & Hedges to my pocket, I set off toward St. Vincent's Hospital. The afternoon was at its peak. The sun was spilling its warmth from the sky and the gutters were thick with fallen leaves, a rich yellow-brown, the color of the finest Virginia tobacco. Once upon a time, council workers would have swept them into piles and burned them, filling the air with the smoky aroma of the season's passing, the exhaust fumes of time's speeding chariot. But not any more. Now, in accordance with Environment Protection Authority ordinances, the incineration of vegetable waste material within the greater metropolitan area was prohibited. The leaves would rot to a mucous mulch and be flushed down the stormwater drains into Port Phillip Bay.

Something similar would happen to me if I didn't start making some serious plans. So far, my career trajectory from union researcher to electorate official to ministerial adviser was less the product of driving ambition than an incremental advance through the ranks of the party. And look where it had led me. Cooling my heels in Water, writing policy analyses for a minister who rarely read them. Spending my working hours in the company of engineers, men whose idea of intellectual stimulation was to calculate the flow-through rate of a sewage tunnel.

Brian Morrison's little consultancy hardly represented a major opportunity, especially considering the task involved. And the idea that my decision might in some way affect the outcome of the bid was, of course, absurd. If anything was going to convince me to accept his proposition, it was the prospect of getting Red down from Sydney, if only for a couple of days.

My intimacy with Red was fading, eroded by the passage of time and the exigencies of absentee parenthood. Intimacy requires habit, the sharing of daily routines. For a time, when his mother was off pursuing her career, Red and I had lived a kind of shared bachelor existence, camping out amid our dirty dishes in the vestiges of the family home. I still missed that time, missed driving him to school, picking his socks off the floor, bickering. I also yearned for the paternal bit, the chance to offer advice and point directions. To swing a bit of fatherly lead.

Wendy would make the big decisions, that was inevitable and accepted. His school, his choice of friends, they were outside my power. But why should everything be that way? If Brian was fair dinkum, if the payoff for my cooperation was that Red would get bumped to the prize possie in the fun run, then maybe his proposition was worth considering.

Prompted by such thoughts, my ruminations turned to my own childhood. When I was about eight or nine, my father was the licensee of the Carter's Arms Hotel in Northcote. Occasionally, Aborigines would come in off the street, one or two at a time, into the public bar. Not really black blacks like the ones in the Jolliffe cartoons in *Pix* and *Post* at the barber's shop; these were lighter skinned men. But you could see it straightaway, that touch of the tar brush. Half-castes, my father called them, the first time I ever heard the word.

"They make trouble," Dad said, mouthing the orthodoxies of the age. "It's not always their fault, but if you let the races mix you get trouble. Just look at America." And so we did, on television almost every night. Snarling police dogs, night-sticks, water cannon. "They can't handle the grog like normal people. It's their genes."

But my father was, in his way, an advocate of equal rights. At least the right to get legless, regardless of race or creed. He wouldn't serve them over the bar but he'd sell them bottles at the back door.

Royal Reserve Port, Seppelt's Solero Sherry, tawny muscat. "Better that than aftershave," he told the regulars. We didn't stock aftershave.

I felt sorry for them. And, in some obscure way, my pity gave me a sense of superiority. Not just toward the half-castes, poor unfortunates who couldn't help the way they were, but also toward my father. And particularly toward the regulars in the public bar, the men whose way of life Dad was defending. Barstool philosophers with scruples so finely honed they couldn't share as much as a slop-soaked bar towel and a threadbare carpet with men of a different hue.

These reflections got me as far as St. Patrick's Cathedral, its steeples aimed at the heavens like a thicket of Gothic missiles. In the forecourt stood yet another statue: Daniel O'Connell, Irish patriot and political agitator. *The Liberator,* read the inscription chiseled into his plinth. Another troublemaker from a race notoriously incapable of holding its liquor.

Unlike their dark-skinned cousins in more northerly parts of the country, Melbourne's Koories were a tiny, almost invisible minority. Four or five thousand souls in a population of nearly three million. And Ambrose Buchanan, for all his firebrand reputation, was not originally from these parts. So, even if he insisted on playing hardball, it remained to be seen what local support he could muster. Especially if he went treading on the toes of the Talbots. For all of Brian's big-picture scenarios, an experienced operator like Buchanan would be unlikely to let rhetoric get in the way of a deal, if one was offered. I flicked my stub into a pile of leaves, half-hoping for a tongue of flame and a wisp of smoke.

Reaching Victoria Parade, I crossed to the private consulting rooms next to St. Vincent's. The customary cluster of smokers lurked at the entrance. You had to admire them, puffing away, undeterred by the irony of the location. Admire them? Hell, I joined them. I still had ten minutes up my sleeve and might as well spend them exercising my lungs in the great outdoors.

There were four other smokers. A brace of gossiping nurses in plastic smocks and white running shoes, a tradesman in khaki overalls and a sales assistant from the hospital florist with a dusting of pollen on the sleeve of her chunky-knit sweater. She was no more than nineteen, young enough to know better. Gripping her cigarette fiercely between lacquered fingernails, she sucked at it hungrily with fleshy, over-glossed lips. A name tag was pinned to her bosom, the lettering too far away to read. Sharon, I bet myself. Or Krystal.

Patronizing bastard, I thought, lighting up one of my own guilty pleasures. What makes you think you're so superior? Just as I lit up, a woman emerged from the building and joined us, energetically hunting in a black leather handbag that hung by a strap from her shoulder.

Somewhere in her mid-thirties, quite a nice age for the time of year, she was dressed in a professional but slightly haphazard way, as if she had better things to worry about than her grooming. Her dark maroon pants-suit complemented her tall, slim build, and her disc earrings exactly matched the gold buttons on her jacket, but she wore very little make-up and errant strands kept escaping from the tortoiseshell combs that pinned back her dark brown hair. Hospital administrator, I bet myself. Healthcare professional. Corporate Services. Strategic Planning. Something quite senior.

Lest I appeared to be staring, I averted my gaze. "Ten," I said to myself, lighting up.

Reflected in the plate-glass window of the florist shop, the woman continued to ferret in her bag. A look of mild exasperation furrowed her brow. She let the bag drop to her side and turned to leave. It seemed she hadn't checked her supplies before slipping outside for a smoke. Fortunately for her, there was a Good Samaritan in the vicinity. I cleared my throat, thumbed open my gaspers and extended the pack.

She hesitated for a moment. Then, with an apologetic little grimace, she took one. "Pathetic, isn't it?" she said.

I shrugged. Sure it was. But it was why we were standing there, after all.

Close up, there was something vaguely outdoorsy about her. A slight tan. A hint of muscularity. A definite self-sufficiency. A girl, I could tell, who knew how to change a tire. A bushwalker, perhaps?

A Girl Scout, but one with a vice. The combination was appealing. I made a flame.

As she leaned forward to accept it, she held my gaze, making her own assessment. Her seal brown eyes had little crow's-feet in the corners. There was laughter in them. Not mockery but a wry, playful humor. They were grown-up eyes. I liked them. They'd seen a lot but they didn't give much away. I could've looked into them for a long, long time.

She kissed three little puffs out of her cigarette, just enough to get it burning. She wore, I noticed, no wedding ring. Not that I had any particular reason to notice, but there you are. Nodding thanks, she tucked one of those nomadic strands behind her ear and took a step backward. Half-turned toward the street, her stance was both casual and slightly self-conscious.

They say you can read a woman by the way she smokes a cigarette. I could read this one like a book. It was called *Woman Smoking a Cigarette*. I wanted to say something, but didn't know what. Certainly nothing banal or obvious or gormless. Nothing that might prematurely reveal my true nature.

A steady tide of pedestrians streamed past, entering and leaving the hospital. The pregnant women and children with plaster-encased limbs weren't so bad, but when a skeletal old geezer with an intercom in his throat wheezed past in a walker, moving at the speed of an emphysemic snail, I tracked his progress with fascinated revulsion.

Turning to share this cautionary vision with my fellow desperado, she of the Dunhill-colored hiking suit, I found that I had left my run too late. She was already stubbing her half-smoked cigarette in a planter box of sand. With a brisk nod in my general direction, she hurried into the building.

The nurses and the blokes in overalls, too, were extinguishing themselves and drifting back to duty. So Sharon and I stood there alone, smoking our cigarettes and thinking our thoughts. I can't vouch for Sharon, but I was thinking about love. It was a mystery I'd been contemplating for quite some time.

For most of the previous year I'd been investing my emotional reserves and bodily fluids in what had turned out to be a losing proposition. Claire was my first serious relationship since the end of my marriage, an apparently ideal match who arrived in my life complete with a large libido, a small business and a four-year-old daughter. And when her ex-husband came knocking on the door, wanting to see little Gracie, I encouraged such visits. How could I do otherwise? I, too, was an access father, snatching time with my child only when the opportunity arose and his mother acquiesced.

Claire, however, acquiesced to more than just parental access. Full conjugal relations, it transpired, were also resumed. "It just sort of happened," she told me, like that explained everything.

Single again, I was no longer sure who I missed the most, the mother or the daughter. Gracie at least had the sensitivity to shed a tear when I said goodbye. Claire merely congratulated me on how well I was taking it.

So well did I take it that within three months my cigarette consumption had gone through the roof and all my trousers had gone tight around the waist.

Burying my butt in the mass grave, I headed inside. Even as I turned to go, another smoker was taking my place. We brave few, sentries at mortality's gate. As I waited for the lift, I scanned the directory of tenants, a *memento mori* in moveable plastic letters. Gastroenterologists. Urologists. Neuro-ophthalmologists. Colorectal surgeons. A cardiothoracic specialist. I didn't like the sound of that one.

Telling myself I was doing the right thing, I boarded the lift and pressed the button for the ninth floor. Nine. The same number as my total remaining cigarettes.

6

DR. BERNARD MANNE, although described on the honor-roll downstairs as a consultant physician, was essentially a general practitioner. The fact that his surgery was located in this hotbed of specialization was a matter of convenience rather than a claim to professional eminence. Most of Bernie's regular patients worked, like me, in the immediate area and he had built up a lucrative little practice ministering to our many and varied medical needs.

Apart from the usual collection of dog-eared *National Geographics* and long-defunct *Business Weekly*s, I found the waiting room empty. "Go right in," said the receptionist. "The doctor is waiting."

Except the doctor wasn't Doctor Manne. It wasn't any kind of man at all, in fact. It was the neglectful smoker from downstairs. She was sitting at Bernie's desk, scanning a file as though looking for something incriminating. Hello, I thought, they've caught up with Bernie at last.

I cleared my throat in the open doorway and the woman looked my way. As she did so, her face broke out in a smile that was both totally spontaneous and utterly infectious. She had a wide, generous mouth and, now that I could see them more clearly, it occurred to me that those creases at the edges of her eyes were sneaky little laugh lines. She recognized me from downstairs but didn't say so.

"Mr. Whelan?" she said.

I didn't deny it.

She stood up and stuck out her hand. "I'm Phillipa Verstak. I'm looking after the practice until Dr. Manne has recovered." Her voice was quiet but authoritative, as though she was accustomed to dealing with your more diffident category of patient.

"Verstak?" I said. A name from my childhood. "Any relation?" To Tanya Verstak, Miss Australia 1961, famous at the time as the first New Australian to win the title. White Russian, we were told. Whatever that meant.

Dr. Phillipa Verstak merely gave a polite shake of her head. It was an obvious question, one she had probably been asked all her life.

Her grip was firm and warm. As I took it, I found myself glancing surreptitiously at her other hand. She still wasn't wearing a wedding ring. Meaning that she hadn't got married in the lift on the way upstairs. Or perhaps that she found a ring inconvenient during certain sorts of medical procedures. Or meaning nothing at all. She probably had a mature and ongoing commitment to a colorectal ophthalmologist with whom she resided in a mock-Tudor home in Doncaster with their 3.4 children. If so, he was a cheapskate. Apart from the earrings, she wore no jewelry at all.

"Recovered?" I said. Bernie had given me my annual grease-and-oil change only the previous week. He'd just come back from a Stress Management conference in Noumea and was glowing with the kind of well-being that only comes from five days of tax-deductible windsurfing.

"He was kicked by a horse." She'd repinned her hair but a strand had fought its way loose, unnoticed. I wanted to reach over and tuck it behind her ear.

"Not Bijou Deluxe?" I pointed to the framed thoroughbred hanging among Bernie's diplomas and degrees.

Bernie owned Bijou Deluxe in a consortium with three Chinese dental technicians, a copyright lawyer and the shelf company of a master builder. He'd tried to sign me up, rhapsodizing from behind the pile of bloodstock gazettes that littered his desk. Twenty grand, plus stabling and training. "Three wins and two places in seven starts," he said. "You'll never regret it." And nor did I. I passed instead. So did every other horse that Bijou Deluxe subsequently raced.

"I didn't ask its name," she said. "All I know is that Dr. Manne got a bit too close in the mounting enclosure and his jaw will be wired for the next few weeks. The locum service asked me to stand in for him. Of course, if you'd rather wait until he returns . . ."

There was no question of that. A team of Clydesdales couldn't have dragged me away.

"I'm sure I'll be safe in your hands," I said, and lowered myself into the patient's chair.

Dr. Verstak sat in Bernie's chair with the big window behind. It faced back toward the city, giving out onto the old watchtower of the Eastern Hill fire station. Any moment, bells would sound and men in red braces would slide down a brass pole, rush across the road and douse my burning desire with buckets of water. "What seems to be the problem?" she said.

"I'm just here to pick something up," I said. "Bernie said to drop by today." My file was in clear view on the desk. It was the one she'd been reading when I came in. A snatched smoke and a quick bone-up just before the patient arrives. That's why they call it medical practice. I indicated the file. "Take your time."

I watched her scan the last page, then smile her wry smile. "I see that Dr. Manne has been treating you for nicotine addiction."

"Harsh words," I said. "From a fellow junkie."

"According to this," she said, not looking up, "you're on twenty-five a day. I only smoke four a day."

The woman was in deep denial. A four-a-day smoker relishes the special moment. A four-a-day smoker does not stand in a draughty vestibule, tossing off a quick puff. Botting from strangers. Still, who was I to quibble?

"You're doing better than I am," I said. "But I must say it's unusual to find a doctor who smokes."

"Physician heal thyself and all that," she said, looking up now. "Doesn't do much for my credibility, does it?"

"On the contrary," I said. "I find it refreshing. It probably gives you a more sympathetic appreciation of the patient's situation."

"Perhaps," she said, putting a little professional distance between us. "But we're not here to talk about me, are we?"

"No, of course not," I agreed. "How did you start? I mean being aware of the risks and all."

"You mean that I should've known better?" She sighed, resigned to my curiosity. I'd bought the right to ask, after all. Paid for it with a Benson & Hedges. "By now, we all should know better."

"Humor me," I said. "I'm interested." I was interested, all right, but cigarettes weren't the half of it.

She let out a little exasperated sigh, yet I wasn't entirely convinced that she minded the chance to talk about herself. "I started at university. All those late nights, burning the midnight oil. Actually, I think cigarettes really did help. After I graduated, I didn't smoke for ten years. I started again last New Year's Eve."

I nodded knowingly. "A few convivials, your guard goes down."

"Mortar attack, actually," she said. "I thought I was about to die, so I wasn't too concerned about the long-term effects."

"Mortar attack!" I reeled back in mock horror, assuming she was joking. "I heard things can get pretty hairy at Western Hospital, but I had no idea it was that wild." Western was in Footscray. Little Saigon.

"Phnom Penh, actually." She could see the humor in it, but she hadn't been joking. "I've been working there for the past nine months. Community Aid Abroad. I've only been back a couple of weeks."

That explained the tan and the slight otherworldliness. Our esteemed Foreign Minister had recently taken a break from his full-time job of brown-nosing the Indonesian military to bestow his peace-making skills on benighted Cambodia. Phillipa's job there, I assumed, was part of the attendant aid effort.

"Well you've got the best excuse for backsliding I've ever heard," I said. "It must have been fascinating. Not the mortar attack. The whole experience. Are you going back?"

Take me with you, I thought. After twenty years in the Australian Labor Party, mine-infested paddy-fields didn't frighten me. Not with Dr. Daktari at my side, borrowing my cigarettes.

"Haven't decided yet." She tucked the loose strand of hair back and turned again to my file, terminating the subject. "I see Dr. Manne referred you to an acupuncturist."

"Professor Wu," I said. "From Wuhan. It worked fine for three months. When I started again, I went straight to a pack a day."

"And you tried the ear-clip?"

"Decided I preferred lung cancer to the ribbing I got at work."

"No luck with the hypnotism? Dr. Karpal gets very good results, I understand."

"High recidivism rate. But I lasted nearly a year."

"Nicotine gum?"

"Made everything taste disgusting."

"Yes. It does, doesn't it?"

As we worked our way through my back-catalogue of failed experiments, I got the distinct impression that her interest was not entirely abstract. Cure-swapping is one of the principal by-products of cigarette smoking. "Transcendental meditation. Cold turkey. Weekend retreats. Herbal mouthwash," I said. "You name it, I've tried it. Everything except Smokers Anonymous. I may be desperate and despicable, but I haven't entirely lost my self-respect."

"Let's hope we have more success this time," she said. The medical first-person plural.

"Let's. Should I take my clothes off now?"

"Thanks for the offer," she said. "But this is something you can do by yourself. Be sure to read the instructions very carefully first." She slid open a drawer and took out a small cardboard container.

Nicotine patches. Bernie's latest weapon in his war against my recalcitrant metabolism. Cuts out the middleman, he said. Sends the poison directly to the brain where it's needed, reduces the bitumen in the lungs and assists the addict to break the cigarette habit. On top of which, if I volunteered as a guinea pig for the trial program, I'd get them for free. She handed me the box.

"Nicabate," I read. "Rate-Controlled Nicotine Patches. Bit wimpy, isn't it? Shouldn't it be something like Decimate or Niceradicate?"

"Nick Off," she suggested.

"So where do I stick them?"

She ignored that one. "The dose has been calculated to match your current tolerance level, so it's very important that you don't smoke while wearing the patches. You should be particularly wary of social situations where you might unconsciously accept an offered cigarette."

"Such as mortar attacks," I suggested. "Or while having a drink after work."

"Yes, exactly."

"At Mietta's, for example."

Mietta's was a watering hole in the city. The place to be seen. A place of timeless elegance and ten-dollar aperitifs. The sort of joint where corporate art advisers drank Campari sodas with stockbrokers at one table while a rising soprano displayed her coloratura to the Argentine consul-general at the next. I mentioned it as a provocation, to get a rise. Some of those Community Aid Abroad people had a touch of the hairshirt about them.

"What's wrong with Mietta's?" The woman was being deliberately obtuse. It was driving me wild.

"Ever been there?"

"Of course," she said primly. "Makes a change from the Irish Rover in Phnom Penh."

She rose to her feet, signaling the end of the consultation. "Please call me if you experience any difficulties. I'd appreciate you letting me know how you get on. Side effects and so on."

"Side effects?" I said. Bernie hadn't said anything about side effects.

"Disturbed sleep patterns. Headaches. Mild agitation. An itch."

The itch I already had. Disturbed sleep patterns I could only hope for. "Headaches and agitation," I said. "Sounds like my job."

"Oh?" She opened the door. "What kind of work do you do?"

I sucked in my stomach. "Special consultant to the Olympic bid," I said. It wasn't exactly brain surgery but it sounded a lot sexier than plumber's apprentice.

As I slipped the Nicabate box into my pocket, my fingers closed around the packet of Benson & Hedges. "Eleven," said a voice in my head.

7

THE PHONE STARTED RINGING at eight on Saturday morning, dragging me from the arms of anesthesia with the voice of an insistent stranger.

"Are you the yellow 1979 Daihatsu Charade auto hatchback with six months registration?"

"Huh?"

"The one in the paper?"

"Oh, that." Earlier in the week, I'd booked an advertisement for the Saturday car classifieds. "I need some work," I yawned. I swung my feet over the edge of the bed and rubbed the sleep from my eyes. "I mean *it* needs some work."

A fair bit, really. The diff had gone, the transmission was slipping, the brakes were soft, one of the taillights was kaput and the finish was showing the general ill-effects of long-term on-street parking. But I wasn't telling him that, whoever he was. "$4990," I said. The market price. "Or nearest offer. Available for inspection all day."

He took my address and said he might drop round later. Much later, I hoped. I lay back down and pulled up the bedclothes. The phone rang again. "Are you the yellow Daihatsu Charade . . . ?"

By nine o'clock, I'd fielded six calls. Despairing of a lie-in, I got up and cooked myself breakfast. Cooked as in toasted. Two slices, dry. An orange juice and a serve of hi-fiber lo-taste cereal. Each bowl had more roughage than a coir doormat. In celebration of the weekend, I spoiled myself and demolished two of them. Tea without milk.

Saturday and Sunday were lay days on the personal-training front. Apart from lugging the papers home from the corner store, my only form of weekend exercise was a bit of domestic horticulture. And after I'd gone out into the courtyard and fertilized the lemon tree, even that was taken care of.

There was no lawn to mow, no hedge to trim, no path to sweep. Apart from the brick-paved courtyard, large enough only for my well-tended gin-and-tonic tree and a cast-iron patio setting, there was no garden at all. Nor was there anything else requiring more maintenance than could be done with a kitchen knife and a wet rag.

Handy I was not. A lesson it had taken me seven years to learn, at the cost of many a bruised thumb and bent nail. When Wendy and I went our separate ways, the first thing I did was sell our renovator's-opportunity in West Brunswick and move back to already renovated Fitzroy. A modest two-bedroom terrace in a quiet little street at the city end of Brunswick Street, all for a measly hundred and fifty grand. Worth ten grand less since the real estate market hit an iceberg and sank. But as long as I wasn't planning on moving house, and still had a job that let me keep up the payments, the bank and I were quite content with it.

With breakfast eaten, the papers read, and the first of my potential buyers yet to arrive, I lit a cigarette and rang Wendy. *Choose the right psychological moment to start*, instructed the brochure in the pack of Nicabate patches. *Pick a day when you are less likely to be stressed*. Any day I was required to speak with Wendy definitely did not fulfil that criterion.

I'd rung her the previous evening but found only the answering machine. As a senior corporate executive and the wife of a prominent Sydney lawyer, she obviously had better things to do with her time than return her ex-husband's messages. Even if she did get a substantial staff discount on the cost of the call. "What is it this time?" she said.

Four years we'd been divorced, no fault all round. Don't get me started.

I told her about Brian Morrison's offer. Not the consultancy bit, just the part about Red presenting the torch to the IOC Evaluation Commission. It was short notice, I knew, but what did she think? Red could fly down on Thursday, do the relay bit, stay on for the weekend. He'd miss out on school, I admitted, but going absent for a couple of days in the sixth grade wasn't going to ruin his chances at a Rhodes Scholarship. Assuming, of course, that he wanted to come.

"He won't want to stay the weekend," Wendy said. "He'd miss his rugby game. And that might affect his chances of selection for the state side."

"Red's playing rugby?"

He'd been living in Sydney for a while, so I should've been prepared for this. Still, it was a disturbing development. My little boy, seduced from his roots, wallowing like a brute in the mud, his nose broken, his head up the arse of some future detective-sergeant in the New South Wales drug squad.

"Union, of course," said Wendy. "Not League." The distinction was too fine for me. Something about one being a game for thugs played by gentlemen and vice versa. But it got worse. "Richard thinks Red shows real promise." Richard was the new husband, a Crown prosecutor with an income in the high six figures, a yacht at the Rushcutters Bay marina and considerably more influence than I had on my son's life. "He's been very encouraging."

"So what happened to the cult of the warrior?" I said. "Changed your tune about the rituals of male bonding?"

"Sport has been very good for Red's self-esteem," she said. "Richard doesn't think we should stand in the boy's way."

"Especially not if he's running through the Hyatt ballroom with a flaming torch in his hand," I said. "Can I talk to him?"

She'd have him ring me, she said, when he got home from the junior-league game. But, in principle, she had no objection if he wanted to fly down for a night or two. "Did Brian Morrison say anything about accommodation?"

"I didn't ask," I said. "I assumed he'd stay here."

"With you blowing smoke all over him?"

"I've given up," I said, exhaling away from the phone. "I'm on the patches." Or would be by Wednesday.

"Bit of a dump, isn't it?" she sniffed.

The inference was unwarranted. Red's Melbourne digs may have lacked the water views of his new stepfather's semi-detached at Darling Point, but they were perfectly adequate to his needs. Red had, in fact, been a prime consideration when I bought the house. He had a room of his own and, on the three or four occasions a year his mother's schedule permitted Red to stay with his father in Melbourne, he found all of his familiar things waiting for him.

Okay, so he'd outgrown the Masters of the Universe pillowcase and no longer played with Skeletor and the other inhabitants of Castle Grayskull. But the movie posters from the video rental store were reasonably up-to-date, his skateboard was in perfect working condition and several pairs of clean socks were standing by if required. And, if he climbed onto the window sill and held his head at the right angle, he could see right over the neighboring rooftops as far as the high-rise Housing Commission flats on the other side of Brunswick Street.

The rest of the house, too, wasn't exactly a slum. Luxurious, even, if you counted the adjustable shower nozzle and the microwave oven. The mortgage was certainly top-class and managed to hoover up a fair whack of my salary, what was left after I shipped four hundred dollars a month north for child support. Not that I regretted a penny of it. It probably paid for the upkeep on Wendy and Richard's new in-ground pool, thereby preventing Red from getting chlorine poisoning.

"Ask him to call me, please," I said to her. "If he wants to do it, I need to confirm with Brian Morrison asap." As soon as Wendy rang off, the first of my customers arrived.

The Daihatsu, I'd decided, was not worth the expense of fixing. The arithmetic just didn't add up. More often than not, I trammed it or walked to work. Even with a permit, finding a parking spot was practically impossible. Registration, insurance, repairs, tickets. All up, for a man in my situation, car ownership was a losing proposition. Cab vouchers and an occasional dip in the departmental carpool would, I'd decided, see to my transport needs. Selling the Daihatsu would be a mutually beneficial congruence of private and public policy.

Three weeks earlier, I'd put a handwritten For Sale notice on the board in the staff lunchroom at Water Supply, and stuck up photocopies around the office. The only expression of interest had come from the shop steward in Faults & Emergencies. He took my details and said he'd ring to arrange an inspection time but never called back. Perhaps I'd have more luck with my ad in the newspaper.

My first callers were a young couple with a newborn baby, looking for a second car so she could take the little mite to the baby health center while hubby was at work. She was exhausted and the two of them looked like they didn't have two pennies to rub together. They stared blankly under the hood, whispered to each other about the broken taillight and asked vague questions about the mileage. When they left without asking for a test-drive, I was relieved.

Invidious business, selling a car privately. Even before I'd begun, I was having second thoughts.

"Watch the brakes," I warned the next caller, a young buck in skin-tight stonewash. I had him pegged as a spotter for a dealer, but that didn't stop me talking down the merchandise. He left the keys to his own car in lieu and took the Charade for a quick burn around the block.

"The shockers are shot," he said on his return. "Four grand. Take it or leave it." I may have lacked the killer instinct of a true used-car salesman, but I wasn't that much of a soft touch. I left it.

The rest of the day was spent fielding a steady but tepid stream of shoppers. Fathers with teenage daughters. Wary migrants. First-car buyers on a budget. More spotters. Every time it took off on a test-drive, I broke out in a mild sweat and braced myself for the distant sound of impact.

In between, I pottered around the house, dusting Red's room

and listening to the football on the radio. In preparation for *Quit Day*, as the Nicabate brochure referred to it, I cleared away all the ashtrays. More saucers than ashtrays, really. The real ashtrays had been disposed of long ago. As a method of fortifying the intent to give up cigarettes, ashtray removal was, in my experience, far from foolproof.

Nor was the news on the football front encouraging. Fitzroy started behind and stayed that way all day, thrashed by Melbourne out at VFL Park. No joy for Denis, either. The Swans were demolished in the third quarter by a resurgent St. Kilda. Not even the home-ground advantage helped.

By five o'clock, I'd had seven inspections, four test-drives and no sale. With each new caller, I felt worse. Not only had I failed to make a sale, I felt like a huckster attempting to palm off an agglomeration of mechanical deficiencies as a functioning automobile. First thing the next morning, I decided, I would shop it around the car-yards. The return would be five hundred dollars lower but I'd sleep easier at night. It wasn't as if I really needed the money, after all. Wasn't I about to pick up an easy five grand, courtesy of Brian Morrison and the MOB?

That's when my final caller turned up. A nondescript, rather taciturn bloke with a brown cardigan and a stammer. Undeterred by the vehicle's catalogue of deficiencies, he insisted that he was s-still interested, s-subject to a t-test-drive. Which he t-took, leaving a single key on a leather braid. "It's the g-green Camimirra at the end of the s-street," he said and burbled off in the Charade.

I put on a Roy Orbison album and ironed some shirts and, after twenty minutes, began to w-wonder just how f-far my potential buyer had gone. Perhaps he'd hit a mechanical snag. Or another vehicle. When he hadn't returned in three-quarters of an hour, I started to get toey. I needed cigarettes anyway, so I left a note and wandered down to Brunswick Street.

A few hundred meters down the hill, it was all cafes and patisseries and bookshops. Up my end, close to the housing project, the tone was still defiantly downmarket. Smelly derelicts in crap-encrusted overcoats dozed on the tram stop outside the Little Sisters of the Poor. The drone of post-match commentary leaked from the Rob Roy Hotel. The crusty whiff of old souvlaki hung in the air. Across the road, at the foot of the flats, Chinese fathers pushed little girls in ornate chiffon dresses on the swings in the playground and turbo-heads with soapy forearms washed their GT-XLs in the carpark.

Cars crawled past anonymously or throbbed by with the windows down and the stereo up. But none of them was a butter yellow Daihatsu Charade with a busted taillight, *Any Reasonable Offer Considered*. I bought cigarettes at the Asian grocery, lit up in the odor of sesame oil and overripe jackfruit, and went back home.

Nobody was waiting, so I took the key on the leather braid down to the green Camira parked at the end of the street. It was a poor fit and, as I jiggled in the lock, a bloke opened the door of the nearest house. "Right there, are you, mate?" he said, and I knew immediately that I'd been dudded. That Mr. Stammers had given me a useless key in exchange for my 1979 Japanese hatchback with 67,000 on the clock and a bald spare tire.

Hardly worth his trouble, really, but not a bad deal from my point of view, considering the piece of shit was fully insured for a replacement value of five grand. If it stayed stolen, was chopped up for spare parts or pushed off a cliff in the Wombat State Forest, I'd be laughing.

The Fitzroy cop shop was near the flats, a cream brick attachment at the rear of the town hall. I waited another hour, then went over and reported my tragic loss. The duty officer, a buzz-cut lug fresh from the academy, gave me some superfluous advice and a piece of paper for the insurance company. It was a story that got me a good laugh at Faye and Leo's dinner party that night.

Faye and Leo were neighbors who lived in a big terrace on the other side of my back lane. Their son Tarquin was the same age as Red, and the two boys had been friends since back when they were in kindergarten together. Faye was a gourmet cook and an inveterate matchmaker. At seven-thirty, I dug up a bottle of Mount Ida shiraz, nicked across the lane and knocked on her back door.

"Only the lonely," I hummed, knocking on the back door. "Dum, dum, dum, dewy, dum, dum."

This time, Faye was well wide of the mark. Wide being the operative word. Her candidate was a generously proportioned children's book illustrator with a laugh like a flock of seagulls being sucked backward into the engine of a jumbo jet. A real tryer, she insisted on reading my palm over the poached pears and praline parfait. I had, she said, a particularly pronounced love-line. When I finally succeeded in retrieving my hand, I suggested we all walk down to the tapas bars in Johnston Street for a nightcap. Once there, I managed to flee unnoticed by slipping off the end of the conga line during a Gypsy Kings number.

Red rang on Sunday morning, gung-ho for the torch relay. "All the other kids at Little Aths are spewing," he said.

Wendy came on the line. "I've decided to come down, too," she said. "I'm due to touch base with the Melbourne office anyway." Lucky them. "And Brian Morrison says the MOB will pay for a suite at the Hyatt."

"You've spoken to Brian?"

"I was talking to Sandra on the phone and Brian just happened to be there." The woman's presumption was unbelievable. A long time ago she presumed to be my wife. "He agrees that the hotel is more convenient from a press-availability point of view. And I thought it'd be a bit of a treat for Red. Something different." From his room at his father's house, for example.

"But . . ." The word froze on my lips and I conceded defeat.

It would've been petulant to do otherwise. She was right about the hotel being an adventure for the kid. Up there on the sixteenth floor, jumping on the beds, ordering room service, souveniring the Do Not Disturb sign, leaving wet towels on the bathroom floor. Rock 'n' roll heaven. If I was Red, I knew what I'd prefer.

"We'll come down Wednesday so Red can visit his grandparents. He hasn't seen them all year. Richard would like to come, too. But he's got a big case."

As distinct from a small penis.

8

FIRST THING MONDAY MORNING I rang Automotive & General and explained my predicament.

A form could be mailed to me, I was informed in the cheeseparing tones characteristic of the insurance industry, but my claim would be processed only after the standard thirty-day waiting period applicable in auto-theft cases. Full details of which could be found on my policy document. If I happened to have a microscope handy. In the meantime, should I require the use of a vehicle, interim arrangements could possibly be made, subject to approval by an assessor. Shoot me the form, I said. Hold the assessor. The exercise will do me good.

And so it did, although the most auspicious moment to commence the patch cure had not yet arrived. There were certain formalities to be transacted before I donned the cloak and dagger of MOB's Secret Emissary to the Renegade Native. The small matter of obtaining the approval of my employer. The man who paid my wages, Angelo Agnelli.

I set off through the mild morning sunshine and walked up the hill past the flats and St. Patrick's to the rear entrance of Parliament House. On the way, I detoured via the hospital consulting rooms, hoping for an accidental encounter with the refreshingly candid

Dr. Phillipa Verstak. Thoughts of her had come to me unbidden on more than one occasion during the weekend and I was disappointed not to find her among the puffers at the portal.

I did, however, find Angelo Agnelli. He was in his parliamentary lair, one of a row of utilitarian, glass-walled cubicles in the vaulted catacombs beneath the Legislative Council. He'd returned from the Canberra confabulation on the weekend, newly conversant with progress on the Perth to Darwin rail link and plans to irrigate the Simpson Desert with overflow from the Tasmanian glacial thaw. Feet on the wood-veneer desk, he was refreshing his memory on a money bill he was about to propel through the Upper House on behalf of the Treasurer.

"As I understand it," he yawned, displaying his bridgework and the damp splotches in the armpits of his shirt, "we put the state debt on Visa, which we then pay off using our Mastercard."

After two terms in office, Angelo's heart was no longer in it. The first flush of his reforming zeal had generated a certain pale incandescence but now even that feeble light was dimming, exhausted by the recognition that his larger ambitions would remain unrealized. He would, he had belatedly come to understand, never be Attorney General. At forty-five, Angelo was a man with a fluorescent future behind him.

Even his boyish good looks were beginning to go. With remarkable speed, his chubby cheeks had hit the downhill slope to jowldom and his well-cultivated bella figura was beginning to take on the faded aspect of a run-down resort hotel. Angelo, I didn't doubt, remained firmly on the side of the angels but the only song the heavenly host had been singing in his ear lately was the current balance on his parliamentary superannuation.

"Godfather," I said. "I've had an offer you can't refuse."

He leaned back and folded his hands over his paunch. "It's this fucking fitness jag you're on," he said. "Now you've gone and got yourself drafted into the Woeful McKenzie All Stars."

"Woeful's already spoken to you?" My decision, apparently, was a foregone conclusion.

"Told me at caucus this morning." Angelo and Woeful were factional allies, each reliant on the other for his place in Cabinet. "Woeful McKenzie's a fucking idiot. And if the Olympic bid needs your help, we must be in deep shit. But I've told Woeful he can have you for a week. Any longer and he'll have to start paying you out of his own budget."

"A week'll do it," I said. Three days, tops.

Ange stood up, took his jacket off the back of his chair and handed it to me. "What's happening with the union negotiations?"

"Same as usual," I said, helping him into his jacket. "SFA. Nothing the bureaucrats can't handle. The Missos are all talk, anyway."

He did up his button and shot his cuffs. Mr. Minister. "Play your cards right with this one, you might do yourself a bit of good with Hugh Knowles & Co." Pausing briefly on his way out the door, he laid a fatherly hand on my shoulder. "Time you were thinking about the future, Murray."

With that worryingly ambiguous advice ringing in my ears, I strolled the short distance to the Old Treasury Building, soaking up the sunshine and a couple of cubic meters of carcinogenic vapor. General Gordon looked down disapprovingly. What would he know? He was dead.

Brian Morrison's base of operations was on the top floor, up where the heritage carpeting ran out and the real work got done. It was less an office than a command center, a bunker with a view. A dozen or so gray metal desks squeezed into the room. The paintwork was peeling and the lights hung by chains from the ceiling. Piles of press releases and media kits covered every surface, computer consoles glowed, phones rang and staff bustled. With the exception of Brian, they were all female. But then Brian was always a firm believer in getting the best man for the job, especially if he was in charge.

The man himself was standing at a white-board, the Darth Vader of Community Relations, mapping a media schedule with a woman I recognized as the former political roundsperson for the *Sun*. Taped to the wall behind them were front-page stories on the progress of the bid. THUMBS UP FROM IOC BOSS, read one, illustrated by a flattering photograph of Juan Antonio Samaranch. In little more than a year, this ancient gnomic Catalan had become a household name to Melburnians, his every utterance divined for evidence of our city's Olympic prospects. The arrival of any of his IOC associates in town was reported with all the solemnity of a papal visit.

Covering another wall was a large-scale map of the eastern seaboard on which the course of the torch relay was traced in thick red marker pen. A cardboard arrow captioned "Today" pointed to a spot on the Princes Highway halfway between Eden and Disaster Bay.

"Murray," cried Brian, as if my arrival was a complete surprise. "Great news, mate. It's all fixed."

Rummaging briefly among the paperwork littering one of the desks, he thrust a document into my hand. The torch-relay schedule for the following Thursday. Redmond Whelan, 8 P.M., Hyatt Hotel ballroom. Brian instantly replaced it with my letter of agreement, ready for signature. It was one of those vague "duties as agreed" deals, about as legally binding as the fine print on a chewing-gum wrapper. I signed, using Brian's gold-nibbed Mont Blanc. He hastily pocketed the paper and handed me an engraved entree card.

In Honor of the Visit of IOC Evaluation Commissioners
Pascal Abdoulaye, Kim U-ee and Stansislas Dziczkowszczak,
the Board of the MOB invites
MURRAY WHELAN AND GUEST
to Attend a Gala Dinner
at the Savoy Ballroom, Hyatt-on-Collins,
Thursday 26 April, 1990 at 7:30 P.M. RSVP.

"Two hundred dollars per," he said. "I've arranged for it to be deducted from your fee."

From now on, Brian instructed, I was to liaise directly with Denis Dogherty. As for Ambrose Buchanan, Brian suggested we meet informally. Officially, Buchanan was Visiting Lecturer in Identity and Ideology in the Faculty of Dispossession and Displacement at Footscray Institute of Technology. But he was only ever on campus on Fridays. In the meantime, he could be found at the Stars Cafe in Gertrude Street, Fitzroy, around about lunchtime.

"Welcome aboard, then," he concluded. "We're relying on you." The beeper on his belt began to vibrate and the mobile phone in his pocket started ringing. Two frighteningly efficient-looking women hovered peripherally with items to be actioned.

"Find your own way out, can you?" Brian said.

As I reached the ground-floor hallway, a tottering aristocrat was being feted into the exhibition room by an entourage of suits. *"Par ici, Monsieur,"* I heard someone say. *"S'il vous plait."* As the doors closed behind them, a second voice spoke. *"Manuyangka nyiyarlangurlu, jarntungku marda, yankirrirli . . ."*

It sounded pretty convincing to me. But then I don't speak French.

9

LUNCHTIME, by any reasonable estimate, was still at least an hour away. I lit a cigarette and headed for the City Club. After pigging out at Faye's matchmaking dinner and sleeping most of Sunday, I was in need of a solid workout.

I did a double round of sets on the super circuit, jogged a couple of kilometers on the treadmill and was warming down when Holly Deloite came and stood beside the bike. She was wearing shorts and a polo top with a penguin stitched on the pocket. Even her knees looked fit. "Um," she said, sheepishly. "Sorry about the other day."

"Magilla Gorilla?" I exhaled, knees pumping, thirty-seven seconds left on the clock, T-shirt plastered to me like a wet Kleenex.

She made a face. "I used to go out with the guy, can you believe it? His name's Steve Radeski. He worked downstairs at the night-club. You know, Typhoon. Haven't seen him for ages, then he starts turning up here, pestering me. Wants me to go out with him again. I mean, as if."

All her sentences seemed to end on a rising note. A phonetic question mark which compelled a response. Which I was in no position to offer. Merely breathing was difficult enough.

"He's a jerk," she said, shaking her head in disbelief. That she'd ever got involved with him, I supposed. "And he's getting to be a real pain in the butt. If he keeps coming back, he'll get me fired. Garth reckons he frightens the clients."

I dismounted, calves trembling, thighs in spasm. Hoping I wouldn't pass out from the sudden rush of oxygen, I sucked in a lungful of air, flexed my arms, and made muscle. "If he hassles you again, bay-bee," I exhaled, "he'll have me to deal with."

"Gee, that's a relief," she grinned. A thought crossed her mind, leaving its footprints on her forehead. "Um," she said. "You got a car?"

"Uh-huh." Being so easily gulled out of my motor, I'd decided, didn't show me in my best light. And, if you don't have a car, people think you're a crank. "Why?"

Holly smiled again and the crease in her brow went away. "Just wondering," she said. "Need a fresh towel or anything?"

While I changed back into my Hugo Boss, I considered dashing home and slipping into something a little more informal for my meeting with Ambrose. But there was enough bullshit flying around already. Might as well play the part. Besides which, it was already one o'clock. Time to rock. I caught a Number 3 tram in Collins Street, rode past St. Pat's and St. Vincent's and was in Fitzroy in less than ten minutes, my hair still wet from the shower.

The flats rose a sheer twenty stories into the cirrus-streaked sky, throwing a shadow across Gertrude Street. I walked in the shade cast by a row of nineteenth-century buildings, survivors of the slum clearances of the 1950s that had threatened half of Fitzroy with demolition in the name of progress and clean living.

Past the Champion Hotel, a bloodhouse of the more traditional kind. Lingerie Lunches, said the hand-painted sign on the tinted-glass window. Topless Barmaids. Past the Lebanese chicken bar where the chickens were rumored to come with special herbs for those who knew the password. Past the Tai Lai Unisex hair salon and the Commonwealth Bank, filled with single mothers waiting to cash their pension checks. Past the Aboriginal Health Service, formerly the inner-metro clap clinic, with its red, black and yellow facade and its perpetual gaggle of Koories on the front steps.

Long ago, long before the Greek man came, all this land belonged to the black man. Now he had claimed it again. Apart from the Macedonians, the Serbs, the Cambodians, the Ethiopians and the Tongans, this end of Gertrude Street was an exclusively Aboriginal precinct. Darktown, all half a block of it.

The Stars Cafe was a high-ceilinged, linoleum-floored corner room with a self-service counter and pine tables, part of a moldering row of ornately decorated Victorian terraces. Presuming such places still existed, it might have been the cafeteria at a country railway station.

A haze of steam rose from a bain-marie, misting the windows and carrying with it the aroma of vegetable water and baked meat. Two women in aprons stood beside a tea urn, buttering bread in the roar of the dishwashing machine surging through the servery hatch from the kitchen. The place was almost full, thick with the rhubarb of conversation and the clatter of crockery. Aboriginality lay lightly dusted across the clientele, as unmistakable as a pinch of cinnamon.

I recognized Ambrose Buchanan immediately. It wasn't hard. He was the darkest man in the room. His beard was a little longer than in the video, the flecks of white more pronounced, but he still wore the same battered denims and the same air of restless engagement. He was holding court at the end of a long table, leaning back casually in his chair, giving the good oil to a bunch of teenage Koories with bad-boy earrings. They stood there, hanging on his every word. Or maybe just hanging, hands thrust deep into the pockets of their Air Jordan windbreakers. A bulging leather valise, crammed with papers, sat on the floor beside his chair.

As I came through the door, he looked across the room and immediately marked me as being there for him. Either that or a lost businessman who'd mistaken the place for one of those gravlax and goat cheese joints that littered Fitzroy like noxious weeds.

I nodded at him and he nodded back. We held each other's gaze for a moment, then he inclined his head toward the chalkboard menu. I picked up a tray and he returned to his conversation.

The ham salad came with a slice of canned beets and a circle of fresh orange. Bush tucker. At the Stars, even the gastronomic flourishes were survivors. By the time I carried my plate to Ambrose's table, his homeboy disciples were farewelling him with elaborate soul shakes. They leered at me scornfully and loped to another table, all boneless legs and jutting elbows and acquired attitude.

Ambrose extended a leg under the table and pushed out a chair. "Got a call to say someone was coming. Thought I recognized the name."

"Ambrose." I accepted the offered seat, clearing aside a litter of used crockery to make space for my plate. "Didn't think you'd remember me."

"Oh, I remember all right." He tilted back in his seat and scrutinized me thoroughly. "Never saw a man so scared in all my life. "Course you've put on a bit of weight since then, eh?"

"You should talk, graybeard," I said. "Old man of the tribe now, are you?"

Ambrose scratched his whiskers. "Last of the old-time cheeky blackfellers. Come to warn me off, eh?"

"Maybe it's to invite you aboard."

"Your salad's getting warm," he said. I sawed off a couple of mouthfuls of limp lettuce and he studied me as I chewed. "Why you?" he said, after a while. "Any particular reason they sent you?"

Not the reason he thought. I wanted that clear from the outset. "Just lucky, I guess."

"Not planning on calling in any old debts, eh?"

"Didn't know there were any."

"No?" He was skeptical. "So, you're here to tell me what a great thing it'll be for Aboriginal people if Melbourne gets the Olympic Games, eh? To tell me all about the great contribution Koories have made to Australia's sporting history." He jerked his chin at something past my shoulder and I turned to look.

I'd been wondering about the Stars. And there they were. One entire wall of the cafe was lined with sporting trophies. A vast silver array of cups, medallions, shields, pennants and boxing belts. I'd seen engraver's shops with smaller displays. Hung at intervals between the trophies were framed photographs of Aboriginal sporting heroes.

Doug Nichols, rejected by Carlton on account of his color. And the other magical black footballers who came after him. The great Polly Farmer. Syd Jackson, the best half-forward flanker of his generation. The Krakouer brothers. Maurice Rioli. Nicky Winmar. Derek Kickett. Gilbert McAdam. Boxers, too, of course. Lionel Rose, bantamweight champion of the world. Tony Mundine, title-holder in four separate weight divisions. Plenty of others that I didn't recognize, women as well as men.

More than just a tribute to athletic prowess and an extraordinary accumulation of historical mementos, the display was an affirmation of black pride. A collective up-yours to the entire gubba world. When I turned back, Ambrose had taken a manilla folder from his overstuffed portmanteau and put it on the table between us.

"Three," he said.

"Three what?"

"That's the number of indigenous athletes this country has selected to represent it in the ninety years it's been competing in the Olympics."

"Point made," I said. "But it's the view of the MOB that attracting the Games to Australia will radically increase the opportunity for Aboriginal participation." I recited the official formula without pretense at enthusiasm.

"Radically, eh?" Ambrose stroked his whiskers.

"Considerably, then."

"So what do we get? Didgeridoo anthem at the opening ceremony? Exclusive rights to the souvenir boomerang concession? Bit of this sort of thing?" He opened the folder and pushed a photograph across the table, a glossy 8 x 10 print.

Ambrose Buchanan traveled fast and light but that didn't stop him doing his homework. The photo was a true classic. You could date it immediately from the wide lapels and short haircuts, the smug potato-fed faces.

A group of white men was standing around an Aborigine, grinning at the camera, relishing a joke. The black man was the joke. He had a gangly stork-like build and he was so black he looked like he was chiseled out of anthracite. A white singlet hung pathetically from his bony shoulders and baggy white shorts dangled to his knees. Five interlocked rings decorated the chest of his singlet and he held aloft a sputtering Olympic torch. The white men were slapping his back, urging him forward with mocking enthusiasm. He was staring straight into the camera, his teeth dazzling, his eyes pools of bewildered terror.

"This the sort of thing they've got in mind, eh?" Ambrose made it a high rhetorical flourish, loud enough for faces all around the room to turn our way. "Well, fuck that shit."

We were, I implicitly understood, actors in a piece of public theater. I was the gubba in the suit, the snake in the garden, up to no good. Ambrose was the righteous brother, champion of the community, refusing to be drawn into any backroom treachery.

Playing my role, I did my best to look chastened, waiting until our audience turned back to its lunch. "No need for the history lesson," I said. "You've already got them worried. They want to know if you're just going to blow hard in general or if you're planning something in particular."

"This is where I'm supposed to issue a demand for land rights over the proposed baseball stadium, eh?"

"Where the Gunditjmara used to assemble for friendly contests of spear-throwing," I suggested.

"That right? Sounds like we'd better get the lawyers on the job. In the meantime, finish your lettuce and come take a look at this."

Past the kitchen, narrow stairs led downward. Sports posters lined the walls, their edges curling. Dusky-skinned ruckmen taking high marks, runners breasting finishing tapes, high-jumpers clearing crossbars. The muffled thud of reggae rose to meet us as we descended into the pong of sweat and leather.

The basement had windowless cement walls, a floor-level boxing ring, a pair of heavy punching bags suspended from a low ceiling, a speedball and a rack of free weights. An Easter Island statue stood in the corner, feeding towels into an antique twin-tub washing machine.

A young man in a singlet and track pants was sitting on the edge of a press bench, curling barbells. He was maybe twenty years old, medium height, slight build, not an ounce of fat. He wore a knitted black beanie, pulled down almost to his eyebrows. He might have been a very swarthy Sicilian but for the angle of his cheekbones, the fullness of his lips and the slight flare of his nostrils. The land-rights slogan on his singlet, too, was a dead giveaway. For a boxer, he was slightly built. Somewhere between bantam and fly, I guessed. Rosella weight, budgerigar weight.

We stood at the bottom of the stairs, checking it out. Ambrose was in a frisky mood. He did a quick dance around the heavy bag. Muhammad Ali. Jab, jab.

The arm-curler ignored him, his face impassive, absorbed in his task. His arms pumped mechanically in time with the rastafarian rhythm emanating from a ghetto blaster. I dawdled on the spot, hands in pockets, taking it in. Such as it was. No atrium-roofed pool here, no fluffy towels, no sauna. Just hungry determination and hard training and rising damp. The tape ended and the curler finished his set and returned the weights to their rack.

Ambrose danced over. "You're Darcy Anderson, aren't you? Ernest's cousin? I'm Ambrose Buchanan."

Darcy bobbed his head, nodding listlessly, eyes downturned. The name Anderson rang a distant bell in the back of my mind. I couldn't quite place it, but I felt for the kid, living in the shadow of some high-achieving relation.

"So how's it going?" Ambrose picked up a barbell, tested its heft.

Young Darcy had the eloquence of the true athlete. "Orright," he shrugged. "I 'spose."

The Easter Island statue dropped the lid on the washer and kicked it into juddering action. Ambrose shadow-boxed, beckoning him over.

Maxie was built like Samoa after the cyclone, his brow a solid ridge of ancient scar tissue. He was some sort of islander mix. Part Polynesian, part Melanesian, part brick shithouse. He crossed the gym with the proprietary waddle of a troll in its lair, the subterranean servant of some volcano god. Ambrose danced close and swung wide, knuckles balled. Maxie raised a languid hand and absorbed the punch in his open palm, smothering Ambrose's fist in fingers the size of bread rolls.

"This is Murray Whelan," said Ambrose. "Maxie's in charge down here. He used to box with Sharman's." Taking all comers in a traveling tent show. Five quid to any mug lair who could knock him down.

Maxie let go of Ambrose's fist and extended his massive hand. I took it tentatively and found it as soft as a feather pillow. I pumped it once and let go before it smothered my entire arm. "Now don't you go disturbing this man's training, Ambrose," he growled.

Darcy picked up a rope and started skipping on the spot. The rope was taped together at the handles and the spot was worn shiny from a million shuffling footfalls. We watched him get into his stride, his spidery legs flying.

"He's dead keen," rumbled Maxie. "In here at lunchtime, nights."

"What class does he box in?" I said, trying to pretend I knew what I was talking about.

"Box?" Maxie stared at me blankly. "Darcy couldn't box to save his life. Triathlon, that's his sport." He mimed the actions — running, cycling, swimming. "Rated third in the state, seventh nationally. Working himself up for the national titles. Wouldn't hurt a fly. Would you, Darce?"

Darcy pounded on, oblivious, sweat beading on his upper lip. I grinned stupidly, tripped up on a ready stereotype.

"Murray here's from that MOB mob," Ambrose told Maxie. "The Olympic bid, y'know."

"That right?" Maxie looked at me anew. "What are our chances?"

"You'd better ask Ambrose that," I said.

"I'd say it's still an open question, eh?" Ambrose nodded toward Darcy. "Doin' okay, is he?"

Maxie shrugged, a tectonic realignment of continent-sized

shoulder blades. "Reckon he'd have a better chance if that jailbird cousin of his kept away."

Ambrose frowned. "Deadly's out, eh?"

Darcy pounded on the spot, mind turned inward. Maxie gave a disgusted grunt. "Been hangin' round, trying to buddy-up to young Darce here. Goin' the long-lost cuz. Bad news, that one. I run him off."

"Yeah, well." Ambrose started dancing again, sparring backward, out of Maxie's impassive range. "Better you than me."

We went back upstairs and helped ourselves to tea at the urn. The lunch rush was over, the crowd thinning. Our table had been cleared and wiped and Ambrose's folder set back in place. We sat down and I waited for the pitch. Ambrose gazed toward the trophy cabinet and adopted a pensive air.

"I have a dream," he said at last. "As they say in Pitjantjatjara. A Koori Institute of Sport. State-of-the-art equipment. Culturally appropriate residential facilities. Scholarships. All tailored to the specific needs of the indigenous athlete."

For fifteen minutes, without drawing breath, he pitched his proposition. Spoke of how sport had once been a ticket out of the native reserves. How blacks played in a world of white games, white rules, white officials and selectors, never partners in the enterprise. How discrimination persisted. How difficult some found success, particularly when it took them away from their families. How an Aboriginal Sports Institute could maximize the potential of future generations of indigenous athletes.

He didn't need to sell me. If the MOB was worried about Australia's race-relations image among the sporting world's heavy-hitters, an Aboriginal Institute of Sport would be a very smart card to play. Incorporate the idea in the bid prospectus, have the state pitch in a bit of seeding money, talk up the national focus and slide the whole thing sideways to the feds. A bargain, considering the potential pay-off. A win-win situation, I could hear Brian Morrison calling it.

"Well worth exploring," I said when Ambrose finally shut up. "If we get the Games."

"If? You don't sound too confident. We were hoping for a bit more enthusiasm."

"We?"

He jerked his chin across the room to where his young acolytes were hunkered down at a table of their peers, bullshitting and smoking cigarettes. "The community," he said. "Young people angry and frustrated at the lack of opportunity." From where I was sitting, the community looked about as angry as a swarm of enraged tree sloths. Not that it mattered. High-pressure tactics wouldn't be needed to sell this idea. It was a stroke of marketing genius.

"It would need to be adequately resourced to work properly," I said. "The MOB would need to make representation to Woeful McKenzie, the Sports Minister. Get him to run it up to Cabinet for in-principle approval. Before that, some basic issues need to be sorted out. Funding issues, federal-state issues, management issues. Of course, I'll need some costings first."

Ambrose was glazing over. "You're the bureaucrat," he said. He opened his file and dug out a page of jottings. Big-picture stuff, no detail. "I see my old mate Pascal Abdoulaye is due in town."

I stared at him blankly. A newspaper clipping emerged from the file. IOC CHIEFS TO RECEIVE RELAY TORCH. Ah, yes, I remembered. The Evaluation Commission honcho. One of Samaranch's point men. As seen on my invitation card. "You know him?"

"He's the Senegalese ambassador to the European Community. I was on an anti-apartheid committee with him in Brussels. Maybe I could catch up with him at this thing with the kids."

My heart sank. "The torch relay?" I said, knowing what was coming next.

"That's the one. How come you haven't got a Koori kid handing over the torch, eh?"

Ah shit, I thought. Can't argue with that. Why hadn't Brian Morrison thought of it? "Good idea," I said, unenthusiastically. Red's disappointment, I felt sure, would not be fatal. Yet another fuck-up by good old Dad. "Got someone in mind?"

Ambrose's hand twitched absently, flicking the offer into oblivion. "Save the tokenism for the Talbots," he said. "As they say in Wurundjeri. I'm more interested in this Sports Institute. You think the MOB might buy the idea?"

"I'm just the messenger boy," I said. "But, personally, I think they'd be mad if they didn't. Got a number I can call you on?"

"You're in me office now," he said.

And that was it. A perfectly civilized discussion. Apart from an initial bit of pro-forma chest beating, Ambrose had been a pussycat. His proposition wasn't a threat. It was a golden opportunity. Brian Morrison's hysterics had been entirely unwarranted. If the MOB knocked back a winning idea like this Aboriginal Sports Institute, it didn't deserve to win the bid. All it need do was stick its imprimatur on the thing until seeding funds could be found. For very little money, the country could buy itself a shitload of goodwill with the gnomes of the IOC. And probably quite a few gold medals in the long term, considering the sporting potential of the Aboriginal population.

Maybe even one in triathloning. If synchronized swimming and curling could make the Olympic program, the pedal-run-swim combo was definitely in the race. As I waited at the tram stop on Gertrude Street, the conscientious young Darcy emerged from the side door of the Stars, a sports bag slung over his shoulder. Casually wading through the stream of slow-moving traffic, he headed across the street. Busy tanning my lungs in the sunshine, I paid him little attention. It was the other guys that caught my attention.

They were coming through the screen of trees between the undercroft of the high-rise and the street. It was little more than a scrubby cluster of shrubs designed to enhance the environment a little for the residents of the flats. Mostly it just accumulated scraps of litter. There were four of them, pissing around, kicking a can along in front of them and swearing loudly enough for the sound to carry across the street.

Skinheads were not a common sight in Melbourne. These ones must have bought their outfits from some British bovver-boy catalogue. Close-cropped hair, jeans turned up at the cuff, high-lace

Doc Martens, rolling gait. As they burst through the bushes, an Asian woman was coming along the footpath, pushing a child in a stroller. Before she could react, they had her surrounded. "Ching-chong-chonkie," sang one, clearly the spokesman of the group.

The woman attempted to ignore them, continuing on her way with as much dignity as possible. The child in the stroller was about eighteen months old. Its tiny cheeks were framed by a furry little hat with bear's ears. The skinheads pranced about making ching-chong noises, trying to get a rise out of the woman, but going no further. Even if they'd had the guts, they wouldn't have dared. Not in this neighborhood, not in broad daylight.

Already a couple of drinkers had spilled out of the hotel across the road and were watching the show, standing on the footpath with glasses of beer in their hands. The Asian woman turned into the flats just as Darcy cleared the traffic and reached the footpath. Looking for fresh game, the skinheads moved to block his path.

"You a dago or an Abo?" the gang's leading intellectual shouted. He probably lived in one of the leafier suburbs and decided to become a skinhead after the gloss went off train-surfing. Didn't want to waste his private school education.

Darcy shouldered him aside, disregarding the taunts. "Hey," yelled the skinhead. "We're talkin' to you."

As they started after the Koori, reinforcements joined the jeering crowd at the door of the hotel across the road, waving their pool cues for emphasis. "Piss off, you wankers," came a shout. From a safe distance, the skins lobbed a barrage of double-fingered salutes and incoherent witticisms. If not quite good natured, the exchange almost had a sporting quality, like it was a familiar game in which all the players were reprising old moves. Even by the debased standards of local street theater, it was a sorry spectacle. Maybe this happened every afternoon at about this time.

As quickly as it started, it was all over. Darcy had vanished into the housing estate beyond the flats. The skins clomped back the way they had come. The drinkers returned to the bar. I drew hard on my cigarette and flicked it into the gutter, leaning off the curb to signal an oncoming tram.

The meeting with Ambrose Buchanan had gone well. The easiest five grand a man ever made, paperwork pending. I was out of Water for the duration and Red's grip on the butane baton was secure. All was well with the world. The tram glided to a halt, brakes hissing, and I climbed aboard.

With one hand I found my Zone One All Day ticket, with the other the box of Nicabate. The psychological moment, I resolved, had arrived. Taking my seat, I undid two shirt buttons, tore open one of the little sealed envelopes and attached a patch to my midriff. This was going to be a piece of piss.

And so it would have been if, less than twelve hours later, young Darcy Anderson wasn't flat on his back on a slab in the morgue.

10

THE MINISTERIAL SUITE at the Department of Sport, Recreation, Racing and the Olympics was a snug berth for a couple of old Port Melbourne lads. Strolling distance to both parliament and the bid headquarters. Nice view across the Treasury Gardens. Comfortably clubbish brown leather furniture. A Skytel dish on the roof to keep the minister appraised of trackside conditions and starting prices. A well-stocked liquor cabinet. The only thing missing was the smell of cigars and the little pictures of bulldogs in derby hats playing snooker.

Denis Dogherty, more terrier than bulldog, raised his head from the paperwork on Woeful McKenzie's desk, pushed his glasses up onto his brow and massaged the bridge of his nose between thumb and forefinger. He looked like a wizened child at a school desk too big for him. "Park your carcass," he said. "Take the load."

I stood instead at the window. He came around the desk and joined me, nodding north in the general direction of Parliament House.

"Question Time," he said. "The boss'll be up on his feet right now, explaining to the opposition why the Totalisator Agency Board found it necessary to pre-purchase a ten-year supply of potato chips for its corporate hospitality box at Moonee Valley racecourse."

"And why did it?" I asked.

"Invite a few clients around for a drink," he said. "Nothing worse than running out of chips." He spoke with neither humor nor rancor, a man who would rather be somewhere else.

A cool change was blowing in from the south, a smear of gray that herded the stratocumulus before it as it advanced. Down below in the gardens a breeze rippled the leaves and gently swayed the branches. A couple more weeks and the color would be gone. Woody skeletons would thrust their fingers into a leaden sky. Denis nodded contemplatively down at the traffic crawling along Wellington Parade.

"Mug's Alley. That's what we used to call it. You had to be a mug to park there. A thieves' paradise. Bold as brass, they were. Come back, you'd find your wheels gone. Radio stripped, the works. All in broad daylight, too."

He shook his head. Not just in disbelief at such barefaced larceny, I suspected, but also at the passing of a more innocent time. Denis Dogherty had seen quite a few seasons come and go, and not all of them from the twelfth-floor window of a Minister of the Crown. He didn't have a political philosophy, at least none I'd ever heard him bother to articulate. He had a memory and he had a class. It made little difference that the class had changed beyond recognition and that the memory, too, was far from reliable.

"Ancient history," I said affably. "Which we will be if we don't win this bid."

Denis came out of his reverie. He marched back behind the desk and sat down beneath a framed photograph of the finish of the 1989 Cox Plate. Stylish Century and Empire Rose neck-and-neck at the post, courtesy of the Bloodstock Council of Victoria. "So," he said. "This Ambrose Buchanan going to be a fly in the ointment?"

"Not unless he's playing his cards very close to his chest." I gave him a detailed rundown of our conversation at the Stars.

"An Aboriginal Institute of Sport?" He chewed the idea over, nodding to himself. "You ever see that photo of Lionel Rose as a kid, barefoot beside a tin humpy? When he wins the world title, the bloody hypocrites turn around and give him a civic reception. Like that makes it all right. Criminal the way those people were treated. Maybe we could call it the Lionel Rose Institute."

"So you agree it's a good idea?"

"It's the sort of thing that floss merchant Brian Morrison should've come up with months ago. Christ knows he gets paid enough." Deserting the sinking ship had done nothing to endear Brian to Denis.

"Probably," I said. "But he should buy this. It's obviously well worth supporting."

Denis looked at me like I'd arrived with the last fall of rain. "Unfortunately, mate," he said, "merit is not sufficient grounds for making it onto the Olympic shopping list."

Obviously not. It never is, whatever the list. "I don't just mean for altruistic reasons," I said. "It's also a great selling point."

Denis rubbed his eyes and tried to hide his exasperation. "That's what everyone says about their pet project, Murray. And this late in the piece, four months to go till the decision, it's difficult to get the MOB to pick up any new proposal, no matter how marketable."

By the look of it, my little consultancy was going to be the shortest job in the history of employment. "So I go back and tell Ambrose Buchanan thanks but no thanks?"

"Not necessarily," he said. "But if we want to get this thing up, we'll need a bit of leverage."

"Leverage? What sort of leverage?"

"This sort." He picked up the phone and punched in a number. His combative instincts were kicking in. Whatever else he was doing, he was enjoying himself.

"Brian," he said into the phone. "Bad news, mate. Got Murray Whelan here with me, just back from talking to Ambrose Buchanan. You were right to expect trouble. Apparently Ambrose knows our African IOC. All part of the international brotherhood of the dusky-hued. Anyway, he's threatening to get into the bloke's ear, piss on our parade if we don't meet his demands. Wants our support for an Aboriginal Institute of Sport . . . Yeah, not a bad idea in itself . . . yeah . . ."

He leaned back in Woeful's big office chair and smiled conspiratorially as he listened to Brian's response. Tiberius on the telephone. "He mentioned the torch relay, too. High potential there for a media stunt. Just the sort of thing that gets international press coverage . . ."

On top of Woeful's credenza was a football on a little wooden rack, some sort of presentation number, covered in autographs. My hands found it and started tossing it back and forth between them.

Denis was laying it on with a trowel. "A very vulnerable time, especially with the Evaluation Commission in town . . . Ambrose could probably round up a war party of young Koories if he really wanted to make a pain in the arse of himself . . . Blackmail? Couldn't agree with you more . . ." He tipped me a broad wink. I flipped the ball end over end, going with the play.

For ten minutes they conferred, mapping out a way to get us off the hook. As I listened, I worked up a good spin. Just as I got the ball to balance on the tip of my forefinger, Denis hung up.

"This is the deal," he said. "You write up the proposal for the MOB's consideration. Brian does the spade-work to get it accepted as a matter of urgency. The MOB submits a formal request for government support. We lash it to the raft of projects to be considered by Cabinet on Thursday. If it goes through, Hugh Knowles can announce it at the big dinner that night."

"You certainly don't muck around, do you?" I said, genuinely impressed.

"You'd better not, either," he said. "If we're going to make the Cabinet agenda deadline, I'll need a draft submission by close of business today. Copy to Brian for distribution to MOB management. And he wants you on deck for their breakfast meeting tomorrow morning, in case of questions. Eight-thirty. Broad brushstrokes."

Given the notice, they'd be lucky to get a thin undercoat. "Anything else?" I said. Land-speed record? Four-minute mile?

Denis was back on his feet. "Use my office, save going back to

Water. I'll be over at the House, clueing Woeful up. Giving him his post-match rubdown."

He'd need one. The Liberals had the smell of blood and were cutting up rough, sure that power was about to drop into their waiting laps. Unless we won the bid, of course. All bets would be off if we won the bid. On his way out the door, Denis introduced me to Woeful's private secretary. "Carmel here'll do any typing you need for this, won't you, love?"

Carmel was one of those public-service perennials, the basilisk at the minister's door. A fifty-year-old Kim Novak who made the trains run on time and the tea for the boys in the backroom with equal equanimity. If she didn't know where the bodies were buried, I was prepared to bet, she had a pretty fair idea where the receipts for the shovels were filed. She was sharp as a tack, gave nothing away, typed 100 wpm and sized me up at a glance. "I'll stay until six," she said. "No later."

Denis paused in the doorway. "No longer than two pages. No more than half a million in seeding funds. And, for Chrissake, either kick that frigging football or put it back where it belongs."

Denis's office was a small, glass-walled work-station just down the corridor. He kept a neat desk, everything shipshape and Bristol fashion. I raided the stationery cupboard for pens and notepads and proceeded to make a mess of it. Tempus fugit, as they say in Walpiri.

For the next three hours, I gave free rein to my most creative bureaucratic faculties. Like an economist, I worked backward, fabricating arguments to fit my conclusions, bolstering them with statistics plucked from thin air. Employing the usual organizational models, an occasional phone call, a pocket calculator and a damp finger held up to the wind, I sketched a hypothetical management structure, ballparked a budget and identified plausible funding mechanisms for a High Intensity Training Program for Indigenous Athletes.

Properly speaking, such an endeavor was a federal matter. Properly speaking, a thorough feasibility study was required. Properly speaking, community consultation was the order of the day. But this wasn't a proper proposition. This was rabbit-and-hat territory, a pump-priming exercise. The bells and whistles could come later. Even if we lost the bid, the thing would at least get an airing. In the meantime, it was abracadabra rules.

By six o'clock, my little piece of embroidery had been typed and duplicated. The requisite number of copies had been dispatched to the Cabinet office for distribution with the weekly agenda papers, subject to the Premier's approval, and others sat in a neat pile on Woeful's desk. Five minutes after Carmel put the cover over her word-processor and headed for the train home, Denis returned from Parliament House. He reported that he'd had a word with the minister who, in turn, had cornered the Premier and requested that the matter be listed for consideration by Cabinet at its Thursday meeting.

Under the circumstances, Denis thought, it was the best result possible. "The Cabinet agenda's chock-a-block with budget issues at the moment, what with the Treasurer leaving his wallet in his other trousers. And the Premier's never been keen on last-minute inclusions. But he's agreed to think about it overnight, tell Woeful his decision in the morning."

Not a bad afternoon's mischief. Apart from the Premier's okay, only one matter remained outstanding. "Feel like a drink?" I said.

"You'd be all carrot juice and mineral water these days, wouldn't you?" said Denis. "A man with his sights on the big league." He took cans and chilled glasses from the well-stocked bar fridge built into the credenza. "Want a chip? There's plenty."

Normally, the first sip of beer had me reaching for a cigarette. This time, I realized with astonishment, I felt no such impulse. Cigarettes were a concept, an abstraction, an idea with which I was familiar. But I did not crave one, even mildly.

Four hours had passed since my last cigarette and, until the hops hit my mouth, I hadn't even noticed. Despite the wussy name, these Nicabate band-aids packed a real wallop. I touched the magic patch through the fabric of my shirt, giving it an encouraging pat. "Nothing on tonight?" I asked. "Game Fishing Association presentation night? Jockey Club smoker? Dancing the bossa nova with Don Pablo Cardena?"

In our racket, our evenings were rarely our own. Squiring the boss to social functions was all part of the gig, a continuous round of catered dinners and mail-order chitchat, feigned enthusiasms and set-piece speeches. Back at Ethnic Affairs, I'd often found myself at such events four or five times a week, consoled only by the free linguini, too much retsina and the fact that no one was waiting at home.

Denis loosened his tie. "Quiet night at home with Marjorie, for once," he said. "Cup of cocoa and beddy-byes."

We sat on the clubby brown sofa, sipped our beers, ate salt 'n' vinegar chips from the packet and watched the gloaming settle gently over the gardens.

"You ever drink at the Pier Hotel?" I said, just chewing the fat. "My old man had the licence there for a while. We lived upstairs."

Eighteen months at the Pier while I was still in short pants were my sole claim to roots in the Port Melbourne community, a way-station in my childhood migration around the watering holes of Melbourne.

"That right?" said Denis, interested. "I'll admit to the occasional beer there, although the Sandridge was the wharfies' pub. So when was this?"

"Late fifties," I said. "You lot at the Stevedores were in the news all the time. More strikes than a bowling alley, they used to say. I was just a little kid at the time. You remember the Eclipse?"

"The picture theater? Where the 7-Eleven is now? 'Course I do. Every Saturday, rain or shine. Cowboys and Itchybums, lollies ten for a penny."

Very ancient history. The wooden workingmen's cottages of the old seaside suburb had long been transformed into the pastel-tinted, marine-themed abodes of advertising executives and fashion designers. The only lollies they still sold in Port Melbourne were individually wrapped Ferrero-Rocher hazelnut truffles. Still, you take your nostalgia where you find it.

"And when it was your birthday," I recalled, "they'd put your name up on the screen. Happened to me when I turned eight."

"No, that was the Port Cinema," he said. "They had the upstairs at the Eclipse, the dress circle. Me and Woeful used to meet the girls there. Just after the war, this was. We couldn't go round to the house, pick them up. Old Mother Boag didn't like the idea of her girls going out with a couple of red-raggers. Fearsome pious, she was. Pope on the wall, Mass at Saint Joey's every Sunday. But a real battler. Worked at the Swallow & Ariell biscuit factory after the girls' dad was killed in the war. Burma Railway, just like Woeful's. You got fleas or something?"

One of my hands was running circles around the nicotine patch. The other was scratching my armpit. I desisted immediately, went to the fridge and cracked another couple of cans. "That's right," I said, remembering. "I heard that you and Woeful were married to sisters."

"Beth and Marjorie Boag," he nodded. "The belles of Bay Street. There was a third one, Irene. The little sister. Married a migrant, funny sort of bloke. Fell off a ladder and died, she did. Tragic."

So much for my reminiscences of historic Port Melbourne. We lapsed into silence. Me toying with my can, Denis staring pensively into the night. He drained his glass and stood up. "Time, gentlemen," he said. "Time."

We rode down in the lift together, me headed for the ground floor, Denis for the carpark. "See you in the morning after the MOB meeting," he said. "We'll have the word from the Premier by then and you can brief Woeful in detail. You all right?"

"Yeah," I said. "Why?"

"You seem a bit keyed-up, that's all."

"I'm fine," I said, wondering what he meant. Apart from a little tingling in the scalp, I felt buoyant.

"Take care," he said, as I stepped into the foyer.

"You, too," I told the gap in the closing doors.

But Denis's course was already set. And, besides, I don't think he heard me. He should have gone home.

11

A RESTLESS ENERGY was jiggling its hands in my pockets. Mild agitation, Doctor Phillipa had warned. A side effect of the mysterious osmosis at work in my shirt.

The evening rush hour had finished and the darkening streets were almost deserted. I stood for a moment, considering my options. Across the road, in the syrupy dusk of the gardens, a pair of Japanese honeymooners were trying to tempt a possum from a tree, timidly waving bread rolls at the foliage. The Windsor was just up the road, the favored watering hole of Parliament House staffers and press gallery leak-sniffers. A man would need to be desperate to seek company there. A more compelling alternative suggested itself to me.

I turned down Flinders Lane, the slope of the hill adding momentum to my pace. No hurry, I told myself. The chance that I would find Dr. Phillipa Verstak in the lounge at Mietta's at seven o'clock on a Monday evening was a very long shot indeed. Still, nothing ventured. Wire-caged posters at the rear of the *Herald* building carried the latest news. PRINCE EDWARD — I'M NOT GAY. That was a weight off my mind.

Flinders Lane was once the heart of Melbourne's rag trade. But the whir of the sewing machine was no longer heard there, nor the rattle of wire coat hangers on garment racks. Now it was all tribal art galleries, pasta bars and the entrances of multistory carparks. At Rosati, its tiled interior as vast as Milan railway station and as empty as an Etruscan tomb, bored waiters in floor-length aprons lounged against the bar. A hundred meters down the hill, I turned up a laneway that led toward Collins Street.

Sheer walls rose on either side, punctured only by the service entrance of the Hyatt Hotel. Sitting in the loading bay was a garbage skip the size of a shipping container, surrounded by plastic milk crates and empty detergent drums. Fixed to the wall beside the staff entrance was a row of metal benches. Usually, they were occupied by hotel employees who had nicked outside for a quick smoke. Evidence of this fact could be seen in the butts that littered the cobblestones. I looked down at them with the disgust of a reformed man.

The seats were vacant except for a waiter in a dinner suit. He stood up as I approached, shifting his weight from foot to foot and running a finger around the inside of his collar like an impatient bridegroom. He wasn't smoking, I realized, but waiting for someone, peering impatiently up the steps toward the door marked Strictly Staff Only. As I got closer, I recognized him.

It was Holly Deloite's insistent ex, the thick-stemmed Steve Radeski. Dressed not as a waiter, I realized, but a bouncer. A crowd-control supervisor, an event-management security consultant, a chucker-outer. Professional muscle.

But not, in the half-light of the alleyway, the most frightening example of his metier. He was a few centimeters shorter than me and I found something almost comical about the posturing way he held himself, legs bowed, arms dangling. Bulging slightly in a hand-me-down dinner suit, he looked too dumb to be seriously dangerous.

His hair was thinning. His ponytail was greasy and lank. He had a rash of some sort, pinhead pustules which pitted his cheeks and inched up his neck past the over-tight collar of his dress shirt. He looked like he'd been using Manuel Noriega's dermatologist and Clive James's tailor.

What on earth, I couldn't help but wonder, did a gorgeous girl like Holly ever see in a meatloaf like this? With that thought, a sudden wave of irritation welled up within me. Just where did this strutting bonehead get off, thrusting his unwanted attentions upon women? One woman, anyway. One that I knew about. This was the sort of bloke who gave blokedom a bad name. And what was he doing here, lurking about the staff exit? He couldn't by any chance be waiting for Holly to come off her shift upstairs, could he?

"Steve, isn't it?" I heard myself saying. "Steve Radeski?"

Bigfoot's eyes flicked over me, indifferent. You meet a lot of people in the hospitality industry, you can't be expected to remember them all.

"You know Holly Deloite, right?"

He stared, triangulating the content of the question with known associates. It was a lengthy process. "Yeah," he finally admitted. "Why?"

"Not waiting for her now, by any chance?" It came out as a challenge.

"Could be," he said, stepping closer. "Who wants to know?"

"A friend of Holly's," I said. "Trying to save you some trouble."

The penny finally dropped. "You're that fucken lawyer, aren't you?"

Radeski suddenly seemed a lot bigger, more bulked-up, less pathetic. It was like someone was inflating him with air. His jaw muscles bulged. The veins in his neck were pulsing like compressor hose. I began to have second thoughts. Maybe I should have expressed myself better, made some light conversation, built a little rapport, eased into the issue gradually.

"Where do you fucken get off?" he demanded.

"Now listen here," I said, hearing what sounded like fatuous pomposity echo up the ominously empty alley. "I'm just trying to do you a favor, that's all."

But he didn't want any favors. He stuck his face in mine. His breath smelled of sour milk and the whites of his eyes had a muddy liverish tinge in the stark fluorescent light spilling from the loading bay. "The fuck you think you are?"

Rational discourse was clearly out of the question. My fight-or-flee reflex kicked in, making my underpants decidedly nervous. Anything to placate him. "Sorry," I babbled. "My mistake." I began to back away, showing him the palms of my hands. The universal gesture of submission. The international sign of the chicken.

Groveling cut no ice. This guy had a serious anger-management problem. His ugly mug was contorted with blind rage. He was on a hair trigger and I'd just pulled it. A low growl came from the back of his throat. His nostrils flared. He lowered his head.

I turned to run but it was too late. He charged. The top of his head hit me square in the middle of the chest. "Oomph," I said as the air rushed from my lungs. My feet lifted off the ground. I flew backward and slammed against the garbage skip.

I was boxed in, trapped in the narrow gap between the wall of the loading dock and the side of the Dumpster. Radeski took a backward step and lowered his head, preparing to head-butt me again.

My courage — what little I still possessed — deserted me. This was no way to die. Liverpool-kissed to death in a back alley. And for what? For being a meddling busybody. "Please!" I blurted, the only supplication my breathless lungs could manage. Please don't kill me. Please don't crush the life from my worthless body, O Mighty One. "Please!"

"Police? Where?" Radeski paused and glanced over his shoulder, checking for evidence of the constabulary.

In that split second, I dived sideways. Agile as a hysterical mountain goat, I clambered up the stack of milk crates and jumped onto the rim of the open Dumpster. The metal was thick with grease and my feet skittered out from beneath me. I flew sideways, the heel of my shoe connecting with the slotted lever arm propping open the lid of the skip. A rancid stink rose to meet me and my shoulder hit a bag of garbage. It burst, spewing its contents. A buffeting pillow of fetid air pressed down upon me and a great echoing crash exploded in my ears. The lid of the Dumpster slammed shut.

I lay in total darkness, panting, my ears ringing. The Dumpster vibrated like a gong. My shoulder throbbed. A disgusting stench filled my nostrils, part table scraps, part toxic waste.

Rolling onto my knees, I groped about blindly for a means of self-defense. Slimy plastic brushed my skin. I gagged on the overwhelming smell. Reaching up into the dark, I felt for the lid. It pressed down, cold to the touch. Shin-deep in bags of trash, I backed into a corner and braced myself for the worst.

Worst? Just how bad was it going to get? There I'd been, strolling peaceably along, minding my own business, en route to a quiet drink in the elegant surrounds of Mietta's cocktail lounge. Now here I was, trapped in a giant garbage bin, about to have my features rearranged by a psychopath in a penguin suit.

Right. Things had gone far enough. Grievous bodily harm was one thing. But being suffocated by the smell of room-service leftovers? That was too much. The laneway was a public thoroughfare. Somebody must have heard the Dumpster lid crashing shut. Christ knows I still could, resonating like a tidal wave in my Eustachian tubes.

A place the size of the Hyatt must have hundreds of employees. Sooner or later, one of them would pop outside for a smoke. Or somebody would arrive for work. Night shift on the front desk. A bellboy. Anybody. If Psycho Steve was still there, surely he wasn't mad enough to bash me in front of witnesses.

The silence continued. I crouched motionless, suspecting a trick. Time passed. Palms flat on the lid, I bore upward. It must have weighed half a ton. A narrow crack appeared. I peered out into the lane. Steve Radeski was swaggering away, hands dangling at his hips like a gunslinger, ponytail dangling between his shoulder blades. Arsehole.

My strength gave out and the gap closed. I banged the metal with my balled fist and got a futile hollow ring. A dull ache mustered its forces in my frontal lobes. What I needed was a lever, something to prop the lid open while I squeezed through the gap. All this trash, there had to be something that would do the job.

I fumbled in my pockets and found that I still had my cigarette lighter. I flicked it on and looked around. Apart from a scatter of paper litter, the rubbish was bagged up. I tore at the flimsy plastic, spilling out the contents. After I'd gutted half a dozen of the bags, I struck another light and examined the result.

No doubt about it. It was garbage all right. Five-star crap. Evian bottles. Individual pot-sized serves of grain mustard. Cigar stubs, Romeo y Julieta, full coronas. A soup-stained banquet menu: Timbale of Tasmanian Scallops, Rack of Herbed Lamb, A Macedonia of Seasonal Fruits. Wilted gladioli. The foil from a first-class airline ticket: Melbourne–Amsterdam return. An empty condom packet. Top-shelf brand, ribbed for her sensual pleasure. *This Week in Melbourne.*

I searched with my feet, kicking bags open, banging on the Dumpster wall as I went, yelling at the top of my lungs. Stomp, stomp. Something hard struck my shin. It felt promising, wooden by the heft of it, about as long as my arm and half as thick. A chair leg. Imitation Regency. Someone had been breaking up the hotel furniture. Thank Christ for rock bands. It was just what I needed.

One hand braced against the lid of my steel sarcophagus, I thrust the lever into the gap. Then, pulling downward with my right hand, I swung my left leg into the narrow opening and over the rim of the skip. Gradually, I managed to wriggle the rest of my body into the slot until I was sandwiched between the lid and the rim of the skip, my cheek pressed against the greasy metal. One side of me hung inside, the other outside.

"Right there, are you, mate?" said a voice.

Horizontally headlocked, I stared into the night. Not five paces away, sitting on a milk crate on the apron of the loading dock, was a fat guy in kitchen whites, smoking a cigarette.

"How long you been there?" I grunted, my chest compressed between the skip and its lid.

He languidly raised his cigarette and let me see that it had just been lit. Holding the chair leg in place long enough to prevent my fingers being crushed, I swung both legs over the edge and dropped to the ground. "No, no. Don't get up," I said. "I'll be right."

Dignity is an overrated virtue. I brushed my lapels, dusted off my knees, buffed my shoes on the back of my trousers, detached a cold canapé from my shirt front and adjusted my tie. The pudgy smoker sat with his elbows on his knees, an ironic smile on his face, silently observing my toilette.

"You see that guy attack me?"

The smoker looked at me like I'd been prematurely released back into the community. He said nothing.

I found myself agreeing with him. Let's not mention this to anyone, I suggested to myself. Worse things happen at Party Conference. What I needed was a drink. And a cigarette. Quitting could wait until tomorrow. Fuck the nicotine, I could do with the consolation.

"This hotel is a disgrace," I said. "Lousy decor, poor housekeeping and no little mint on my pillow."

Unbuttoning my shirt, I tore off the adhesive patch and tossed it on the ground.

12

COLLINS STREET SEEMED TO THINK it was the Rue de Montparnasse. Fairy lights twinkled in the trees, horse-drawn carriages plied the tourist trade and the baroque facade of the Old Treasury glowed like a honeyed lie in the middle distance. Dodging a steaming pile of manure, I made my way to Alfred Place and the sober facade of Mietta's, the most elegant gin joint in town.

A faint odor of refuse still clung to my apparel and my hands were streaked with grease. Flitting through the deserted vestibule, I ducked under the stairs and into the gents' lavatory. This relic of a bygone era had been preserved intact since before the Great War, its vitreous enamel as crackled as celadon china and stained the color of hundred-year-old eggs. The water was cold as permafrost and the soap as thin as a communion wafer, but I had the place to myself.

In the bleary glow of the single 25-watt bulb, my Hugo looked more like a science-fiction award than a six-hundred-dollar suit of clothes. My tie, flecked with what I hoped was chocolate mousse, was beyond redemption. Discarding it in the used-towel bin, I sponged down my jacket, scrubbed the smear of grease from my forehead, ran wet fingers through my hair and examined myself in the mirror above the chalky marble washstand. Only the manly scent of coffee dregs and wet ashes remained to suggest the nature of my recent misadventure. Presentably raffish, I decided. Devil-may-care. Now for a cigarette.

The vending machine was in the foyer, butted against the payphone at the entrance to the lounge. Tearing the cellophane off the pack with my teeth, I fed the change into the slot and dialed the Hyatt Club, reading the number off my membership card. Smoking Causes Lung Cancer, declared the warning on the pack. Life is a Terminal Condition.

"Is Holly Deloite there?" I inquired. "Can I please speak to her?" Yes and no, came the answer. Holly was presently taking a class. Could someone else help?

I didn't see how, given that her ex-boyfriend's bad behavior had already jeopardized her employment. Leaving a message that he was lurking about the hotel, assaulting patrons, could only exacerbate her problems. I said I'd call back later, rang off and went into the lounge.

The house style at Mietta's was *belle époque*. Urns of orchids on pedestals, flock wallpaper hung with over-framed oils, the windows swathed in more washed silk than the bustle on Nellie Melba's wedding gown. The furniture was an eccentric mix of mismatched antiques, all deployed around a concert grand with a vase of hydrangeas on the lid and a marble negro kneeling beside the keyboard with a basket of fruit on his head. The eponymous proprietress was standing by the cash register, surveying her domain with a purse-lipped hauteur more suited to the headmistress of the Presbyterian Ladies College than to a saloon keeper.

Apart from all that furniture, she didn't have much to look at. Scarcely a dozen customers were scattered around the room, the last of the late-working office crowd. Three or four couples, chatting in low undertones or toying silently with their drinks. By the fireplace, a bright little blaze of conversation, two trim women in after-five, three men in dark suits and careful ties, looking like they'd come straight from chambers or the counting house. A solitary drinker propped at the bar, thumbing through a back copy of the *New Yorker*.

No sign of Dr. Verstak. And probably a good thing too, given that I was in no fit state to conduct a seduction. The only suit I could see myself pressing that night was the one I was wearing. A tuxedoed maitre d' materialized, looked at me like I was something the cat dragged in, led me to an obscure nook and ushered me into a low-slung wing-back horsehair-upholstered chair last seen in Colonel Mustard's library. I ordered a double whisky, single malt, water on the side, and lit a cigarette.

Every cigarette has its purpose. This one served many. Recompense for injury received. A balm to my bruised ego. A prayer of thanks for deliverance. A reward for a day's work well done. A healing draught from the well of solace. A sensual pleasure. An affectation appropriate to the surroundings. A warranted act of self-indulgence. An existential affirmation.

Try getting all that from a nicotine patch. I downed my drink, straight up, and signaled for another. When I reached for my wallet to pay, I found the invitation card to the IOC dinner. Three courses and a showband in the company of their excellencies Pascal Abdoulaye, Kim U-ee and Stansislas Dziczkowszczak, imminent envoys from the cloud-swathed heights of Olympus. Recipients of the sacred fire, to be carried hither by my own fleet-footed progeny, bearer of the city's fondest hopes.

For which I would need a dining companion. A woman, preferably. I considered the possibilities. It didn't have to be a date, to adopt an odious Americanism. There was no reason I couldn't invite any one of a dozen women. Workmates, past and present. Party comrades. Old flames. Ex-wives. God, wouldn't that be a bummer. I sipped my drink and gave the matter some thought.

You didn't really think that Phillipa Verstak would be here, I told myself. Sitting alone with her legs crossed and an enigmatic half-smile playing across her lips. You didn't really imagine her turning quickly away as you came through the door, then turning back and saying "Of course I remember" and "No, I don't mind" as you invited yourself to sit down, reaching across to light her cigarette, your eyes meeting. Of course not. That would be ridiculous. Absurd. Pathetic.

Little gusts of conversation and the tinkle of glasses wafted across from the congenial fivesome sitting by the unlit fireplace. The talk was of European aviation. *"The Flying Dutchman,"* groaned a male voice and the others all whinnied. I envied them their easy sociability and lit another cigarette.

"We'll miss the curtain if we don't hurry," warbled one of the women. This initiated a bout of general fussing and fidgeting and finishing of drinks. Suddenly they were all on their feet. One of the men, a bony, angular fellow with so much self-regard he didn't even need to show it, beckoned the waiter and whispered pontifically into his ear. Then they were gone.

After a while, my watch told me it was pushing eight. Beyond that, it didn't have much else to say. The booze started doing its job. I gave my lungs a good fumigation. Pretty soon I was feeling quite a bit more chipper. The possibility of dinner canvassed itself. Something Chinese, I thought. One of the more affordable provinces.

That's when she arrived. Appeared in the doorway, just like that. In a skirt this time, knee-length. Black hose, nice calves. A high-collared teal-blue blouse, a fringed Carmen scarf around her shoulders, pinned in place with a silver brooch. Clutch purse. All dressed up for a night out. Make-up, even. Lipstick. Yum-yum. A little breathless, slightly flustered.

She scanned the room. Her mouth tightened with irritation then quickly relaxed into relief. She hadn't noticed me, back there in the corner.

She hesitated, trying to make up her mind. The maitre d' did that for her, leading her to a place not a million miles from mine. She'd scarcely sat down before her hand was in her purse.

Gotcha!

She reached for the book of matches in the ashtray on the little marquetry table in front of her. But I got there first. "Say something in Cambodian," I said.

She accepted the offered light, again holding my gaze. Kiss, kiss. Puff, puff. *"Neuv m'dohm nih mian miin reu te?"*

Sing-song tones, rising and falling. Pretty convincing, I

thought. Especially the long, vibrating vowel at the tail end. "What's it mean?"

"Stick out your tongue," she said. "And say 'Ahhh.'"

Then the waiter was at her shoulder. "Excuse me, madam," he said. "But if you're the lady with the opera party, your friends said they couldn't wait any longer."

"Thank you," she said. "I'll have a Glenfiddich, no ice." A warranted indulgence. "It's been that sort of day."

"Mine, too," I said. Particularly the last half-hour. "Do you mind?"

She didn't have the energy to resist. "The man with the patches, isn't it? So, do they work?"

"Murray," I reminded her. "Ask me next week." I lit a cigarette. "I haven't found the right psychological moment."

"Pathetic, aren't we?" She eased back into her seat, relaxing now.

I liked the *we*. Nothing medicinal about it, this time. "Didn't know they played opera on Mondays," I said. "Or whatever it is they do to opera."

"Preview night," she said, going with it. "A friend works for a big sponsor, got free tickets. *Tristan and Isolde*. To tell the truth, I'm a bit relieved. Wagner's a bit heavy going, don't you think?"

I nodded sagely. The old fucking Nazi. "I'm more of a Bizet man myself," I said, playing to the shawl. "Puccini. That sort of thing." Goofy on Ice.

Her drink arrived and she took a decent belt. Hard liquor. Hot dog. Doctor, doctor, gimme the news. "I was thinking of having a bite to eat," I said, gesturing vaguely in the direction of the bar. "Do you feel like . . ."

"I've already eaten, thanks. Couldn't face three hours of Wagner on an empty stomach."

She yawned, put the back of her hand over her mouth. "Sorry," she said. "I was on emergency-room duty at the Alfred last night. Worked until 2 A.M."

"Long hours," I agreed. I was a very agreeable fellow. Just what the doctor ordered. She hadn't said if this friend with the freebies was male or female. The fivesome was three boys, two girls. Odds were it was a he. But he couldn't be that much of a friend if he left without her.

But let's not talk about him, I thought. Let's talk about her. And me.

"You must tell me all about Cambodia," I said, searching for common ground beyond operaphobia and cigarette addiction. "I used to work at Ethnic Affairs. Had a bit of contact with the In-dochinese community here in Melbourne." Angelo opened a festival once. Tet. My job was to see he didn't do anything offensive.

"Perhaps some other time."

Not quite the brush-off. She *was* dog-tired. I could see it. But there was something I definitely needed to know. "If you don't mind me asking," I said, coming right out with it. "Are you by any chance married or otherwise involved at the moment?"

She took her time, languidly swirling the liquid in her glass. "Why do you ask?"

"So I won't ask you anything inappropriate."

"Such as?"

The entree card was in my hand. "I know it's short notice and all, but there's this big Olympic dinner on Thursday . . ."

I felt the old visceral clutch. Apart from anything else, there was the doctor-patient ethical stuff. Not that she was my doctor. Bernie was my doctor and I wouldn't dream of asking Bernie out.

But she was smiling. "I'll see you there," she said.

"Really?" If I had a tail, I would've wagged it. "You'll come?"

"I already am. Rodney, the one with the opera tickets, he's some-thing to do with the Olympics, too. I'm going with him."

If I was your friend, I wanted to say, I wouldn't have left you for *Tristan and Isolde*. Either of them. I'd be here with my magic flute, working up a little *Così fan tutte*. Something to do with the Olympics, eh? Him and half of Melbourne.

She yawned again. "Sorry," she smiled, heavy lidded. "'Scuse me."

"Sure," I shrugged.

She looked a shade off-color. "Can you smell something?"

"I think the water in the flower vases needs changing."

She finished her drink. "I think I'll make the most of my reprieve, get an early night."

"Very sensible." I was in with a chance. Look at the opposition. One of three chinless wonders. We parted at the door.

"Good luck," she said. I didn't think she just meant quitting smoking.

Dinner was a Hokkien mee at the Nam Loong. Five dollars fifty and you couldn't do it cheaper at home. Strips of red-cooked pork in the window, a melamine bowl and teacup, a bucket of chopsticks on every table and Cantonese caterwauling from the kitchen. Stuffed with noodles and jasmine tea, I waddled back up to the Collins Street tram stop. The footpath was thick with moviegoers headed for *Death Warrant* and *Robocop 2*. Evidence that, even at eight-thirty on a Monday night, the vibrancy of our city's cultural life yielded to none. As we clattered past the Old Treasury, I noticed that upstairs lights were still blazing.

Work, you bastards, I silently urged. Do whatever it takes. The barbarians are at the gate, nudging it open with the doors of their Rolls-Royces. Win us this bid or Labor's fate is sealed. Win it and we will set our house in order. Lose it and in will rush the Liberals, and with them all that is grasping, avaricious, mean-spirited, cynical, arrogant, self-righteous, punishing, hypocritical, pompous and cruel.

Nothing like a feed of Chinese to get the proletarian juices flowing.

I bought milk and bread at the souvlaki joint on the corner and walked up the narrow street to my humble abode, meeting its emptiness with fortitude sufficient unto the day. The red light was blinking on the answering machine. Brian Morrison reminding me of the morning's meeting with the MOB.

I showered off the remnant *bouquet de Dumpster* and balled Hugo into a supermarket carry bag, ready for the dry cleaner. I'd missed *Four Corners* and there was nothing left on television, so I set the alarm for seven and hit the hay early.

As sleep's dark pool rose to meet me, laughing piccaninnies splashing among its lily pads, a faint presence crept toward me through the night, scattering the X-ray barramundi. Wugga wugga, it went. Wugga wugga. Kjuk kjuk kjuk.

The fucking police helicopter. It passed overhead, low enough to rattle the window glass. Then came the sirens. First ambulance, then police. Then more police.

Trouble at the flats. Again. Police over-reaction. Again. You could bet they never hovered above silvertail Toorak at chimney height, setting the cookware rattling and terrifying the companion animals. Nor were they patrolling city laneways, protecting innocent ministerial advisers from the steroid-deranged psychopathic ex-boyfriends of pulchritudinous aerobics instructors. Never around when you needed them. Wugga wugga, they went, interminably.

I buried my head in my pillow and embraced the darkness.

"Say 'Ahh,' " she said. "And tell me where it hurts."

13

THE CLOCK RADIO WOKE ME at three minutes past seven with what was left of the hourly news bulletin: *". . . outside the Fitzroy flats last night. Police have so far been unable to establish a motive for the fatal attack. They believe the man, a local resident, may have been the victim of a gang bashing and are appealing for witnesses."*

The reporter's voice came at me through the fug of waking. It was not until my feet were on the floor and the news had shifted to Canberra that I fully registered the meaning of her words. A street killing in Fitzroy last night? Well, that explained the police helicopter, I thought, as I groped my way toward the shaving mirror and the low-fat milk.

A bit of a worry, a lethal bashing only streets away. But this was Fitzroy, after all. And thus had it ever been. In a perverse way, there was even something comforting about the persistence of crime in Melbourne's oldest suburb. A victory of tradition over the forces of gentrification.

Today was the day, I swore over my high-fiber cereal. Yesterday was a false dawn; my relapse was due to circumstances beyond my control. It was now or never. I stood naked before the mirror, scraped the remnants of adhesive off my solar plexus and carefully attached a new Nicabate patch. I shaved and dressed. Then, as my tea brewed,

I field-stripped my thirteen remaining cigarettes and washed the tobacco down the sink. Take that, you bastards.

Bright-eyed and bushy-tailed, I stepped out into the dawning day. The morning was fresh with promise. The sky above the flats glowed with the first flush of sunrise. Pink, gray and yellow streaked the clouds, marbling them like the layers of some outrageous confectionery. Sunlight struck the dewy lawns of the Exhibition Gardens, transforming them into a carpet of diamonds. The air was crisp and invigorating. I breathed deep and felt it doing me good.

As I walked toward the city, I mentally marshaled my arguments for the Aboriginal Institute of Sport. I also recalled the words of the news bulletin. *The victim of a gang bashing.* What the fuck did that mean?

Fitzroy didn't have gangs. Not any more. This wasn't the 1920s when razor-toting larrikins tore the pickets off fences and beat each other insensible at all-in brawls. Nor was it Bedford-Stuyvesant, or South Central LA with its ethnic warfare and drive-by shootings. We still had our rough edges, our greatcoated winos and barefoot ferals, our ferret-faced teenage mothers and lingerie lunches, our dumb-fuck rev-heads and back-lane chop shops. But these were no more than the embellishments of urbanity, bait for a suburban gentry in search of inner-city authenticity. In reality, the corner pub had given way to the sushi bar and the futon factory. And racial differences were just so much local color. In contemporary Fitzroy, street violence was rarer than an oven-roasted artichoke heart.

The front doors of the Old Treasury were not yet open for business, so I pressed the night bell and waited on the doorstep, watching an endless flow of commuters emerge from Parliament station. At the kiosk on the footpath, newspaper posters hung in their wire racks. BEATEN TO DEATH. COUP FEARS IN KREMLIN. Both the morning dailies were, by the look of it, leading with bad news about the government.

One of Brian Morrison's efficiency women opened the door, led me upstairs to the first floor, offered me coffee and deposited me in a small conference room almost identical to the one in which I had lunched with Denis and Woeful the previous Friday. On the table was a large, lushly produced book with a cloth-bound slipcover embossed with the MOB logo. It was a copy of the city's formal proposal to the IOC, a paean to Melbourne's pre-eminent suitability to stage the Olympic Games.

Each sport had a chapter, replete with technical specifications, projected attendance figures and unimpeded hyperbole. Even culture got a run: shots of string quartets and white-faced mimes were interspersed with cross-hatched rock wallabies and a bearded Aborigine I was sure I had once seen at the Victoria Market, sitting cross-legged on the asphalt with a didgeridoo, busking for coins beside the hot-donut wagon.

I flipped through the book and drained two cups of coffee. The door-opening woman reappeared and delivered a photocopied memo. The words were mine, but the signature belonged to Brian Morrison. It confirmed that Denis Dogherty's game plan was running exactly to schedule.

The Aboriginal Institute of Sport was now an initiative of the MOB Department of Government, Corporate and Community Relations. The board was urged to commit itself to the project as part of the total Olympic package and to request government endorsement. As I finished reading, Brian opened the door.

"The board is studying it now," he said. No hello, no nothing. "I wheel you in, you give it a general boost, answer any questions. Ready to rip?"

As ready as I'd ever be. Talk about a cowboy outfit, this MOB was the original pearl-handled capgun. We went along the corridor and stopped at a door. Brian reached for the handle, paused, furrowed his brow and drew me back a couple of steps. "What do you know about this killing at the flats last night?"

"I heard the flying pig and lots of sirens," I shrugged. "The radio said some poor prick got himself beaten to death."

"Some poor *Koori* prick." He paused expectantly. Suddenly I was the resident expert on dead Aborigines. "No negative fallout for us, I hope."

"Well, I didn't kill him, if that's what you mean."

"Ha. Ha. You know perfectly well what I mean."

"He wasn't in police custody at the time, was he?"

Brian smirked and eased the door open. "Let's be thankful for small mercies."

We went into a room with Victorian-era wallpaper and French windows overlooking Collins Street. A long conference table ran its length. Sitting around it were about a dozen men, each looking like he'd been born wearing a suit.

This was the force at the core of the MOB. The business worthies and marketing experts and superannuated sports officials in whom the city had invested its highest hopes. In whose hands rested the future of the Labor government. Men who regarded spending other people's money as their highest public duty. Men far too important to wash their own socks or iron their own shirts. Pulse-takers and decision-makers. The only woman in the room was taking minutes. It was pretty much as I'd expected.

Hugh Knowles, the big banana, was seated at the far end of the table. He was a flinty-eyed man in his late fifties with a crown of pepper-and-salt hair. According to the finance pages, he possessed an air of quiet authority. For my money, he had all the charisma of an actuary.

Flanking Knowles was one of the men I had seen in the lounge at Mietta's. The horse-faced one who had whispered to the waiter, then bolted for the opera. Phillipa's friend. My rival. He had about him the alertly oleaginous air of a professional courtier.

I adopted a suitably deferential demeanor and stood at the end of the table while Brian introduced me as a special consultant on Aboriginal matters. The room responded with a collective look of such profound sympathy that he might equally have told them I was dying of leukemia. He sat down and I went into my shtick.

"The proposal currently before you provides a unique opportunity to project a positive international image of Australia's race relations. It will also serve to further enhance support for the bid from the Aboriginal community." Blah, blah. And so on and so forth, about five minutes' worth, including manicured thumbnail costings. "Any questions."

There was a long silence, then Knowles's greasy sidekick leaned forward. "Downside?" he said.

I sucked my cheeks and gave it a count of ten. Brian had no doubt spread a little quiet terror, talked up the threat angle. My job was to show them the stick but not to wave it about. "Failure to grasp this opportunity could be construed as lack of commitment to racial justice by a certain member of the Evaluation Commission due in town this week."

The darkie, not to put too fine a point on it. You could hear the creases falling out of their underpants. There was a minute but distinct shifting of bodies in chairs as attention was transferred from me to the far end of the table. Hugh Knowles cleared his throat. When he spoke, his voice was barely audible. A flat, lockjaw monotone.

"Thank you, very much," he said. "Mr. Whelan."

And that was it. Brian was out of his seat like a rocket, piloting me through the door, easing it shut behind him as gently as if stepping from a nursery.

"Great work, mate," he declared in a reverential half-whisper. "It's a foregone conclusion. You can sense the enthusiasm. Call me in an hour." He slapped me on the shoulder and slithered back inside.

Go figure.

As I stepped outside, I suddenly realized that I hadn't so much as thought about a cigarette since leaving home. It was a realization that filled me with a pleasure as satisfying as any smoke could provide. A pleasure that lasted just about as long as it took me to cross the street to the news kiosk and read the front page of the *Sun*.

The unconscious body of a 22-year-old student, Darcy Anderson, was discovered lying in the undercroft of the Gertrude Street flats at about 10 P.M. He was rushed to St. Vincent's Hospital where he died a short time later of severe head injuries. A promising triathlete, Anderson was training at the Stars gymnasium shortly before his death.

The story was illustrated with a photo of the crime scene and rounded off with the "Crime Stoppers" hotline number.

Jesus Christ. So this was the dead Koori that Brian was wondering about. Darcy Anderson. The kid in the gym. This wasn't just some anonymous punch-up at the flats. This was somebody I could put a face to. Somebody I had spoken with, if only to say hello. This was also a death with wider implications.

The nearest phone was a hundred yards down the street in the glass-roofed plaza at Collins Place. I waited my turn, thinking that maybe it was time I got myself a mobile. Became a proper wanker.

Ken Sproule was senior adviser to the Minister for Police. Our respective masters did not exactly see eye-to-eye but Ken didn't hold that against me. Ken was a crafty little fixer with a keen sense of the nuances and a man who tried not to make more enemies than absolutely necessary. If he saw any mileage in it, he could even be helpful.

"You know I can't talk about police operational matters," he said. "Even if it did happen in your front yard."

I wasn't calling on behalf of the Fitzroy branch of Neighborhood Watch, I explained, but because I was doing a spot of Koori cajoling for the Olympic bid. "Not a convenient time for young Aboriginal athletes to start getting themselves killed," I said. "Just tell me it wasn't racially motivated."

Under the circumstances, Ken was prepared to be a tad more forthcoming. "Sorry, mate," he said. "But I'm afraid that's exactly what it looks like. A gang of skinheads were seen trying to pick a fight with him in the street yesterday afternoon, very close to where he later had his head smashed against a concrete pillar. Homicide are out there now, trying to track them down. Unfortunately, our informants aren't what you might call the world's most reliable witnesses. Piss-heads from the Royal Hotel across the road. All of them well tanked, most with prior convictions. Apart from the haircuts, none of them can describe these alleged skinheads for shit."

"I can." I told him what I'd seen the previous afternoon.

"Why didn't you fucking well say so," he said. "Hold on a tick."

While I was standing there with the phone in my hand, I looked across the plaza and saw Hugh Knowles striding manfully toward the entrance of one of the office towers. His briefcase bearer, Dr. Phillipa's friend, trotted at his heels. Knowles, not missing a beat, fed himself into one of the revolving doors. His hoplite was not so adroit. The rubber edge of the door hit him in the face and he reeled back, clutching his nose.

"What's so funny?" said Ken Sproule. He'd been onto the cops. They wanted a contact number. I told him they could get me at Woeful McKenzie's office and he rang off, telling me to expect their call.

It was ten o'clock. Time to connect with Denis. I headed back toward Spring Street. Up ahead, some sort of press conference was happening in front of the Old Treasury, a knot of cameras and note-book-toting hacks milling at the foot of the terrace. As I reached the corner, the ruck parted and I saw the object of their attention.

A hand-painted banner had been unfurled across the front of the building. NO OLYMPICS WITHOUT JUSTICE, it read. Lined up behind it, arms folded in an attitude of truculent militancy, stood a row of young Koories. In front of it, speaking into a megaphone, was Ambrose Buchanan. He was in full oratorical flight, his words ringing across the intersection.

"If racist thugs believe they can attack Aboriginal people," he declared, "it's because institutions like the one behind us are prepared to tolerate their activities. Until we get justice for Aboriginal people, how can we be expected to support this country's bid for the Olympics?"

He thrust his fist into the air and began to chant, his slogan echoed by the bumfluff brigade behind him. *No Olympics without Justice. No Olympics without Justice.*

14

MY HEART, never reliably buoyant, sank.

But I knew immediately what I must do. What any reasonable, thinking, politically aware member of the Labor Party would do under the circumstances. I left the scene. Quickly. Concealed in a thicket of pedestrians, I continued on my way toward the Sports Ministry.

By the time I reached the next corner, the banner was being rolled up, the Young Panthers had stuck their clenched fists in the pockets of their windbreakers and the hacks had closed their notebooks. Having made the media deadlines, Ambrose and crew clearly had no intention of hanging around the Old Treasury steps all day.

Keener than ever to speak with Denis, I hurried upstairs to Woeful McKenzie's office. The minister was closeted with his departmental head and Denis was nowhere in sight. According to Carmel, he hadn't arrived at work yet. While I waited for him, I borrowed his desk and rang Brian Morrison.

Brian came down the line at me with the unstoppable enthusiasm of a fire hose. "We got the green light," he crowed. "Soon as Cabinet okays the funding, Knowles'll make the announcement. Great work, mate."

"Looked out your window recently?"

"Buchanan?" he said. "Plus two men and a dog. The only thing that little tantrum will achieve is to undermine his credibility. We kept our part of the bargain and Ambrose Buchanan has no legitimate reason to go bitching."

"You don't think this killing in Fitzroy could make us look bad? The cops think race was a factor."

"Crime happens everywhere, mate. The IOC members understand that. Christ, the IOC from Uganda used to run the army for Idi Amin. What's one killing more or less to someone like him? Our job is to demonstrate that such things are an aberration. To counter any residual perception that this is a racist society. Which this institute project will help achieve. A project that we now own, thanks to you. Soon as Charlie Talbot gets back from Africa, the local community can add its stamp of approval. You've stitched up Ambrose Buchanan beautifully, Murray."

Not an achievement in which I felt I could take much pride. It didn't seem the ideal moment to confess that Denis and I had somewhat overstated Ambrose Buchanan's negotiating stance on the institute matter. Fabricated it, actually. "So what should I tell Buchanan?"

"As of now, he's out of the loop, irrelevant. And your job is to work with Denis, advance the proposal through Cabinet so Hugh Knowles can announce it at the dinner on Thursday night. Far as I'm concerned, you can tell Ambrose Buchanan to go to buggery."

Instead, I called the Water bureaucrats to get a progress report on the union negotiations. Progress was not progressing. It was, in fact, regressing. After months of bluster, the union had called a snap strike. Effective as of midday, all maintenance crews were off the job.

Being the first strike ever in the history of the metropolitan water utility, this was embarrassing news for Angelo Agnelli. Fortunately for me, it had not happened on my watch. For the next few days, at least, it was not my problem. And, with any luck, it would all be over by the time I returned. Leaving a few well-chosen words of encouragement for the minister, I pleaded pressing Olympic business and rang off.

By now, it was past ten-thirty and Denis still hadn't clocked on for the day. I rang around Parliament House, thinking maybe there'd been some misunderstanding about where we would meet. He wasn't there either. I was trying to make up my mind whether or not to wait when Woeful's door opened. His departmental head emerged, carrying a bundle of files, and disappeared down the corridor.

"Due at the Premier's in ten minutes," Carmel warbled.

Woeful lumbered out and stood at her desk. "Where's Denis?" he demanded.

Carmel shook her head and shrugged. "I've just had Marj Dogherty on the line, wanting to know if he had to go up the bush or interstate or anything on short notice." She handed Woeful a sheet of paper, his copy of my Cabinet submission on the Aboriginal Sports Institute.

Woeful pushed his eyebrows together, scanning the page. "Not that I know of," he grunted. "Why?"

Carmel's confidential secretary eyes slid across to me. They slid back to Woeful. I must have passed the credentials committee. But only just. She lowered her voice. "Apparently he didn't go home last night."

"How do you mean, didn't go home?"

"Didn't go home," she repeated. She tapped the face of her watch. Chop, chop.

Woeful hesitated, suspended between two demands. "Well," he growled. "How am I supposed to know where he is?" The sheet of paper became a cylinder in his hands. He slapped it against his open palm a couple of times, deliberating.

Then he noticed me. "Thought you were supposed to be squaring things off with that Ambrose Buchanan. I look out my window this morning, there he is, across the road, shitting on the MOB's doorstep. Bloody big help you turned out to be."

True. "This kid getting killed last night didn't help."

The big man sighed gloomily. "Terrible business."

Poor old Woeful, I thought. The last vestige of that vanished era when the ranks of the Labor Party were filled with such men. Shearers, engine drivers, coal miners. A time that still informed our collective mythology. But a time long gone. Only accident and inertia and the obscure functioning of factional hydraulics had allowed Woeful to rise as far as he had. And the talents of his trusty henchman, Denis Dogherty.

Nobody, least of all Woeful himself, ever pretended that managerial talent had anything to do with it. By rights, he belonged in a museum. Either that or serving out the twilight of his career lunching with the trustees of the Tennis Center and appointing his cronies to the Bookmakers Registration Board. Not bearing the full weight of the party's hopes and the people's Olympic expectations.

"According to Ken Sproule, the cops think it was racially motivated."

Woeful's shoulders sank another inch. "Just what we need." He peered at me suspiciously. "Mate of Sproule's, are you?"

"Strictly business," I protested, hand on heart. The Minister for Police, Ken Sproule's master, was Woeful's most powerful adversary in caucus, Gil Methven. "Wouldn't trust him as far as I could throw him."

"Bloody well hope so," said Woeful, apparently mollified. "Haven't seen Denis this morning, by any chance?"

I shook my head. "Not since we left here last night. Said he was going home. I'm looking for him myself, check progress on the Cabinet item." I indicated the paper in his hand.

Woeful nodded absently, like he'd already forgotten the question. He looked down at the cylinder of paper and gave a resigned shrug. "Suppose I'd better do what I'm told, then. Go give the Premier a nudge." He set off, bear-like, toward the lifts.

"What'll I tell Marj?" called Carmel after him. He vanished around the corner, making no reply.

"Denis ever done this sort of thing before?" I asked her. "Not go home?"

She stared at me across the rampart of her desk, blank-faced. What she saw was a person of uncertain status. A man who trafficked with the minions of Gil Methven. As far as she was concerned, Denis

Dogherty's domestic arrangements were not the subject of office gossip. And she was right. It was none of my business. A man might not go home for any number of reasons.

At that point, the phone rang. It was for me. The police. Carmel arched her eyebrows and switched the call through to Denis's desk.

The voice identified itself as Detective Senior Constable Carol Sonderlund who stated that she was calling in relation to the incident in Fitzroy overnight. While the police appreciated my offer to help identify possible offenders in the matter, my assistance would not be required. Adequate descriptions of the individuals concerned had been subsequently obtained from a number of people who had seen them in the vicinity the previous afternoon.

This dose of wary legalese suggested that I was getting the full benefit of Ken Sproule's clout at police HQ. "You really think the skinheads killed Darcy Anderson?" I said, fishing for information. "They didn't strike me as being up to it."

"We'll determine that when we interview the persons concerned," said Sonderlund.

So they hadn't picked them up yet. "Any other suspects?"

I didn't really expect an answer and I didn't get one. Denis's desk calendar was sitting beside the phone. I flipped it open and checked the previous night. No appointment was listed. Inquiries were continuing, Detective Sonderlund advised me, and the police were optimistic of an early arrest.

When I went back to the minister's office, Carmel was speaking softly into the phone. "I'm sure there's a simple explanation, Marj." As I came in, she put her hand over the mouthpiece. "I'll let him know you called," she told me. She took her hand off the phone and waited for me to leave.

Fair enough. The punctuality of a member of Woeful McKenzie's staff was hardly my affair. My actual employer, *pro tem*, was the MOB. And, so far, I had met my contractual obligations to them. Nobody was paying me to sit around twiddling my thumbs waiting on a missed appointment. An appointment which was now unnecessary since I'd spoken to the minister myself and confirmed that the matter was in hand.

I went to the gym.

Holly Deloite was wiping the glass display cabinet behind the reception desk. The electric blue of her leotard exactly matched the color of the window-cleaning fluid. Her eyes were a slightly paler tint. She opened them very wide.

"You're kidding!" She put down her pump-pack of Windex. "Steve Radeski threw you in a Dumpster?"

"Not threw," I said. "Shut. After I threw myself, trying to get away. Soon as I opened my mouth, he went absolutely batshit. Tried to kill me, I swear. If he's not on steroids, I'm Mr. Universe."

"He's definitely on something," she confirmed. "Must be. In the six weeks I've been in Queensland, he's really bulked up. Stacked on, like, thirty-five kilos. Which is, like, crazy. I mean it's not like he's competing any more."

"What would he compete in?" I said. "The pan-galactic dick-head titles?"

She got all defensive then, probably because she could tell I was wondering what she'd ever seen in the guy. "Believe it or not," she said. "Steve Radeski used to be an Olympic athlete. Almost, anyway. He was in the national weightlifting squad. Not one of the really big ones, either. Eighty-kilo class." I currently weighed slightly more than that. "He used to be a pretty nice guy."

"Well, he isn't any more," I said. "He's a maniac. And, if I were you, I'd be worried about him hanging around this place." Suddenly I was back *in loco parentis*. "And not just because he might get you fired."

Holly drew back her shoulders and fired a rapid volley of cleaner onto the counter top. "Don't worry about me." Squirt, squirt. Wipe. Wipe. "I can handle Steve Radeski."

"Excuse me," called an American accent from behind a rack of pedal-pushers. "Do you have this in my size?"

"You be careful," I warned. "Or I won't join your aerobics class."

Holly darted a quick glance around the gym, then leaned across the counter and gave me a peck on the cheek. "You're very sweet to worry," she said. "Coming!"

Sweet? I didn't want to be sweet. I wanted to be feared. I wanted to be desired. I wanted the body of a twenty-year-old. I changed into my shorts, set the resistance dial on the exercise bike to Tour de France and climbed aboard. I took a deep breath and filled my lungs with air. It was fourteen hours since my last cigarette and I wanted to see what those babies could do.

The patch on my midriff was definitely working, foxing my nicotine receptors with its surreptitious hex. The thought of cigarettes had scarcely entered my brain all morning. Cigarettes were a thing of the past. For cigarettes I felt nothing at all. Perhaps a slight nostalgia, a remembrance of things past. But, beyond that, nothing. *Nada. Niente.* What I did feel, by the time I'd run to the top of the Empire State Building on the Stairmaster and rowed the length of the Amazon on the rowing machine, was gut-churning sick.

All morning, ever since my song-and-dance routine before the MOB bigwigs, a teensy jitter had been creeping up on me. A faint standuppishness at the nape of the neck. A slight cerebral pulsation. Now, my bloodstream pulsing with nicotine and lactic acid, I definitely needed a little lie down.

I staggered into the sauna and fell naked onto the top row of roasted cedar planks. A purging heat enveloped me, rich with the koala-fart aroma of eucalyptus oil. Sweat gushed from my pores, sluicing away the toxins in a great, cleansing torrent. Gradually, my stomach settled. I lay there, my brain twitching, thinking about Ambrose Buchanan.

He'd had been pretty fast off the mark. Even a pissy little demonstration like the one on the Old Treasury steps took a bit of organizing. Paint the banner. Find the megaphone. Round up the usual suspects. Which suggested that he'd been planning all along to come out against the bid at the first opportunity. Which made it look like he'd been jerking my string with his Aboriginal Institute of Sport idea. If so, he'd shot himself in the foot, handing a great PR opportunity to the MOB even as he planned to attack it. Not a smart move, on the face of it.

Perhaps he didn't expect us to deliver. The white establishment didn't usually fall over itself in its haste to implement suggestions from black activists. As far as Ambrose knew, the MOB hadn't yet even considered his proposal, let alone snapped it up and taken it over. Quite possibly, he had simply assumed he would get the customary run-around and acted accordingly.

No Olympics without Justice. Was that an ambit claim, a coverall slogan that encompassed the entire wider agenda? Or did it refer specifically to the Darcy Anderson case? Ambrose's sound bite blamed racist thugs. Was he referring to the skinheads, or making a general polemical point? With the police hot on the trail of the suburban bovver boys, how could Brother Ambrose justify his inference that the MOB was somehow complicit in Darcy Anderson's death? Surely that was just polemic.

By the time I got under the shower, my bones had turned to rubber. As I wafted back through the gym, Holly hailed me. "Um," she said, tentatively. "I was wondering if you could do me a favor."

"Sure," I said. "Name it."

Unfortunately, she did. "It's just that there's some CDs and stuff, a cassette player, that I left at this person's place when I went to Queensland. Anyway, I really need them back for this new aerobics routine I'm working on. Only I haven't, like, got a car at the moment and I was just wondering . . ."

"You need a lift?"

"It's not far. Heidelberg."

A twenty-minute run, hardly a major excursion. On the other hand, I didn't actually have a car. "Um." I prevaricated, thinking that my stolen car story would sound like a bullshit excuse.

"Of course, if it's not convenient."

It was all I could do not to laugh. I'd seen better pouts on a two-year-old. "Somebody else is using my car at the moment," I said. "But I could probably borrow one from the pool at work."

"Great." She brightened immediately. "Is tonight after work okay?"

What the hell, I thought. It wasn't every day that a gorgeous young gym bunny tried to twist me around her little finger. And it wasn't like I was expecting Michelle Pfeiffer around for a candle-lit dinner, after all. Or even Doctor Phillipa Verstak for that matter. And Heidelberg wasn't Wheelers Hill or Hoppers Crossing or Patterson Lakes, some godforsaken suburban dormitory an hour away.

"You finish at eight?" I said. "Right?"

Downstairs in the food court, I sat at the bar with a bowl of rabbit food and a bottle of Evian. My personal contribution to the national current-account deficit. "See that," said the barman. The picture on the big-screen television showed a pillar of water gushing high into the air, a great white geyser exploding from the middle of a residential street. "Some idiot driving around town, running over fire hydrants."

I cocked my ear to the voice-over. Over two thousand homes were currently without water in the western suburbs and emergency tankers had been rushed to parts of Hampton and Glen Waverley.

For a moment, I was tempted to call Water Supply and find out what was going on. I dismissed the thought. For a few days at least, they could get along without me. I lingered over my lettuce, sipped my spring water, then set an unhurried course for the nearest black-fellers' camp.

15

IT WAS ONE OF THOSE DAYS when you can almost see the point of golf. A day not to be stuck indoors, chained to a desk.

I headed down the sunny side of Exhibition Street and into the Carlton Gardens. The Ideal Home Show had just opened and young couples on their lunchbreak hurried past, hand in hand, in hot pursuit of fresh kitchen ideas and new bathroom solutions. Their destination, the resplendent cupola of the Exhibition Building, floated above the treetops like a Valkyrie's bra cup. The sky was a cloudless vault, but in the deep shade of the Moreton Bay figs there was a damp chill in the air that sent a shiver down my spine.

I broke back out into the sunshine and turned down Gertrude Street toward the Stars Cafe. At a piss-drenched phone booth outside the Champion Hotel, I rang Sport for a word with Denis.

Still no show. But there was a message from Woeful. The Premier had okayed the agenda inclusion request. And could I come to Woeful's office at Parliament House at five, no reason given.

Further down the street, the perennial cluster of malingerers on the steps of the Aboriginal Health Service eyed me impassively as I walked by. Across the road, the flats looked exactly as they had the previous day. Nothing suggested that a young man had been beaten to death there less than eighteen hours earlier. I half-expected signs of police activity. Doorknocking uniforms, latex-gloved forensic pathologists, homicide dicks with narrow ties and gruff manners. As it was, nothing out of the usual marked Darcy Anderson's passing.

Almost nothing. The Stars was closed. Black crepe paper was taped around the windows and a hand-printed notice was pinned to the door. "In memoriam Darcy Kevin Anderson. Closed until Thursday." Somebody back up the road at the Health Service could probably point me in the general direction of Ambrose Buchanan, but I wasn't inclined to ask. Under the circumstances, it wasn't a good time to go pushing a bureaucratic wheelbarrow around the neighborhood.

Ambrose Buchanan would keep. I bought a coffee to go and a copy of the city edition of the *Herald* and walked them up to the tram stop opposite St. Vincent's consulting rooms. There was nothing for me at Sport, I was avoiding Water and I still had some time to kill before Woeful wanted me at Parliament House. Sooner or later, Phillipa Verstak would come outside for a cigarette and I'd catch her in the act, pretend I just happened to be passing. In the meantime, I sat in the sunshine, ate my lunch and read the paper.

So far, the press spin on the Olympic bid had been unanimously positive. Today was no different. Ambrose Buchanan's little demo on the Old Treasury steps didn't rate a mention, despite the photo opportunity. The *Herald* led instead with a full-page piece about fuck-ups in the public transport ticketing system. Millions Wasted Shock Horror. To compound the damage, the story was a leak from the Transport Workers Federation, a factional game-play by our comrades in the union movement. Yet another of the thousand self-inflicted cuts from which we were slowly dying.

The Labor Party, I thought. It's a great life as long as you don't weaken. Across the road, shifts of smokers came and went. I regarded them with benign condescension. I, too, used to do that. Filthy habit.

Darcy's death got a spread on page five with a photo of the flats and a picture of the victim on a surf-ski, courtesy of the *Warrnambool Advertiser*. They were running the sportsman angle, first Aboriginal to compete at national level in a triathlon, great future cut tragically short. An act of random violence, the nature of the injuries indicating that he had been slammed backward with considerable force, striking his head against a concrete pillar and dying almost instantly.

A sidebar canvassed resident reactions, playing up the mean-streets angle. A real little morale-booster for the local residents. The Fitzroy flats were no Shangri La, apparently. Shades of the Bronx. Made you wonder why their looming presence never managed to put a dent in local real estate prices. It got to be three o'clock and I'd read the dismal rag from cover to cover twice and still there was no sign of Phillipa.

Now that I thought about it, as far as I could recall, I'd never met a doctor socially. A couple of bulldozer nurses at the Health Employees Federation was as close as I'd ever come, but they didn't count. Doctors and nurses were not in the same class, not by a long calcium carbonate.

Medicine was more a caste than a profession. Socially incompetent alcoholics, most of them. Higher than normal suicide rate. The most lucrative of the money-harvesting professions. Only the law came anywhere near it. Forget Ms. Verstak, I told myself. You'd need to be a barrister earning a minimum of two hundred grand to stand any hope at all. Or a mining company executive, holder of the key to the executive washroom, chief pocket pisser to Hugh Knowles.

Feeling like a love-struck schoolboy, I ambled back toward the city. As I passed St. Patrick's I was tempted to go inside, examine the architecture, make sure Daniel Mannix was still in his crypt. Instead, I turned down Cathedral Place, cut across an empty building site and tapped on the door of the portable site office in the middle of the pot-holed asphalt expanse which was the government carpark.

Theoretically, ministerial advisers were entitled to the use of a fleet vehicle, if, as and when required, subject to availability and ongoing priorities. As often as not, getting a car was like drawing teeth. I knocked more in hope than certainty.

Fortunately, the dispatch officer recognized me. He'd been Angelo's driver for a while back at Ethnic Affairs, a military type in the agreeable sense. A bit of a finagler. He was bored out of his brain and it took very little persuasion to get him on the phone and initiate proceedings for the issuance of telephone approval from the transport wallah at Water. He probably thought I was headed out to hunt the hydrant kneecapper or direct a tanker run to dehydrated pensioners at the Maidstone old folks home. He was right. I should have been doing something. I just didn't know what.

In due course and the fullness of time, approval was obtained and I was issued with the keys of a white Toyota Corolla with red government plates. The previous user had left a tape in the cassette player. *The Eagles' Greatest Hits.* A powerful argument for the need to downsize the public service. The radio was tuned to the ABC and as I pulled out of the lot the announcer crossed to the newsroom for an update.

Gorbachev was threatening armed intervention in response to Lithuania's unilateral declaration of independence. KGB troops were moving into Vilnius. Ambrose Buchanan made the number two spot, warning that the bid would draw international attention to high Aboriginal mortality rates. This was followed by a police appeal for witnesses in the Darcy Anderson case, a sure sign they weren't making much progress. Dermott Brereton was up before the tribunal on a striking charge, cited on video evidence. Again. The weather outlook was fine and mild.

City traffic was at a crawl. It took me fifteen minutes to get to the underground carpark at the Hyatt and another ten to find a spot. There was a fifteen-dollar minimum charge, daylight robbery. By the time I'd argued the toss with the carpark attendant and walked back up the hill to Parliament House the sunshine was all but gone.

Woeful's office was a glass-walled cubicle in the arched vaults below the Legislative Council. It was a small, functional space with barely enough room to swing a chihuahua. Especially when there were visitors.

Woeful had two of them. The lanky one with the dour face, perched on his chair like a praying mantis, was Gil Methven, the Police Minister. The short one, backed against the bookcase, hands deep in his pockets and doing his best to conceal his glee, was his aide, Ken Sproule. Woeful was hunkered down behind his desk, cornered, looking even more dismal than usual. He saw me arrive and beckoned me inside.

The atmosphere was poisonous. Ken inched to one side, making room for me beside him. Methven ignored me. You could have cut the air with a knife. Woeful was doing the talking.

"He told her he'd be working late last night, so she didn't wait up. She thought he might've been trying to ring but couldn't get through because one of the grandkids knocked the phone off the hook and she hadn't noticed. She's frantic with worry. Called all the hospitals. Been ringing the office every five minutes to see if he's turned up."

Gil was a hard man of the right and not noted for his sense of compassion. He spoke with a hoarse, sandpapery rasp that made him sound like he'd been screaming at his subordinates all afternoon. He probably had. "We can give it to Missing Persons," he said bluntly. "But there's nothing they can do until the morning."

"What are you saying?" grumbled Woeful. "That I should go back to his wife and tell her not to do anything?"

"Gil's just laying it out for you." Ken spoke soothingly. "Once it's official, it's out of our hands. Word goes around. Lots of different people start shaking the tree, you never know what might fall out. You've got absolutely no idea where he might be?"

Woeful spread his palms and shrugged morosely. Going to Gil Methven for help must have required considerable effort. The pair had been bitter factional foes since the dawn of time and Methven had publicly questioned Woeful's fitness as a minister on more than one occasion.

"Hasn't got a girlfriend, has he?" rasped Methven.

Woeful bristled. "He's been happily married for thirty-five years." As if that had anything to do with it.

"We're not trying to pry," said Ken.

Woeful fixed his jaw. "Definitely nothing on the side. I'd know if there was."

"Nervous breakdown?" said Methven. "Out of his depth at work?"

Woeful snorted contemptuously. Nervous breakdowns were for nervous Nellies. "What you're really saying is that he's been promoted above his level of competence. Like me."

Again, Ken hastened to pour oil on the waters. "You've got a lot on your plate, Woeful, that's all. This Olympic business, we're all hanging on the outcome. A conscientious bloke like Denis, it'd be no reflection on him if it all got a bit overwhelming. And these things do tend to happen out of the blue, no warning."

Woeful looked a long way from convinced. "Put it like that," he said, grudgingly.

Gil Methven looked at me sideways. "You're Agnelli's bum boy, right, Wheeler, something like that?"

A lifetime in the Labor Party had inured me to such childish name-calling. After the last election, Agnelli had helped marshal the caucus numbers to deny Gil the deputy premiership, so I knew his remarks weren't personal. I rose above them.

"You must be mistaking me for somebody else," I said. "Someone easily intimidated by a pompous arsehole."

"Now that we've got all that off our chests," said Ken cheerfully. "Woeful says you were the last one to speak to Denis last night."

"We left the office together," I said. "About seven."

"He say where he was going?"

"Home," I said. "And I'm no expert, but he didn't look like a man on the brink of a nervous breakdown."

Woeful shot me a grateful glance and I realized why I was there. In Denis's absence, Woeful wanted a witness to his dealings with Gil Methven.

"Orright," said the Police Minister. "Either the wife reports it now, or she waits until the morning. If she decides to wait, Ken here can have a few discreet inquiries made."

Woeful made a noise in the back of his throat. "What's that supposed to mean?"

Methven slowly unfolded his legs and stood up. "You were the one came to me," he said. "You don't want my help, fine."

The bells began to ring for a division. A continuous, insistent jangle, penetrating as a dentist's drill. It filled the tiny office, on and on. When at last Woeful spoke, he all but choked on his words. "I appreciate this, Gil. I really do. I'll talk to Marjorie, suggest she waits."

We in the Victorian branch of the ALP may have lacked the viscous cohesion of the New South Wales Right, but we were not entirely without a sense of solidarity. Factional differences were sharp in our decline, but they were not yet cutthroat. If one of the boys goes missing, you send out a friendly search party.

The two ministers went upstairs, each taking a different route. "Nice work," I said to Ken.

He agreed. "When you've got 'em by the short and curlies."

"So what are you going to do about finding Denis?"

"Fucked if I know," he shrugged.

16

HOLLY LOOKED EDIBLE. An absolute muffin. Thigh-length V-neck sweater over her Lycra work-out suit, her ponytail threaded through the back of a suede-billed Nike baseball cap. She brought an empty sports bag with her, tossed it in the back seat, and we headed north through the suburban night. Her effervescence filled the car like a well-shaken bottle of Gatorade.

"I really appreciate this," she said.

"My pleasure. Beats sitting around the old folks home, dribbling in my rocking chair."

"C'mon. You're only as old as you feel."

I didn't feel a day over a hundred. But we old codgers must take our pleasures where we find them. I couldn't help but notice that, every time we stopped at a red light, I copped envious glances from men in other cars. Holly's buoyant mood was infectious. I told her about the Charade and we laughed like drains. "I mean, why bother to steal a car like that?" she said. "No offense."

As we conjured up the possibilities — getaway car for a poor-box robbery, a criminal mastermind with low self-esteem — I was thinking what a good idea this had turned out to be. Like a kind of chaste date, I told myself, sneaking guilty sideways looks. Fun, until

I asked about our destination. "So who's this friend?" I asked. "The one with your CDs?"

She didn't bat an eyelid, the little vixen. "Steve, of course," she said. "Who else?"

"Steve Radeski? That fucking steroid-deranged lunatic?" My foot hit the brake so hard we almost went into a tailspin. "No way." I flicked on the turn signal.

"Chill out, Murray," said Holly. "He won't be there. I made sure of that. He's at work. Some shitty disco in Northcote. I checked. Honest."

"You sure?"

She crossed her heart and hoped to die.

I flicked the indicator off. "You must really want this stuff."

"It's not that. It's, you know, the principle. I want him to realize it's totally over between us. So he stops hassling me."

I could see her point, sort of. "Yeah, but what if he's home?"

"He won't be. I rang the place, The Climber. Checked he'd be there. Eight till two, they said."

"Yeah, but just say he's there." A hundred kilos of chemically fueled aggression.

"He won't be," she insisted. "Anyway, I can handle him."

"It's not you I'm worried about," I said. "I'm not trained for this sort of work. Maybe you should have got somebody else to drive you."

"Like who?"

"I don't know. One of those guys I see hitting on you all the time in the gym." Young blokes with well-defined pectorals. Old blokes with access to private security firms.

"Maybe I prefer to do the hitting."

What could I say to that? It had to be bullshit, but she knew she had me. "Okay. He's not there, but ten of his muscle-bound ape mates are."

"No mates," she said. "It's his father's house."

"Don't tell me," I said. "A sweet-tempered four-foot rose enthusiast who cries when he has to kill an aphid."

"A crabby old tyrant who used to run a weight gym," she said. "And thinks the world's out to get him. But don't worry. He won't be there either. He had a stroke and Steve put him in a home."

"What a great family. How did you get mixed up with this lot?"

She set her heels on the edge of the seat, tucked her knees under her chin, hugged her shins and gave me the full ball of wax. How she met Steve at his father's gym while touting her résumé around the suburban sweat shops, looking for casual work. "Across the road from the Rosanna railway station, it was. One of those old-style places, just free weights and crash mats and a few ratty old pressing benches. Didn't even have aerobics. Real Charles Atlas stuff."

The historical reference surprised me. Charles Atlas was back there with Bob Menzies and Queen Victoria.

Holly saw me smile. "Amaze your friends," she said. "You ninety-pound weakling. Anyway, the gym's not there any more. Got taken over by Fit 'n' Well before they went bankrupt. I don't think old Rudy Radeski was much of a businessman."

Although there was no opening for newly registered aerobics instructors in the Radeski family gymnasium, Steve soon found other ways of making himself useful to Holly. "He was a very good lover." She tucked one knee under her chin, hugging her shin. "You know."

I told her I could vaguely remember the concept.

"This was, like, before the steroids, right?" she hastened to re-assure me. "Back when he was normal."

I found it hard to imagine Steve Radeski as normal but I took her word for it. "A normal weightlifter?"

"A better than average weightlifter. You're just prejudiced. It's a perfectly legitimate sport."

"Like aerobics?"

"Aerobics isn't a sport," she said. "It's an activity."

Anyway, she continued. It was Steve who alerted her to the vacancy at the City Club. This was when he was working downstairs at the Typhoon nightclub. They might have even moved in together if it hadn't been for Steve's father. "They were, like, pretty close-knit because his mother died when he was little and his dad brought him up after that, just the two of them." A widower, his business overtaken by new trends, the old man had become possessive of his son. "He reckoned I was a distraction. Probably thought I was sapping Steve's strength or something."

I could see old man Radeski's point. "Were you?" I said. "Sapping his strength?"

"Let's just say I gave as good as I got."

Together the Radeskis concentrated their energies on getting Steve into the national weightlifting squad. Both were ecstatic when he finally made the cut. But their satisfaction was not long-lived.

"Steve reckoned he'd been victimized, that it was all politics. That everybody was using steroids and the federation just needed a scapegoat. After he was kicked out, he didn't know what to do. Just sat around all day feeling sorry for himself, arguing with Rudy, losing condition. That's when things between us started going off the rails. He just didn't care any more. Lost his job at Typhoon. Even lost interest in you-know-what."

I nodded sympathetically. To lose interest in you-know-what with Holly Deloite a man would need to be in a bad way. To compound the situation, the father had suffered his stroke. "Steve wanted to look after him at home but it was hopeless, so he had to put him in a home. He's pretty old anyway," she explained. "Sixty-something."

Geriatric. Just as she told me this, we drove past the Olympic Hotel where my father took the licence after the Carter's Arms. We lived there for nearly five years, all through my adolescence. Unexpectedly, I had a sudden sense of fellow-feeling for Steve Radeski. I, too, was the only son of a widowed father with lousy business acumen. The carpark of the Olympic was now occupied by a Kentucky Fried franchise. Too late for us, the Colonel.

Unlike Rudy Radeski, fortunately, my father had projected none of his own displaced ambitions onto me. The life of a hotelkeeper left him with few illusions, scant time and even less energy. And I took care to do as little as possible to excite his expectations.

And, unlike old man Radeski, my father was not moldering in

some hospice bed. He was living on Bribie Island, fishing every day from his aluminum runabout and studying the stock market with the eye of a man who has finally cracked the code. From a publican who had managed to go broke in five different hotels, he had transformed himself into a late-blooming Midas, parlaying the proceeds from the sale of his last pub into a healthy little nest egg. First it was macadamia nuts, then avocado farms, then resort development. The old fox had even contrived to unload his Qintex shares before the crash of '87, after doubling his dough.

Eventually, I supposed, there would be full-care retirement villages to think about. But later, not now. At seventy-seven, he was showing every sign of living forever.

Sympathy, Holly was explaining, has its limits. Hers ran out when Steve tried to clobber her. "That was a big mistake. He should have known better," she said, setting her jaw.

So she'd cut her emotional losses, changed the lock on her flat and left him to wallow in self-pity. When the job-exchange opportunity came up, she jumped at it. Used the six weeks in Queensland to make a clean emotional break. But now, Steve suddenly reappears, acting like he's got some prior claim. Fronting up at her workplace, demanding you-know-what. Almost getting her the sack. Understandably, a girl decides she wants her things back, wants it understood that what's past is past.

Traffic was thin on the divided road, fast moving, and we had the run of the lights. We passed indoor cricket centers and discount furniture showrooms and warehouses lit like nuclear power plants. Heidelberg wasn't much further, two, three kilometers. As the road dipped and narrowed to cross the Darebin Creek, I asked for directions. "Next left," said Holly. "Liberty Parade."

"Thought you said he lived in Heidelberg?"

"West Heidelberg," she said. "Same thing."

Not where I came from it wasn't. Heidelberg was a leafy middle-class neighborhood where famous landscape painters once daubed masterpieces *en plein air* on the wooded banks of the Yarra. West Heidelberg, on the other hand, was an experiment gone wrong.

Originally built to accommodate the athletes at the 1956 Olympics, it was hailed at the time as a model of modular housing. A vision of the future where those displaced by inner-urban slum clearances could breathe the life-giving air of suburbia. Within ten years, it was a wasteland of broken fences, ravaged lawns and teenage thuggery.

That, at least, was how I first encountered it, back when it peopled my adolescent imagination with terrors such as the Fletcher brothers who carried knives to school, set fire to Preston Town Hall while the mayoral ball was in progress and eventually graduated to the exercise yard at Pentridge prison, five minutes up the road.

Things had changed, of course, in the two decades since I lived just across the Darebin Creek. A more house-proud ethos had taken root. As we continued past streets named for half-forgotten battle-grounds in far distant lands — Tobruk, Narvik, Wewak — we found ourselves in a working-class neighborhood as respectable as any in the city, all picket fences and native gardens. But, despite the applied decoration, the houses were still near-identical boxes, biscuits from the same cutter. Three or four standard designs, street after street, varied only by the occasional three-story walk-up.

We passed a row of shops set back behind a lawn, the approximation of a village square. All were closed but for the hamburger joint, some battling immigrant's grim purchase on prosperity. Holly directed me down a cul-de-sac and I pulled into the curb.

The Radeski residence was unlikely to rate a feature in *House & Garden*. One of the standard boxes, it squatted behind a rectangle of neglected lawn, the windows dark. The untended lavender hedge had grown woody with neglect and the flowerbeds were choked with weeds. Even the houses on either side were dark, with not even the flicker of television to betray life inside.

"How are you going to get in?" I said.

"Easy." Holly grabbed her sports bag. "Back in a couple of minutes." She bounded up the short path toward the front door.

White-painted rocks about the size of bowling balls lined the path and, as I watched, she picked one up and lobbed it through the frosted glass panel of the front door. With an abrupt clatter, the panel collapsed into a pile of shards. She turned, brushed her palms together, tossed me a smirk and let herself into the house.

Ah, the course of love gone wrong. Doubtless she planned to break every ornament in the place. Nothing to do with me, of course, I was just the wheel man. I slid down in my seat, waiting for the neighbors to appear, alarms to sound. Nothing happened. I unsnapped my seatbelt and twiddled the dial of the car radio. A panel of academics was discussing the future of the Warsaw Pact. Madonna was living in the material world.

No more noises emerged from the house. Smashing down the front door had, it seemed, satisfied Holly's vengeful urges. I stepped out of the car and stretched my legs. The night was cool and very dark. Two streets away, a rev-head gunned his motor and laid rubber. A dog barked. As a kid, I wouldn't have been caught dead in this neighborhood after sunset. Now the idea seemed just plain silly. Even the animal population had lost its feral edge. A sleek-furred cat appeared from nowhere, mewing expectantly. I reached down and it ran its tail through my hand. "What's your name, kitty cat?"

The moggie arched its back with pleasure and rubbed itself against my leg. Obviously not a female. It went up the driveway and I went with it, following it around the side to the backyard, killing time.

Along the side fence, tomato stakes were splayed against each other in disarray. A screened porch had been added to the back of the house, its rafters extending to form a pergola shrouded in a tangled mass of overgrown passionfruit vines. A carpet of rotting leaves squelched damply underfoot and the stem of a rotary clothes hoist loomed out of the murk. The driveway extended back to an old aluminum garage, half-buried under creepers, the buckled metal doors sagging on their hinges. I could just make out a small white sedan, the same model as the one I was driving. A jungle of overgrown shrubs swallowed the cat.

Something smacked against my forehead. An old hanging

basket, suspended from the pergola. As I backed away, an arm snaked around my neck, squeezing my windpipe and jerking my head backward. "Gotcha," a voice hissed in my ear.

Jesus, I thought. It's on again.

Reflexively, I drove both my elbows backward, hard.

"Oomph." Breath rushed past my ear and the choke-hold slackened.

I wrenched free and ran, glancing backward over my shoulder. Whoever he was, he was definitely not Steve Radeski. This bloke was much less solidly built. He was wearing a black tracksuit with the hood up and the drawstring pulled tight around his face. That was as much as I could see. A ninja, I thought. Some martial arts dickhead.

He came at me fast, shoulder down. My feet skidded and I slammed into the metal post of the clothes hoist.

"Take it easy," warned a voice, another shape in the darkness, black on black. He wasn't talking to me.

The two shapes circled, indistinct presences in the darkness. The ninja had something in his hand. He swung wide and it whistled through the air. A blow hit my ribs, a jolt of electricity. He swung again and I dodged sideways. Something struck the clothes hoist and a dull wooden note sounded.

You let your guard down, I thought. Get taken in by a bit of crazy paving and some potted geraniums, start thinking that you can just go wandering around West Heidelberg at night, devil-may-care. This is what happens.

I reached up and grabbed the radial bar of the Hills Hoist, kicking out. My heels connected and I swung backward, recoiling from the impact. The clothesline spun on its axis and I felt a shudder run through the crossbar. "Fucken hell," yelped the voice.

My feet hit the ground running and I darted for the side of the house. Not fast enough. A blow struck the back of my knees and I pitched forward through the air. It was a short flight, no frills. No movie, not even a cup of coffee. When I hit the screen door of the porch, it splintered off its hinges and thwacked flat on the ground, me sprawled on top of it.

I was going to suffer. It was going to be brutal and ugly. I went foetal, arms curled around my head.

"Murray!" shouted Holly from somewhere inside the house.

A white radiance seared through my clenched eyelids. I opened my eyes. Two dark shapes loomed above me, staring down. One of them, his head surrounded by a halo of light, was Darcy Anderson.

"Hey," he said, irritably. "You're not Steve Radeski."

I was staring upward into the unshaded globe of the porch light. One hundred watts, its sudden incandescence sent hallucinatory worms wriggling across my field of vision. Darcy Anderson's face came in and out of focus.

Not Darcy Anderson, I realized. Similar face, but older and harder. Unmistakable Aboriginal features, burning with malice. Whoever he was, he held a fence picket in his hand and spoke in a staccato burst. "Where is he? Where's Radeski?"

Standing next to him, staring down in disbelief, was Ambrose Buchanan. He scratched his whiskers. "Murray Whelan?" he said. "The fuck you doing here?"

"Murray!" shouted Holly, somewhere close. "Stop mucking around." I scrambled to my feet. As the back door flew open, the two Koories melted back into the darkness. Holly appeared in the doorway, her eyes wide with alarm.

"Come quick," she said. "There's a body in here."

17

THE BACK DOOR OPENED directly into the kitchen, a fifties Formica job that had seen better days. Vinyl floor tiles and a flickering fluorescent tube. Radeski was a man of simple tastes and prodigious appetite. Either that, or he was doing the catering for the Mormon Tabernacle Choir.

Bulk foodstuffs were piled everywhere. Twenty-five-kilo sacks of rice, hessian bags bulging with potatoes. Cardboard boxes of tuna in brine, plain label. Plastic pails full of something called Megamix 5000, whey protein isolate. Cartons of eggs. Innumerable bottles, vials and jars. Amino acids, creotone monohydrates, ginseng, mineral extracts, an alphabet of vitamins.

Holly charged ahead, through swinging doors, into the lounge room. Not that Radeski had been doing much lounging. Apart from a row of built-in shelves, there was no furniture. Bolted to one wall was a slotted metal frame, some sort of home-made gym equipment. On the floor beside it lay a pile of round weights, like a collection of oversize phonograph records, heavy metal favorites. A press bench sat under the frame, the lifting bar fully loaded. At a glance, Radeski was pressing something in the vicinity of 450 pounds. The air reeked of sweat and the parmesan tang of dried vomit.

We kept going. On the faded floral Axminster beside the front door, surrounded by broken glass, lay a cheap boom box and Holly's blue bag, spilling audio tapes and dog-eared paperbacks. Bruce Springsteen. *The Power of One.* Past a telephone table, a short hallway led to the bedrooms, one front, one back. Holly stopped at a door. "It's Rudy's room. I was on my way out when I thought I heard something."

The matrimonial bedroom. Neat, musty, old-fashioned, the curtains drawn, dust showing on the glass top of the triple-mirrored dressing-table. The double bed was covered with a cream candlewick bedspread. Hanging above it on the wall in a cheap gilded frame was a picture of the Sacred Heart of Jesus.

"Jesus Christ," I said.

Jesus didn't say anything. Surprised, probably. He and I hadn't been on speaking terms for quite some time. He merely bared his inflamed aorta and stared down with his long-suffering eyes. What he beheld was a sight to see.

"Jesus," I said again. "Denis!"

Denis Dogherty was lying immobile on the bed, his dark tie knotted at the collar of his corduroy shirt, his shoes neatly laced. His spectacles, neatly folded, peeped from the breast pocket of his jacket. A dark stain leaked from his right ear and crusted on the pillow beneath his head. Pink foam flecked his lips. His skin was pallid and waxy. His eyes were closed. I sank to my knees beside the bed and peered into his face. The hair on the back of his head was matted and sticky with blood.

"Denis," I said, taking him by the shoulders. "Can you hear me?" His eyelids fluttered and his cheek twitched. The foam on his lips bubbled and he emitted an almost inaudible groan.

"He's alive," blurted Holly in a gush of relief. "I thought he was dead. Scared the shit out of me." Then, confused, "You know him?"

"I work with him." But not for much longer, by the look of it. He did not respond to my voice. I shook him gently, powerless, not knowing what to do. His breath was so faint I thought it had stopped.

Holly was back in the hall, furiously jiggling the receiver. "Shit," she yelled. "Cut off. Steve mustn't have paid the bill. Typical." She reappeared at the door. "There's a phone booth at the shops." She took off, tossing her voice behind her. "I'll get an ambulance."

"Take the car," I called after her but she kept going, her feet crunching glass, her footfalls receding down the path.

You didn't need to be Dr. Kildare to see that Denis was in a bad way. I withdrew my hand, sticky with blood. He'd been lying there for some time, that much was apparent. I thumbed back an eyelid. The white was a filigree of ruptured capillaries, the pupil fully dilated. Whatever that meant.

Snatches of first-aid crowded my brain. Immobilize the patient. No problem there. Keep the victim warm. I laid the back of my hand on his cheeks, found them cool to the touch, tugged the bedspread across his chest and legs. Clear the airways. Don't let the patient choke on his own tongue. Remove dentures, if applicable.

Sticking two fingers between his teeth, I probed his mouth, chanting his name over and over like a mantra. "Denis. Denis. Denis." His head felt as fragile as an eggshell in the palm of my hand.

Something moved at the door. Ambrose Buchanan's face appeared. "What's happening, eh?" He crept into the room and stared down at us.

"You tell me," I said sharply.

He took umbrage at the accusation. "We don't know anything about this," he protested. "Do we, Deadly?"

He moved aside and the ninja sidled into the room, pushing back his hood. Deadly. The name suited him. Early thirties, a bandanna tight across his skull, pirate-style. Medium height, lithe, slippery. Orangy-brown freckles smeared across his cheeks. A red, black and yellow stud in one lobe. Reform-school tats on the back of his sinewy hands. Three shades lighter than Ambrose. Good-looking in a careless, surly sort of way. But speedy, jittery. Deadly.

He jerked his chin at Denis, excited, delighted. "See," he bragged. "Told ya."

"Told him what?" A dull ache spread through my side where the picket had connected. "If you did this, I'll kill you. I swear I will."

Deadly sneered. "Think I'd still be hangin' round if I done this?"

He didn't mind if I thought he was violent, he just didn't want anyone thinking he was stupid. Anyway, my good opinion was irrelevant. He was more intent on proving some point to Buchanan, citing Denis as evidence. "Told ya Radeski was fucking crazy," he said.

My fingers were still in Denis's mouth. As far as I could tell, his teeth were all his own. Not bad for a bloke of his vintage. His generation often had them all pulled out by the time they were twenty-one, rotten or not. Save trouble later.

"Urghhl." Denis dry-retched, coughing bile. His hand came up, ropy-veined, and pawed at my chest. "Stevie?" His voice was a faint whisper, his eyes open but fighting for focus. "That you?"

"It's Murray." I put my hand in the nape of his neck. "Murray Whelan. Hang in there, mate. You'll be right. Ambulance on its way."

He winced and something like panic crossed his face. "You won't mention Woeful, will you?" Fresh blood dribbled from his nose and he started to cough.

"Okay," I nodded. Anything to calm him.

He was no child to be so easily placated. His fingers became a claw, grabbing at my shirt, drawing my face down to his. "Promise me you'll keep Woeful's name out of this."

"Promise," I swore, startled at his vehemence. "I won't mention Woeful."

He relaxed his grip and subsided onto the bed. His body went limp and his eyes closed. "It's up to you now, Murray," he whispered.

"I understand." I didn't have the foggiest idea what he was talking about. Neither did he, probably. He must have been in shock. "What happened, mate?"

"Stevie." His mouth went slack and he slipped again into unconsciousness.

Ambrose and Deadly were standing at the foot of the bed. "See," said Deadly again. "Told ya." He prowled, a simmering presence, teetering on the edge of violence. He slid open a drawer and started prodding around inside.

Ambrose nudged him away and shut the drawer. "Woeful?" he said. "Is he talking about Woeful McKenzie?"

"He works for him." I put my ear to Denis's chest. I didn't know what else to do. His heartbeat was faint, slow, distant.

"You a mate of Radeski's?" demanded Deadly. "So where is he then?" He was a madman, bouncing all over the place, cranked up. The bedroom felt crowded, as claustrophobic as a Christmas sale.

I ignored him, staring up at Ambrose Buchanan from my knees beside the bed. "What's going on, Ambrose? Why are you here? What do you want with Steve Radeski?"

Running feet thudded in the street, approaching fast. Beyond them rose the distant wail of a siren. Deadly backed into the doorway, tugging Ambrose's sleeve. "C'mon, bro. Let's get out of here."

Ambrose looked down at me, his face a plea for forbearance. He raised his open palm, swearing an oath. "This isn't down to us, dead set." He backed away reluctantly, drawn by Deadly's insistence. "Later, eh? I'll explain later."

A hollow gurgle came from deep in Denis Dogherty's chest. His breath was infinitely faint. The back door slapped softly against its frame. Holly's feet pounded up the hallway. A siren moved closer, rising and falling in the distance.

18

"ON ITS WAY," Holly gulped, flushed from the sprint. Lolly legs, the fat tongues of her white trainers sticking out above the laces. "How is he?"

The ambulance woop-wooped into the street and she again dashed off. I could hear her at the front door, hastily clearing away the broken glass. Then the paramedics arrived. Well-practiced young men who had Denis in a spinal brace and out of the house on a gurney in under two minutes.

He had sustained his injuries, the ambos estimated, quite some time before. Perhaps as much as twenty-four hours. His skull was fractured and he'd lost great deal of blood from a gash at the back of the head. When they lifted him off the bed, we found that blood had saturated the pillow and soaked down into the mattress.

I told them what I knew. Which, apart from his name, wasn't much. It was all there in his wallet, anyway.

My request to ride to the hospital in the back of the ambulance was politely but firmly refused. Nor should I follow in my own car, I was told. We were to wait there for the police. They were definite about that.

It all happened very quickly. Holly and I stood on the footpath and watched the flashing light disappear around the corner. The cluster of curious youths which had materialized as if by magic at the sound of the siren vanished just as abruptly. Suddenly everything seemed remarkably quiet, as though the planet had been struck by some inexplicable catastrophe and we were the sole survivors.

As the burst of activity ended, shock gave way to bafflement. My hand went into my pocket, looking for a cigarette. We don't do that any more, I told it. But it wished we still did.

"This is really weird," said Holly, the mistress of understatement. "Steve's a fuck-up, I know, but I can't believe he'd do something like that. Who is that old guy, anyway? Why was he here? Did he tell you what happened?"

Very good questions. "His name is Denis Dogherty," I said. "He works for the Minister for Sport."

That exhausted my supply of answers. And did nothing to explain how he had come to be lying, unconscious and bleeding, in the deserted house of a banned ex-weightlifter. But at least his whereabouts were no longer a mystery. In less than five minutes they'd be wheeling him into the emergency room at the Austin Hospital. Holly was looking considerably chastened. She chewed her bottom lip. "What now?"

"We wait for the cops." And take a quick squiz around the house. Seek enlightenment there.

"Uh oh," said Holly, as we reached the shattered front door. "What about this?"

"Willful damage," I said, sternly. "Breaking and entering."

She took me literally. The color drained from her cheeks.

"Lucky you've got a good lawyer," I said.

She still didn't get it. "Lawyer? You really think I need a lawyer? What lawyer?"

"You gave me the job," I reminded her. "Remember?"

"You think this is funny, do you?" Shirty now, she began brushing crushed glass off the doorstep with the side of her shoe. Touchy, touchy. She was embarrassed, I realized. Not just at her gullibility but at the whole situation. At having lured me here with assertions that all would be well.

"Tell the police the truth," I reassured her. "Under the circumstances, I don't think a busted window is going to upset them."

She said nothing, more interested in picking up plate-sized fragments of broken glass. I went down the hall. There were two doors. The master bedroom where Holly found Denis was on the right. I opened the door on the left.

Little Stevie's bedroom, outgrown but never abandoned. Steam locomotives on the wallpaper and dirty socks on the floor. The bed was seriously unmade, the sheets long unwashed, the greasy pillow flecked with shed hairs, dark pubic curls. Pages from bodybuilding magazines were stuck to the walls, all straining sinews and triangular torsos. Hanging from a nail above the bed was a lifting suit and a truss, a wide leather belt emblazoned with the word "Buffalo." Spilling from beneath the bed was a lurid fan of skin mags, do-it-yourself gynecology.

An overfilled wastepaper basket lay on its side amid the dirty laundry, spilling its trashy contents. Perforated blister packs, empty pill bottles, snap-top glass ampoules, blood-smeared tissues, used hypodermics. Methyltestosterone enanthate. Finaject. Androl 50. Venabol. One of the packets had the outline of a chess piece on it. The knight. Equipoise, long-lasting veterinary steroid, said the label.

Back in the front door, Holly was fussing with a broom, unwilling to meet my gaze. I went into the lounge room and took a good look around.

Apart from the gym equipment, there wasn't much to see. Heavy black drapes hung over the windows, making it even more rank and dank than the bedroom. A row of shelves was set into a recess beside the oil heater, collecting dust. On the wall opposite the pressing bench was a full-length mirror. Dead center, about head height, the glass was shattered. A sunburst of cracks radiated from a dark smudge that could only have been blood. It didn't take Einstein to work out whose.

I took a closer look at the shelves. On the middle shelf was a row of photographs, family sporting triumphs. A teenage Steve in a striped jersey, a soccer ball tucked under his arm. Not a bad-looking kid. An old black-and-white shot of a stocky weightlifter in the classic strong-man stance, legs braced, upraised arms holding a hugely weighted bar above his head. Beside it, a group shot. Thirty or so men in blazers staring soberly at the camera. *Polska Druzyna Olimpijska XVI* read the banner hanging behind them.

"Steve's father," I called to Holly. "Was he in the 1956 Olympics?"

"That's how come he came to Australia," she called back. "Never went home. Well, you wouldn't, would you?"

The bottom shelf held books, propped in place by a chipped plaster statuette of the Virgin Mary. I scanned the spines. Not big readers, the Radeskis. *The Guinness Book of Records*, 1979 edition. Half a dozen brown-covered Reader's Digest condensed books. A James A. Michener paperback, *Hawaii*. I remembered the movie. Max von Sydow and Julie Andrews. *Stalin's Crimes against Poland* in hard cover. I flipped open the title page and read the publisher's imprint. The Council of Captive Nations.

Old soldiers of the Cold War. Men from Eastern Europe with dubious war histories and questionable sources of finance. Self-proclaimed community leaders who cultivated their grievances in suburban social clubs with portraits of dead fascists on their pine-paneled walls. Compulsory folk dancing for the young people. The women out in the kitchen doing things with pickled herrings. I'd spent years at Ethnic Affairs avoiding just such characters. Not that it was difficult. Most of them thought the ALP was a communist front.

But Rudy Radeski was no intellectual cold warrior, I could see that, and I read into the presence of *Stalin's Crimes* no more than an exile's rough obeisance to the history of his benighted homeland. Steve's reading, by the look of it, was limited to *Beaver Monthly*.

The top shelf held a row of sporting trophies. Most were towering plinths of gilded plastic, but some were more modest. I reached up and took one down, a small figurine of a woman tennis player frozen in mid-serve. *St. Joseph's Social Club, Mixed Doubles, 1955. Irene Boag.*

Could this be right?

"Steve's mother," I called to Holly. "Do you know how she died?"

"What?" she snapped back, irritably.

I repeated the question. I wasn't sure why I was asking it. The answer was in my hand. One of the belles of Bay Street, racquet poised. The little sister, Denis called her. Married a migrant, funny sort of bloke.

"Accident," called Holly. "Fell off a ladder. Why?"

"Jesus fucking Christ," I muttered, returning the dusty trophy to its place. Denis had pruned a twig off the family tree.

Well, at least one thing was now clearer. Denis Dogherty was Steve Radeski's uncle. Which meant that so too was Woeful McKenzie. Amazing how little I knew about the two of them. Related by marriage to a right-wing refugee.

"Promise you won't tell them about Woeful," Denis had pleaded. And I'd promised. Tell them what? Fucked if I knew. He was probably brain-damaged, picked up by little Stevie and thrown against the mirror. Christ. As if Woeful didn't have enough on his plate without a berko nephew.

Rudy Radeski and Irene Boag. Immigrant lad and local lass. Battlers, hence the West Heidelberg address. Not far from Rosanna, site of the struggling family business. The mother devoutly Catholic, the father carrying it as cultural baggage from the old country. Steve, the only son. First a mummy's boy, then the focus of his father's expectations.

Enough of the pop psychology. Somebody else could sink their forensic scalpel into this little lot. I went through the kitchen and into the backyard, wondering if Ambrose Buchanan and Deadly Deadshit were still lurking about.

But nobody came out of the shadows, not even when I squinted into the darkness of the overgrown garage and confirmed that the white shape was a government-issue Toyota.

Car, mirror, syringes. The scenario was falling into place. Some time after work the previous evening, Denis had driven here to visit his nephew Steve, an immature young man with a short temper, big muscles and a bloodstream full of elephant juice. Steve had decked Denis, then laid him out in the master bedroom. To recover? To die?

Those weren't the only things that remained unclear. What had set Steve off, for example? And why had Denis come calling in the first place? And what about Steve Radeski's more recent visitors, an Aboriginal activist and a petty-crim Koori? My little brown brothers had clearly not popped around for a glass of sherry and a chukka of cribbage. The ache in my ribs told me that much.

I looked at my watch. Ten minutes since the ambulance's departure. Holly returned the white rock to its place beside the front path and swept the broken glass into a pile. She found a pile of newspapers in Steve's bedroom and I squatted beside her, prising jagged fragments out of the old putty of the door and laying them on the paper for her to wrap. We worked in silence, crouched on our haunches. As I carefully laid each piece flat on the newspaper, Holly folded a page over it as precisely as if she was wrapping a birthday present.

The papers were more than a month old, their news as stale as flat beer. Olympic items dominated. The official start of the torch relay, the Prime Minister handing the flaming firebrand to some beaming tacker in a MOB T-shirt. Plans for the proposed new Aquatic Center praised by a Finnish architect. IOC CHIEFS TO RECEIVE RELAY TORCH, the same story that Ambrose Buchanan had shown me, breathless prose about the upcoming Evaluation Commission visit. This item was circled in black marker pen, and the rest of the page was scrawled with hammers and sickles.

"Was Steve using steroids when the two of you were an item?" I said.

"Sometimes." She inclined her head in the direction of the bedroom. "But nothing like that."

"You hear things." I was openly nosy.

She grinned bleakly, emerging from her shell. "Make you a regular stallion, they do." She balled her fist and flexed her forearm.

"That explains the horse on the pack," I said. "Think I should give them a try?"

"Not unless you want your hair to fall out and your nuts to shrivel to the size of raisins."

"That really happens?"

"Acne, mood swings, memory loss. Steve, he'd come out of training, not be able to remember where he left his car. Does wonders for your motivation, though."

I thought of Denis, doctors working on him. I wanted to ring Woeful, wondered how long before the police arrived. "What do you think motivated this?"

"This?" said Holly, somber again, kneeling, wrapping. "Who knows? Nothing probably." The voice of experience.

As I reached up to the top of the door for the last chunk of glass, somebody stuck a red hot poker through my side. Holly saw me wince. "Are you okay?" She stood and put her hand on my arm and looked at me with such sweet concern that I was in immediate danger of trying to take advantage of the situation.

"Indigestion," I said. An old man's complaint. The sort of thing you get eating tagliatelle primavera in the Hyatt food court, watching the seven o'clock news on the television above the bar, lip-reading Ambrose Buchanan as he goes on about No Olympics without Justice.

Holly was looking through the missing panel in the door.

"This should be interesting," she said.

19

FIRST CAME THE UNIFORMS. One male, one female. All clipboards and torches. Aggregate age thirty. They took our names and listened to our explanations and we gave them a guided tour of the premises. Then the second lot arrived. Detectives, this time.

The top dog was a Detective Sergeant named Hendricks. He wore a drab-olive suit and a put-upon manner and had more lines around his eyes than usual for a man in his mid-thirties. Another five years and he'd be out of the force, running his own business, something with plenty of scope for the long lunch. His offsider was much younger, an up-and-comer who looked at Holly a little too wolfishly, in my opinion, for a man on the public payroll in pursuance of his duties.

Either it was a very slow night at the West Heidelberg station, or Denis was in a pretty bad way. Just how bad, the dicks weren't able or prepared to say. They asked us to wait, separating us to avoid the possibility of collusion. Which was fine by me because I didn't have anything to collude in. Not with Holly at any rate.

I did my waiting in the backyard, edgy and tired at the same time, queasy with apprehension and the slow drip from the nicotine teabag taped to my abdomen. A wooden picket lay on the ground beneath the clothes line and as I looked down at it a string of names uncoiled itself in my mind, connections from which I could draw scant comfort. A story from the papers, a name that fitted a face. Deadly. Deadly Ernest. Ernest Anderson.

It was back in the early eighties, if I remembered right, a couple of years after the incident with Reggie and the gun in Merle's kitchen. A prisoner by the name of Ernest Anderson barricaded himself in the maximum-security division of Goulburn Gaol, along with three other serious offenders. Claiming the NSW Armed Robbery Squad had stitched them up, they articulated their demands for a retrial by mutilating themselves with broken glass and setting fire to their mattresses. The prison authorities took their time finding the right key and, by the time the doors were unlocked and the fire doused, Anderson was the only one still alive.

Ambrose Buchanan was prominent in the campaign for a retrial, arguing that Anderson was a victim of institutional racism, that his original conviction had been based on planted evidence and police perjury. Eventually, the courts were compelled to concur that the coppers had shaved a few too many corners in their haste to make a case. In due course, Anderson walked. Not that anybody seriously doubted he was capable of the crime. With a string of priors running all the way back to primary school, Ernest Anderson was unlikely ever to be confused with Nelson Mandela.

It seemed reasonable to assume that this was the same Deadly who had just belted me in the ribs with a picket. None of which explained why he was looking for Steve Radeski. Or why he'd taken such apparently perverse delight in finding Denis bashed insensible. Or why Ambrose Buchanan was squiring him about. And the name Anderson, was there a connection there?

A cigarette, I felt sure, would help me answer these questions, help get the mental processes working a bit more efficiently. I plucked a blade of grass and gnawed it, but somehow it wasn't the same.

Out the front, radios were crackling and car doors slamming. Several more representatives of the law enforcement community arrived. A clot of curious onlookers assembled on the footpath. After they'd poked about inside the house for ten minutes, the detectives got around to talking to us. Hendricks came out into the yard and stood under the clothes hoist and listened while I repeated what I'd already told the uniforms — who I was and how I knew Holly and what I was doing there, about knowing Denis and how he'd been missing all day.

"I understand the victim spoke to you," said the cop when I finally paused to draw breath.

"He only regained consciousness for a few seconds. I asked him what happened and he said, 'Stevie.' Then he passed out again."

"He didn't say anything else?"

This was the tricky bit. "He was pretty far gone," I said. "Incoherent. But he definitely said, 'Stevie.' Apart from that, nothing else made sense. I'm afraid I can't be much more help to you."

That's not quite the way Hendricks saw it. "Anyone else here when you arrived?"

"Far as I know, the house was empty." I did my best not to sound evasive.

"You know where we can find this Steve Radeski?"

I shrugged, just wanting it all to be over. Dreading the prospect of having to ring Woeful, wondering if he was still at the House. "He's a bouncer at some club. The ex-girlfriend knows all about it."

Hendricks sucked his teeth and rubbed the back of his neck. "Can you believe this shit?" he said. It wasn't a question, not even a rhetorical one. Just another night on the job.

"What happens now?" I said.

We went back to the kitchen where Holly was sitting across the table from the wolfish dick. He was wearing a cashmere overcoat and laying on the charm with a silver trowel. "The Climber?" he was saying. "That dump in Northcote, just near the railway line? Bit of a come-down after Typhoon, isn't it?"

This was all getting a bit pally for Hendricks. "We'll be requiring a full statement in due course. And the homicide squad will probably want a word."

"Homicide?" I said, knowing already. Not wanting to know.

"The victim is not expected to recover," said Hendricks.

"Wow," said Holly. "That's terrible."

Detective Lothario stood up and pushed her sports bag across the table. "Don't forget your things, Ms. Deloite."

The boom box was one of those Taiwanese knock-offs, already falling apart. Sixty bucks at Kmart. A lot of trouble for the price.

"What about the front door?" she said.

"We'll let you know." Meaning she'd never hear about it again.

"When?" She missed the point.

"C'mon." I drew her chair back. "I'll drive you home."

But first a cigarette. Just the one. This sort of situation, a surrogate nicotine-delivery system just didn't cut the mustard. This sort of situation, intimations of mortality were essential, burnt offerings were demanded. Even as I asked Holly where she lived, hoping it wasn't Keysborough or Park Orchards or some other twenty-kilometer haul, I was already turning the Toyota into the West Heidelberg shops. The hamburger place was still lit, still empty, the rack of cigarettes visible through the plate-glass window.

Also visible, waiting on the bench at the deserted taxi rank, were Ambrose Buchanan and Deadly Anderson, his hood back up.

First things first. I pushed open the door of the takeout joint, inhaled the smell of fried onions and rancid cooking oil. *Come to Where the Flavor Is.* I named my brand. A filter was between my lips, a burning match in my hand, before I was back on the footpath. It had been almost twenty-four hours, but some things you never forget. As the flame bit into the tobacco and the first rush of smoke hit my exultant lungs, Ambrose Buchanan got up and walked toward me.

Tears welled in my eyes and a cough exploded in my chest. Head spinning, I staggered to the edge of the footpath and spat the lining of my throat into the gutter. I was feeling better already.

"Those things'll kill you, man," said Ambrose. He took out one of his own and lit it. Twenty meters away, his bruiser mate was watching us over his shoulder, one arm draped nonchalantly across the back of the taxi rank bench. "You tell the cops?" he said.

I got my breath back. Used it to inhale some more smoke. "What do you think?"

Buchanan thought I'd behaved pretty much as he'd expected. He acknowledged the fact with a small nod. "So what was that all about?" he said. "Back there."

"Thought you might be able to tell me."

"Nothing to do with us," he swore.

"Yeah, right," I said. "So I just imagined that your dickhead mate over there decked me with a lump of four-by-two."

"That was just a misunderstanding," he said. "Nothing personal."

"Well that's a fucking relief," I said. "What about Denis? Was he a misunderstanding, too?"

He shifted uncomfortably and picked a speck of tobacco off his bottom lip. "Who's Denis?" he said.

"Denis Dogherty. The old bloke bleeding all over the bed."

Buchanan showed me the pale skin of his palms. "Nothing to do with us," he repeated. It was a line I was getting sick of hearing.

"So you said. You also said that you'd explain what you were doing there. Well, here's your big chance. Enlighten me."

Buchanan kept glancing back toward the bench. He was impatient to go. "Not now," he said. "Later."

"Try telling that to the Homicide Squad," I said, fed up with being taken for granted.

Buchanan stopped in his tracks. "What do you mean?"

"Denis Dogherty is expected to die. If that happens, all bets are off. I'll scream like a stuck pig." I looked past him to the taxi stop. "That's Ernest Anderson, isn't it?" I said. "Unless I get a pretty convincing explanation, right now, I'll have no choice but to tell the cops he was there."

Ambrose did not like what he was hearing. He chewed his cigarette and scratched his beard. Eventually, he conceded to my point of view. "Ah, shit," he said. "Give us a minute."

Holly was sitting in the car, wondering why I was taking so long to buy a packet of cigarettes. I went across to her window and asked her to wait while I talked to these men. She started to ask me something but I turned away. Let her do the wondering for once. Ambrose was bent over Deadly, giving him the word. Deadly was reluctant. Listening, resisting, listening some more. As I approached, he shook his head. I couldn't tell if he was refusing or capitulating.

"Murray Whelan," Ambrose said stiffly. "This is Ernest Anderson."

The intricacies of Koori kinship were beyond me. Big Maxie at the Stars gym had talked about Darcy having some jailbird cousin. Deadly had ten years on young Darce and a lot more wear and tear, but there was a definite resemblance. Similar height and build. But something else as well. Something intangible, familial.

Deadly radiated hostility like a three-bar heater on full power, yet his deference to Ambrose was total, so tangible that I felt no fear. What I did feel was a little light-headed, as if the cigarette I was smoking was my very first. I extended my hand. When he shook it, he made sure I knew he was doing me a favor. "They call me Deadly," he said.

"You wouldn't be related to Darcy Anderson, by any chance?" I said. "Deadly."

Buchanan answered for him. "Darcy and Deadly are cousins. Were cousins."

"I'm sorry for your loss." I stripped off my tie, stuffed it into my jacket pocket. "And for some reason I've just lied to the police for you. Dunno why. Must be the company you keep."

The pain in my side had subsided to a dull ache. It only really hurt when I coughed. So I coughed for a bit, wincing at the pain. Deadly smiled. "Thought you was Radeski," he said. "Sneakin' round like that."

"A fence picket wouldn't be much use against Steve Radeski," I said. "Is that why you brought Ambrose along? Reinforcements?"

Ambrose was the real puzzle. What was he doing in the murky milieu of he-men and petty crims? Ambrose Buchanan did not strike me as a man given to cruising the night in such company.

Deadly's attention was focused on the parked car. "Who's the chick?" he said, appreciatively. He pushed his hood back to reveal his corsair bandanna.

"Radeski's ex," I said, starting to get the wheels of reciprocity turning. "She asked me to drive her out here to collect some stuff she left behind when they broke up. That's what she was doing when you jumped out of the shrubbery and went into your Greg Norman impersonation."

Holly stared back at us, expressionless, then turned away. The three of us in a row, Ambrose Buchanan in the middle. The Good, the Bad and the Ugly. All of us hyper as buggery, acting cool. Holly tilted the Toyota's rearview mirror and began studying the skin around her lips.

"So," I said. "Somebody going to tell me what's going on?"

Nobody spoke. A cab cruised into the parking area and approached the rank. The driver craned across his steering wheel, took one look at Ambrose and Deadly, turned off his roof light and kept going.

"You've got to appreciate Deadly's situation," said Ambrose. "He's on a suspended sentence. Any problems with the law and he's straight back inside."

Perry fucking Mason, beard and all. No, that was Ironside.

Whatever. I cleared my throat and hawked into the gutter. An irritable, impatient gesture. Also a necessary one. Bits of my lung kept falling off. I pitched my cigarette away with a grimace of disgust. It was past ten and I still hadn't called Woeful. Holly had finished with her lips. She closed her eyes and tilted her head back, neck like a swan. The silence grew longer.

"I've got things to do," I said, starting to get up.

Ambrose put his hand on my sleeve. "There was this session at the Royal earlier tonight, on account of Darcy. First time I've seen Deadly here in quite a while. Anyhow, he takes me aside, says he knows something. He's prepared to tell you what he told me but only on condition that he doesn't have to talk to the police."

"Something about what?"

"No police?"

In for a penny. I was already withholding information, fuck knows why. An ethical loophole could always be found later, if I needed to renege. "No police."

Ambrose held my eye. The last time he'd given me that look was in Merle's kitchen. Ah shit, I thought. I raised my right hand, three fingers. Scout's honor.

"Tell him," he said.

Deadly Anderson motioned for a cigarette. I gave him one and lit another myself. At the first hit of smoke, a red mist swirled behind my eyes. The veins in my forehead ticked like an alarm clock. Deadly leaned forward, forearms on his thighs. He flicked invisible ash off the end of his smoke. "Got this mate, right. Works at this stud farm up Lancefield. They use these steroids, right." Flick, flick. "So anyway, we've got this line going. He brings the stuff down at the weekend, I deliver it to the buyers." He took his eyes off Holly long enough to check me out, make sure I was keeping up.

These buyers were not, I took it, certified practicing veterinary surgeons. "So you're Radeski's horse steroid connection?"

"Silly prick can't get enough. Joke is, he thinks he's getting the stuff they put in them million-dollar racehorses. Only that shit's not easy to get, even if you work in the stables. Last few weeks, it's been impossible. So me mate gets the labels. Sticks them on this other stuff. They use it to stop pizzle rot." Flick flick.

I had a bit of a flick myself. "Pizzle rot?"

"That's when rams' dicks go rotten and fall off. Happens in wet weather." Flick, flick.

"That's the secret information?" I said, incredulous. I'd stumbled on a phoney steroid trafficking ring run by Koories. "What's this got to do with anything?"

"Shut up for five minutes and I'll fucken tell you," said Deadly. I did as he suggested. Flick, flick. Mollified by my silence, he continued. "I'm supposed to meet Radeski last night, right. Nine o'clock, under the flats near the Royal. Only I'm an hour late. When I turn up there's jacks everywhere. Blue lights flashin'. You name it. So, only natural, I disappear, right."

"And?"

"And then today he heard what happened to Darcy," said Ambrose. "So he came to me."

"You think that Radeski killed Darcy?"

"That sheep shit can't be doing his brain cells any fucken good. Maybe he decided to pay out on Darcy 'cause I wasn't there."

Okay, there was a certain degree of logic in the supposition. Darcy finishes training, shuts up shop at the gym, crosses the road to where hair-trigger Radeski is waiting for a man of a similar build and complexion. Some kind of interaction takes place, Radeski goes batshit, Darcy winds up beaten to death.

"So you decided it's payback time?"

Ambrose jumped to his feet and started pacing in front of us. Addressing the jury. "You got it wrong, Murray. Deadly here just wants to talk to Radeski, ask him where he was last night."

"Why not just tip the cops? Ring them anonymously or something?"

"And have Darcy's name connected with steroids?"

"You think that being killed by a drug-crazed maniac might be bad for Darcy's posthumous reputation?" I said, incredulous. "That's fucking crazy."

"Not just Darcy. Think about it, Murray. Sport is one of the few places Aboriginal people are allowed to be high achievers in this country. Ask the average white person to name an Aborigine, who do you get? An athlete, right. And so far, no Aboriginal sportsman or woman has been associated with steroid use. See what I mean?"

"But nobody's saying Darcy was on steroids," I protested.

"Not yet. But when the cops get involved, things take on a life of their own. Say Radeski didn't do it. But say the cops talk to him and find out where he gets his shit. You see my point. The crap starts flying around, who knows who it sticks to."

"Darce was clean," said Deadly, vehemently. "I never done the wrong thing by Darce. Dead set."

"So, rather than risk your parole, you decided to run your own private homicide investigation?"

"Looked Radeski up in the phone book," asserted Deadly, a man perfectly within his rights. "Waited for him to come home, have a quiet word. Ask him where he was last night. What's wrong with that?"

Except it was me who'd got the quiet word. "Phone book?" I repeated dully, feeling like I'd been hit with one.

If Deadly's suspicions were right, the steroid-crazed nephew of the Minister for the Olympics had not only possibly killed a member of his own family but also a promising young Aboriginal athlete.

"I can fucken read, y'know," muttered Deadly venomously.

"Deadly here can get a little emotional at times," said Buchanan. "That's why I came along with him. But instead of Radeski we found you."

"And Denis Dogherty," I reminded him. "In a state that seems to confirm Deadly's hypothesis about Radeski being homicidal."

"Looks that way. And very convenient for the cops if they can pin Darcy's death on Radeski. Do wonders for their clear-up rate."

"Jesus, Ambrose," I said. "Make up your mind. This morning you claimed that Darcy's death was racially motivated. You said so on television. What about those skinheads?" I kneaded my temples between thumb and forefinger.

"We're talkin' different issues here."

I was in no mood to argue the toss. Deliberately misleading the cops is rarely wise, particularly for someone in my position. Now I was sworn to secrecy. I needed time to think, to give matters more tranquil consideration.

Tranquillity was in short supply at that point. Holly got out of the Toyota, yawned and looked ostentatiously at her watch. Deadly stood up. Holly tilted her head to one side quizzically, then started toward us.

Explaining these two blokes would be hard enough. Introductions were absolutely out of the question. I needed to get rid of them. Just then, another cab turned into the parking area.

I stood and raised my arm, a white man in a suit. As the cab drew into the rank, I jerked its door open. "Radeski's a bouncer at some joint in Northcote called The Climber. Better hurry if you want to beat the cops."

Deadly didn't need to be told twice. He dived into the cab, dragging Ambrose with him. I swung the door shut and the cab pulled away.

20

"ONE MINUTE," I told Holly.

I dropped a coin into the payphone, dialed Parliament House, got put through to the party room and listened while the phone rang off the hook. Then I called directory assistance. The only D. McKenzie given for Port Melbourne was an unlisted number. I tried, I told myself. At least I tried.

"Who were those two?" said Holly when I got back in the car.

"Clients," I said brusquely. "A work-related matter. Where are we going?"

She didn't believe me, but let it go at that. We were going to Carlton, she informed me, where she had a flat in one of those courtyard blocks opposite the cemetery in Lygon Street. She'd been there for a couple of years. Before that, she lived at home with her parents and younger brothers in Pascoe Vale. Her dad was a mechanic at Essendon airport, where he worked for a firm that maintained corporate jets. Her mother was part-time at Qantas catering at Tullamarine, putting individually wrapped muffins on in-flight meal trays.

My mind was working overtime, trying to get an angle on what I'd seen and heard over the previous hour. "Promise you won't tell them about Woeful." Denis had been adamant, made me swear it. Were his words simply the delirious wanderings of a concussed brain? Or had he summoned up some lucidity from the brink of his battered condition?

Buchanan's role was now easier to figure. He was keeping Deadly on a short leash, trying to ensure he didn't make things worse than they already were. Deadly was clearly unlikely to wait around for the formal processes of the law to take their course. If he didn't have revenge in mind before, he was almost certainly looking for it now.

And, for expedience sake, I had just told him where to find it. Shit, Murray.

Maybe Radeski wasn't at this Climber joint, after all. Even better, maybe the police were there already. The cab driver would probably take his time, stop at every yellow light, try for the maximum fare. I was pretty sure I knew where the club was. If I stepped on the gas, we could probably get there first.

I tossed up telling Holly what I was doing, decided against it. It was all too complicated. I wasn't sure what was going on myself. Fortunately, she had lapsed into morose silence. And the most direct route to Carlton lay through Northcote. We practically had to drive past the place.

At one time, the area had specialized in textile and footwear manufacturing, back before wiser heads than mine decided that the country needed fifteen-dollar Indonesian running shoes more than it needed jobs. Most of the factories now lay idle, stripped to a shell. Some operated as samples 'n' seconds outlets where busloads of bargain hunters from Shepparton spent their social security checks on Chinese jimjams and Taiwanese tea towels. Others had been converted to new roles in the leisure and entertainment sector of the service economy.

The Climber was characteristic of the trend. When I first noticed it, maybe two years earlier, it was painted matt black and called Klub Funkk. Next time I drove past, the name had changed to

Silver's, a clear pitch for the more sophisticated end of the blue-collar market. A scalloped awning over the front entrance, Bacardi and Coke by the jug, Chris de Burgh on the turntable.

The facade was now a muted green with a sinuous pattern of darker leaves spelling out the name. The street outside was deserted, no sign of the cops. Ambrose and Ernest were standing on the little strip of carpet under the awning, arguing with the tuxedo-clad doorman behind his loop of red rope.

"Hey," said Holly as I pulled into the carpark across the road, behind the Voularis Emporium. "That's where Steve works. And there are those guys again. What's going on?"

"Back in a minute," I said.

She was beginning to regret recruiting me as a chauffeur. "Think I'll get a taxi the rest of the way home."

"Suit yourself," I said. I knew I was acting strangely but she was the one who got me into this situation, after all. I left her sitting in the car and crossed the street.

The doorman was shaking his head. "Nothink personal, fellers," he was saying, a great big side of halal beef, another live-at-home boy. "Private function. Hens' night. Chicks only." He reached down to adjust the hang of his tackle, then jerked his thumb over his shoulder at a poster beside the ticket-office grille. A chorus line of oiled beefcake, bare torsos in leather posing-pouches, bowties at their naked necks. *The Chessmen.* Seeping through the double doors beyond came the steady throb of a bass line. *The Climber Welcomes Food Barn Social Club.*

"Then fuckenwell get him to come out here," said Deadly.

I grabbed Buchanan by the elbow and waltzed him backward along the footpath. "This is insane," I hissed. "The cops'll be here any minute. C'mon, I'll drive you back to Fitzroy, anywhere you like."

Deadly swung a leg over the stupid little red rope. The doorman put the flat of his palm on the Koori's chest. "I'm warning you, mate," he said. The two of them went eyeball to eyeball. Shit, I thought, this thing's about to go thermonuclear. Without shifting his position, the doorman extended his free hand toward an intercom on the wall. Just as his hand reached it, it spoke. "Security to rear exit. ASAP."

Indecision flashed across the bouncer's face and he swiveled his head, looking past the box office toward the closed double doors, then back at Deadly. The squawk box sounded again, even more urgent. "Security to rear exit. Steve's flipped out."

A wide grin creased Deadly's face and he was over the rope and through the vestibule. The doorman took off after him. Buchanan and I gaped stupidly at each other, shrugged simultaneously and raced after them, my stomach churning at the sudden burst of activity, the rush of adrenaline, the dread of anticipation.

We hit the swinging double doors at a trot and burst into black. Black walls, black ceiling, black floor. A million swirling fragments of light speckled the darkness, thrown by spinning mirror-balls. The thump of amplified music, the raucous clamor of a hundred cheering women standing on their seats or banging their glasses on tables. At their center, a male body in a jockstrap and coconut oil and nothing else, gyrated in a pool of light on a circular stage, mechanically thrusting his groin into the face of an off-duty checkout chick in a sequined cashmere sweater. She squealed with hysterical laughter.

"Macho, macho man," they chanted to the pump of the music. Secret women's business. Christ, no wonder they didn't want any witnesses. All this on a Tuesday night.

Deadly and the bouncer were ploughing through the crowd, headed for the back wall where an exit sign glowed. A knot of male bodies crowded into the gap of a broached doorway. Waiters in cutoff jeans and shredded T-shirts, their bum cheeks hanging out. Barmen in boxer shorts with matching red braces. A fussy little man in shirt sleeves issuing futile instructions.

We fought our way through the scrum and out into a concrete stairwell. A Chessman in an American sailor suit was bent double, spitting broken teeth into a cupped hand. Sprawled on the stairs beside him was a girl with an emerald green miniskirt pushed up around her waist. In one hand she held a shoe. The other hand was pressed to her nose. A torrent of vivid red blood streamed down the front of her blouse into her bare thighs. Her drop-earrings jerked in time with the sobs that racked her body.

Beyond her, Deadly was shouldering open a door into the night. Buchanan took the steps three at a time, me right behind him. We exploded into an empty laneway, a brick wall rearing before us. To the right was the street. To the left, beyond a row of rubbish bins, the alley took a dogleg.

Panting, the pulse in my neck beating a wicked tattoo, I pulled up short. As Ambrose disappeared around the corner, still in hot pursuit, I put my hands on my knees and coughed. Barked like a bloodhound. A voice shouted in my ear. The voice of reason.

Fuck this, it said. Whatever they're paying you, it isn't enough. And it certainly isn't for this kind of crap. Not for chasing psychopathic maniacs through lunatic ladies' lounges. This is none of your business. Get out of here. Immediately. Before even more complications arise. Before the cops arrive and explanations become necessary.

It was good advice. I took it, starting up the laneway at a trot. Deadly and Buchanan could chase Steve Radeski all the way to hell and back if they liked. Not my affair. The dull ache in my chest had become a sharp stitch. Jogging into the carpark, I threaded my way between the rows of cars. Floodlit on the rear wall of the Voularis Emporium was an advertising hoarding. Milka Full-Cream Swiss Chocolate. Purple cartoon cows in an alpine meadow. Black spray paint covered the cows' udders. Milk is Murder, read the graffiti.

The lesbian vegans strike again, I thought. Eyes on the billboard, I didn't see Radeski until I collided with him.

He was crouched at the door of a low-slung Celica, trying to fit a key into the lock. I bounced off him, tripped on a concrete traffic bolster and went down on one knee. In the instant I recognized him, he was looming above me, hugely square-shouldered in his dinner jacket and bowtie. Pumped for action. Mad as a cut snake.

My feet found themselves and I steadied myself against the dented mudguard of the Celica, cornered at a half-crouch. Radeski stared down. Baffled recognition spread across his features. This was it. Again. I was dog meat.

"Why don't you pick on someone your own size?" It was Holly, behind him. He turned. I began to back away.

"Hey, babe," said Radeski. "Wha cha doon here?"

"Don't you 'Hey, babe' me," Holly snarled, coming closer.

Suddenly, she rose vertically into the air.

For a long second she hung there. Then she swiveled, half-turning. Her leg shot outward and her heel slammed into Radeski's solar plexus. There was an audible thud and he teetered on the spot. She landed, light as a feather, and closed the gap between them, her clenched fists pistoning in a blur of flying punches. Radeski reeled backward past me, forearm up, as a swift succession of blows and kicks rained down on him.

An Amazon! I was out for the evening with Sheena, Queen of the fucking Jungle. And thank Christ she was still there, not in some cab, halfway home. She grabbed my arm and hauled me in the direction of the Toyota. "C'mon, cowboy," she yelled. I didn't need any encouragement. Radeski was right behind us, roaring like a bull. No, a ram.

We wrenched open the doors and threw ourselves into the Toyota, my elbow snapping down the lock button as I jammed the key into the ignition. Radeski's forehead pounded into Holly's window, shattering the glass. I gunned the engine and slammed the T-bar into reverse. Rubber screeching, we hurtled backward. I spun the wheel, found drive and floored the pedal. We thudded across the gutter and roared down the street.

21

"wow." Holly pummeled the air, buzzing from the action. "Did you see that? Did you see that?"

What I saw was a police car, coming toward us. I slowed and it passed us. Through the rearview mirror, I watched it pull into the curb at The Climber. At the same time, Steve Radeski's Celica emerged from the carpark and burned off in the opposite direction.

"That's the first time I've ever done anything like that outside the ring." Holly tore off her Nike cap and shook her hair loose. "I didn't think I still had it."

"We'd better go back," I said. My vice-like grip on the steering wheel was easing and color was returning to my knuckles.

"What for?" she said. "They'll pick him up soon enough. There's nothing else we can do." She was on a high, flushed with victory.

And she had a point. The cops probably already had an APB out on Radeski. If he went home, they'd nab him there. If he was headed elsewhere, it surely wouldn't be too difficult to spot a rusted bronze-colored Celica with a peeling vinyl roof and a demented gorilla behind the wheel.

"What *was* that back there?" I said. "Karate? Tae kwon do?"

"Kickboxing. I used to be the northern region Under-17 champion. I'm a bit out of practice, but." She glowed with false modesty, pleased as Punch. Or Judy, I supposed.

"Wow." Now I was saying it. "You saved my life."

"Probably," she said. "You think I'm a real idiot, don't you? For ever getting involved with a guy like that."

"Drugs change people," I said, offering the solace of a meaningless cliché. Although in Steve Radeski's case it might well have been true. The long-term effect on humans of merino penis enhancer had probably not yet been clinically tested.

The dashboard cigarette lighter popped. As I lit up, Holly drew her hand up into the sleeve of her pullover and punched out the shattered passenger-side glass. A trail of crystal scattered behind us, discarded jewels. Wind tore through the car, cold and exhilarating, sending her hair swirling in a halo around her face. "Hope it's insured," she grinned.

We turned into St. George's Road where a wide median strip separated the north-south lanes. Across the divide, a yellow Daihatsu Charade passed us, speeding in the opposite direction. "Wow," said Holly.

She was staring straight through the windscreen. Just up ahead, an immense column of water was gushing from the median strip, towering high into the air and dropping a curtain of water across the road. We hit it and burst out the other side, our hair wet, the cigarette sodden in my mouth.

"Wow," said Holly, droplets glistening on her hair and skin. "What was that?"

"The hydrant bandit strikes again." As I began to explain, Holly half-turned in her seat and studied me. "You're a bit of a dark horse, aren't you?"

"How do you mean?"

"Going into The Climber like that. Trying to capture Steve, single-handed."

If that's what she wanted to think, I wasn't going to contradict her. I shrugged self-effacingly.

"And those guys back at the club, the ones you were talking to at the shops. They looked part-Aboriginal to me." This non sequitur was somehow also a question.

"Which part?" I said.

"Come on," she said. "What's the story?"

"Like I told you. It's work-related. They're helping out with the Olympic bid. Community relations."

"You work for the Olympics?" She narrowed her eyes and regarded me with profound skepticism. "You're bullshitting me, right?"

The closest thing I had to proof was the invitation card to the gala dinner. I wrestled it out of my wallet and handed it over. She read it out loud. *"In Honor of the Visit of IOC Representatives Pascal Abdoulaye, Kim U-ee and Stansislas . . ."* She hit the Pole, the fourteen-letter jaw-breaker. "How do I pronounce this?"

"It's hard to say," I said.

Impossible. Quite beyond me, anyway, a man who'd spent four years at the Ministry for Ethnic Affairs, bending his mouth around all kinds of phonetic contortions and alien nomenclature. Running up and down to the Translation and Information section, making sure that the minister did not utter an inadvertent obscenity when addressing the Khmer Retailers Association or opening the Turkish Senior Citizens Center.

Just one glance at this IOC joker's name and all I could think of was Mr. Mxyzptlk, Evil Genius from the Fifth Dimension in the Superman comics. Or all those unpronounceable Russians in Tolstoy and Turgenev — General Zherkwilkzlovskayachikov and Madame Shlyapnicwitz-Dzhibladze. At least in a novel, you didn't have to try to say them out loud. And Polish was even worse than Russian. All those strzs and cyzks. It was as if successive waves of invaders and occupiers over the centuries had plundered the country of its vowels, leaving only tangled piles of consonants in their wake.

Holly studied the card like it was a priceless artefact. "Mr. Murray Whelan," she read. "Wow. So what are our chances?"

"Pretty good," I told her authoritatively. "Apparently." Something else occurred to me. "You doing anything Thursday night?"

She looked at me sideways, the ironic look. "You're asking me to this?"

"I know it's short notice."

She shrugged. What was the harm? "Sure." She'd have to find somebody to take her last aerobics class of the day, she explained, but otherwise there was no problemo. "Could be fun. Ta."

She turned on the radio and nodded along. That fucking Madonna again. She was everywhere. My fingers drummed a beat on the steering wheel. My mind churned. What an eventful excursion this was.

Holly's flat was on the ground floor of a three-story block of units. Mid-sixties, by the look of it. A white-painted, bagged-brick place behind a thick screen of acacias. All very Costa del Sol. Most of the tenants, she said, were visiting academics at the nearby University of Melbourne. Despite its location near a major freeway feeder, the place had a quiet, almost secluded atmosphere. Straight across the road, behind its stand of raddled cypresses, the Melbourne General Cemetery was as quiet as a graveyard.

I asked if I could use the phone and we went inside. The front door opened directly into the lounge, a cheerful little room with coir matting on the floor, a cane sofa with hibiscus-patterned cushions, a couple of Bangalow palms, a scatter of covers on the CD player — Prince, INXS, Toni Childs. Two half-empty bottles sat on the cane bookcase, Midori and Galliano. A beaded curtain led to the kitchen. Through the bedroom door I could see a double bed piled with folded laundry, a framed poster of a dolphin on the wall. It was a tidy, lived-in little flat with the smell of apple shampoo in the air.

While I used the phone, ringing around Parliament House until I got an answer, Holly put the kettle on. It had just gone ten-thirty and Woeful, I was eventually told, had been called away about an hour before. Some sort of emergency, his current whereabouts unknown. I called the Austin Hospital and learned that Denis Dogherty was in intensive care. No further information was available.

As I was finding this out, Holly thrust a cup of steaming liquid into my hand. "This'll help you relax."

Give up cigarettes, she meant. *Smoker's Infusion.* A half-empty packet of the stuff had been sitting in my pantry for nearly a year. Red clover and dandelion root. The only root I'd had in six months. Useless. Like Holly's front-door lock, a standard Yale-type. Useless, even taking into account the security chain. Radeski would only have to lean on it. She saw me looking. "Why would he come here?"

This from a woman who had just smacked 130 kilograms of concentrated lamburger repeatedly in the chops. "Because he's out of control, Holly, that's why. The guy's a maniac. He's already put one person on the critical list. Plus he just thumped someone back there at The Climber." Not to mention Darcy Anderson. "God only knows what's going on in his mind, what scores he might get it in his head to settle. One thing's for sure, I'd hate to be in his bad books right now."

She stared at me over the rim of her herbal infusion. "You trying to scare the shit out of me?"

"Got anything proper to drink?" I said.

She had Stolichnaya, pronounced vodka, a half bottle of it in the freezer. I tossed down a bracing shot and leaned back on the hibiscus cushions, closed my eyes and pricked my ears to the lizard slither of my bloodstream. Insects crawled under my scalp. A whole fucking zoo of baboons howled in my ears. I ground my teeth and clenched my diaphragm and forced the gastric reflux back down my esophagus. I felt like shit on a stick.

Holly's hand rested on my shoulder, then gently took the cup from my hand. "You look about ready for bed," she whispered.

$$22$$

MY HAND WENT into the crook of her neck, her hair silky between my fingers, and I drew her toward me. Her lips met mine, cool and impassive. A terrible shame welled up within me, the realization that I had betrayed myself as a sleaze. Burning with humiliation, I drew away.

But she followed, maintaining the gentle pressure of the still unbroken kiss, refusing to relinquish it. Her lips softened and opened, drinking me in. She sighed. Our breaths mingled, hers smelling of freshly laundered towels and tasting of Lite 'n' Low. The kiss went on and on forever.

Instantly, magically, we were in the darkened bedroom, hands roaming hungrily, mouths locked together, devouring each other. She wrenched at my shirt, tearing it open. Buttons ricocheted off the walls. My hands went under her sweater, gliding up her sides and over her breasts, slippery smooth beneath a skin-tight sheath of Lycra. A sheath in which there was no breach or opening. My fingers caressed her bodysuit, searching for a means of entry, a point of insinuation. Her firm body molded itself to my touch, at once accessible and inviolable. My hands moved ceaselessly, exploring every slope and mound, every cleft and indentation. I was as long and hard as a Polish surname. No zipper or button, no buckle or clasp could I find. It was like trying to make love to a seal.

Not a seal, a python. Her limbs wound themselves around me. A pythoness, squeezing the breath from me, shedding her skin. In one deft, invisible movement, she peeled off her leotard and was naked. "How did you do that?" I wanted to ask, speechless at the sight. Her breasts, lovely beyond description, filled my hands. I pressed my lips to a ruby nipple and sucked. Smoke filled my lungs.

I exhaled, savoring the exquisite sensuality of it, and reached to suck again. She laughed, leaning back out of my reach, and drew provocatively on her own cigarette. Mine was in a glass ashtray, a cold circle on my bare stomach, the terminus of a sinuous white thread reaching down from the ceiling. Another cigarette, somehow, was already burning between my fingers. She straddled me. Swirling wraiths of gray surrounded her head. She bent low and inhaled, drawing me inside her. A force welled deep in me. I teetered on the brink of eruption.

Stars spun before my eyes. An immense spasm racked my body, expelling all air. Daggers stabbed my chest, jack-knifing me upright. Head in my hands, feet on the floor, I began to cough. Cough upon cough shook my body, a pounding surf inside my lungs. My ribcage was a concrete mixer. Oysters flew from my mouth and nose.

Slowly, the attack abated. I wiped my nose on the back of my arm and rolled back beneath the bedclothes, dragging the sheet up beneath my chin. The digits on the clock radio said it was six-thirty. I believed them. The pale light of dawn was already sneaking around the curtains.

Jesus, was that a dream or what? I was alone. My bed had the same number of people in it as when I had climbed in, seven hours before. After I had said goodnight to Holly and driven home. My chest ached. Likewise my heart. A man could die and nobody would be any the wiser.

The patch on my midriff was smooth to the touch, its toxic cache leaking imperceptibly into my bloodstream. The brochure warned of disturbed sleep patterns. Now I knew what that meant. That mouth, those filter-tips, I could still taste them. Was it really only a dream? Memory darted before me, eluding my grasp.

I dozed until seven. When the alarm sounded, it met no resistance. I hurt too much to sleep. The pack of cigarettes was still in my jacket pocket. They whispered to me from across the room. Just the one, they said. To start the day. After that, I'd be fine.

I went into the bathroom and stood under a scalding shower for as long as the water stayed hot. An ugly purple-black bruise covered the left side of my ribcage, tender to the touch. Replacing the nicotine patch with a fresh one, I shaved, dressed, ate breakfast and still felt ratshit.

The radio was reporting more attacks on water mains. Three during the night, all in the northern suburbs. Despite suggestions of sabotage linked to the current industrial dispute, the union had denied responsibility. Bullshit, I thought. It looked like the Missos had finally figured out a way to make water run uphill. There was no mention of the Darcy Anderson case.

Those damn cigarettes just wouldn't shut up, so I broke them in half and stuffed them down the plughole. All but the last one, which I smoked. It didn't make me feel any better. It was going to be one of those days.

The red light was flashing on the answering machine. I had forgotten to check when I came home. I punched the button and listened to Wendy remind me that she and Red were arriving at noon and would be at the Hyatt if I wanted to see Red. I liked the "if."

I looked up Holly in the phone book. Despite my best efforts to persuade her otherwise, she'd insisted on sleeping at her flat. "I can handle Steve Radeski," she maintained. Having witnessed her combat skills, I found it hard to contradict her. But in the cold light of morning, I thought I should touch base. When I rang her number there was no answer. Don't panic, I thought. Not yet. Maybe she was out jogging. I'd call again later.

I rang Ken Sproule. It took a while to run him to ground but I eventually found him on his mobile. He sounded like he was speaking from the halls of purgatory. "Denis Dogherty died on the operating table at 1 A.M." he said, straight up.

I wished I'd saved those cigarettes.

"They tell me you were on the scene when he was found." It was both a question and a statement. In a case like this, the violent death of a senior government adviser, Ken would take a close personal interest. We compared notes. I told him what I'd told the police. He told me what the police had told him. That Radeski was Denis's nephew. That it looked like a family argument gone wrong. That Woeful had gone straight from Parliament House to the hospital. He was waiting there with Marj Dogherty when they wheeled Denis out of emergency surgery with a sheet over his face.

"Denis Dogherty was quite a character," said Ken. "Despite our political differences, I had a lot of time for him."

Only the first part of his statement was true, but I appreciated the sentiment. The platitudes would soon be flying thick and fast.

"They don't make them like that any more," I said.

"Amen."

For the next ten seconds neither of us said anything.

Then we got back down to it. Steve Radeski was still at large. The squad car sent to pick him up at the nightclub where he worked had missed him. According to the club manager, Radeski was in an agitated state all evening. He fled the place after indecently assaulting a customer and roughing up a male dancer, and had not returned home. "Apparently he's been using some sort of veterinary shit," Sproule said. "Extremely high testosterone content with unknown psychological effects. The homicide boys are scouring the body-building scene, trying to pick up his trail."

Until they collared Radeski, the cops were playing it low-key. "The press might be prepared to cut Woeful some slack. Family tragedy and all that. But the Olympic minister's chief aide being killed by his steroid-abusing nephew is too good a story for them to sit on forever."

"Let's just hope they catch this prick before he does any more damage," I said. "Finding Denis like I did, I feel like I've got a personal stake in the outcome. I'd appreciate knowing about it as soon as he's arrested."

"You got it," said Ken. "Comrade."

"Before you hang up," I said. "Any developments in the Darcy Anderson case?"

"Apart from those blackfellers of yours going on the warpath about the Olympics?" said Ken. "Nothing so far. You wouldn't credit it was so hard to find a handful of skinheads."

"No other suspects?"

"Such as?"

I was almost tempted to share my secret intelligence. But with the police already looking for Radeski there was no immediate reason to break my promise to Deadly. Anyway, I didn't intended to speak to anyone until I had a chance to talk with Woeful. I rang Phillipa Verstak's consulting rooms and made an appointment for my aching chest. Ten was the earliest she could fit me in, the reception-ist told me. Then I rang Holly's place. Still no answer. As I hung up, the phone rang in my hand. It was Carmel, Woeful's private secre-tary. "I don't know if you've heard," she began.

"I have." My tone was more brusque than I intended.

There was an embarrassed silence and when Carmel spoke again it was in her most officious voice. "The minister would like to see you as soon as possible, to brief him on the Aboriginal Institute of Sport matter listed for tomorrow's Cabinet meeting."

Given the situation, it seemed a strange request. "I didn't think he'd be at the office today," I said, surprised.

Carmel softened a little. "I'm not sure it's completely sunk in," she confided. "I don't think he's been to bed yet."

"I'll come straight in," I said.

On the way, I returned the Toyota to the carpool, blaming the destroyed passenger window on vandals. The dispatcher, a different one this time, couldn't have cared less if the Huns and the Visigoths had also had a hand in the matter. He took the keys with a grunt and shoved a damage-report form across the counter at me.

When I got to Sport, Carmel told me to go straight in, her red-rimmed eyes wide with caution. Woeful was behind his desk, brooding like a caged animal. Or so it seemed; the vertical slats of the blinds behind him looked like bars against the brushed-metal sky. "Shut the door," he ordered, his face haggard and unshaven.

I did as I was told, nodding somberly and reciting the stock phrases of condolence. He ran his hand backward over his scalp. I was one of the first. Soon the whole world would be coming at him with such courtesies. "You were there," he stated bluntly.

For what felt like the hundredth time, I told my story. Woeful listened impatiently, cutting me off when I got to the part where Holly ran to the shops to phone for the ambulance. "I was told he spoke to you."

It sounded like an accusation, like I'd stolen something from him. Which I had, in a way. His dying mate's last words. "Well. Out with it." He stared at me intensely, like he was prepared, if necessary, to wring the information out of me. "What'd he say?"

"He mentioned your name." There was some small comfort in that, I hoped.

"What exactly did he say?"

"He was in shock," I said. "But he said, 'Promise you won't tell them about Woeful.' " Or words to that effect.

Woeful tensed. "Tell them what about me?"

"He didn't say. He was in shock. I'm not sure he knew what he was saying." I felt defensive, a trespasser. "I didn't even think it was worth mentioning to the police."

Woeful's eyes narrowed in his big, sad face. If he knew the meaning of Denis's last words, he made no attempt to explain them. "What else did he say?"

"When I asked him what had happened, he said, 'Stevie.' That's all, just 'Stevie.' "

His expression was impassive but his body could not conceal the slight tremor that ran through it. "Stevie," he said, in a voice so low he could have been talking to himself.

Then, abruptly, he swiveled his chair, turning his face to the window. For a long time neither of us spoke. Eventually, the silence grew too uncomfortable. "If there's anything I can do," I said, backing toward the door. "For you. Or for Mrs. Dogherty."

"Marjorie." The word was a sigh, tinged with infinite regret. "She'll never forgive me."

"You did everything you could." Another trite formula.

He spun in his seat. "What would you know about it?"

Weeping politicians were all the rage in those days. The Prime Minister would blubber into his hankie at the first sight of a camera. But Woeful McKenzie was a man of the old school, uncomfortable with the overt expression of deep emotion. I took his belligerence as a sign of grief.

"Denis was a good man," I said. "According to his ex-girlfriend, your nephew had been having problems adjusting to his father's stroke. I guess Denis went out there hoping he could help."

Woeful's tension ebbed a little. "Yes," he said, fastening onto the explanation as though it had just occurred to him. "That accounts for it."

Carmel tapped lightly and put her head around the door. "I've told them to bring your car around." She spoke in a tone that brooked no contradiction. "And canceled your appointments for the rest of the day."

The Aboriginal Institute of Sport had never been more than a pretext. The real reason Woeful had summoned me was to recount Denis's final moments. He could have said so, rather than treating me as an outsider. But, I supposed, that's just what I was.

"Yes," Woeful repeated, turning again to the window. "He was helping Stevie adjust to the difficulties of Rudy's stroke. That explains why he was there."

But not why he'd gone there without informing his wife. Or why Steve Radeski had thrown him against a mirror, put him on a bed and left him to die.

"If there's anything I can do," I said, backing out the door. "Anything at all."

23

ONE THING I COULD DO, short term, was my job.

I went downstairs and headed for the Old Treasury. As I approached, a party of MOB officials emerged from the front door and rushed down the steps to where three identical white Fairlanes were just pulling up. Judging by the solemnity of the fuss, I was witnessing the arrival of the IOC Evaluation Commission. Suppressing the urge to rush forward and fling myself at their feet in supplication, I leaned against a balustrade and cast an appraising eye over the three men whose good impression of Melbourne would decide the outcome of the bid.

The first to emerge from his car was a tall, middle-aged African in an elegant pinstripe suit. He wore an amiably diplomatic expression and carried himself with all the cultivated arrogance of a graduate of the Ecole Nationale d'Administration. Pascal Abdoulaye, no doubt, representative of the International Olympic Committee in Senegal.

His associate, Mr. Kim of Korea, was a squat, muscular man with hooded, predatory eyes and a subdued manner. According to what I'd read in the papers, he was a key player in preparations for the Seoul Olympics. You know, the ones with the persistent background odor of tear gas.

Finally, there appeared a thin, elderly white man with wavy gray hair, a clipped moustache of the same color and heavy square spectacles. He drew himself upright and looked around expectantly, as if for a guard of honor to inspect. Stansislas Unpronounceable, the jaw-breaking Pole.

In a flurry of fervent handshakes and hearty welcomes, they were swept up the steps and through the front door of the MOB HQ. After a respectful pause, I followed. *Welcome to Melbourne,* said the electronic banner in the empty foyer. *"Manuyangka nyiyarlangurlu, jarntungku marda, yankirrirli . . . ,"* said a voice from down the corridor.

Pressing the cosmopolitan flesh was not part of Brian Morrison's job. I found him upstairs in the war room, getting an update on the torch relay. He'd already heard the news about Denis. Shaking his head solemnly, he led me into the office kitchen. Despite his move to the greener pastures of the corporate world, he still retained all the sentimentality of a true Labor man.

"Bloody Denis," he said, prising the lid off a can of instant coffee. "He's really left us in the lurch, going and getting himself killed at a time like this. Who's going to look after Woeful McKenzie now?"

"He's really taking it hard," I agreed. "Seems to blame himself."

"Woeful's done all right for an old wharfie," said Brian. "But he wouldn't have got off the docks without Denis and everybody knows it. Denis was the one with the brains."

"You think this has adverse implications for the bid?" It was an angle I hadn't yet had time to consider.

"Without Denis, Woeful is dead weight," said Brian, handing me a cup of truly terrible coffee. "Which is the last thing we need this close to the big decision. Unless we can find somebody to hold his hand, there's a real danger he'll drop the ball."

I didn't like the way he looked at me when he said that. "Surely Woeful isn't so central to the bid."

"Maybe not," he said. "But it's a risk we can't afford to take. He's been a prominent part of our lobbying. Personally kissed the arse of nearly half the IOC. That sort of thing is not to be underrated in the

Olympic family. Plus, he's got a crucial role in the funding and political side of things. Woeful was never the best choice in the world for the job but he's done reasonably well so far, thanks to Denis. What we've got to do now is find the right person to step into Denis's shoes."

Nature abhors a vacuum, they say. The Labor Party relishes one. Denis Dogherty was barely cold and there we were discussing his replacement. But, if Brian Morrison thought he could induce me to volunteer as Woeful McKenzie's new minder, he could think again. "The Aboriginal Institute of Sport . . . ," I said.

Brian got the message. "Listed for Cabinet tomorrow. In the meantime, your brief is to concentrate on Ambrose Buchanan."

"You told me Buchanan was out of the loop."

"And that's where I want him kept. Apart from a couple of mentions on the bloody ABC, he didn't get any publicity out of that demo yesterday. So now he might decide to pull some stunt with the Evaluation Commission. I want you to stick to him like glue, make sure he keeps his distance." He reached into his pocket and handed me a small booklet, the Evaluation Commission itinerary: *Visit to Melbourne Olympic Bid, Inc. River Cruise of Proposed Olympic Village at Docklands. Luncheon with Lord Mayor. Tour of Museum of Sport. Inspection of Main Stadium. Sailing on the Bay. At Home with the Australian IOC member. Cocktails with the Foreign Minister.*

Etcetera and so on. The full schedule for a three-day, red-carpet, chauffeur-driven, fully escorted, all-expenses-paid tour of the world's most livable city for Messrs. Abdoulaye, Kim and Dziczkowszczak.

"And I'm supposed to make sure that Buchanan doesn't buttonhole these blokes as they inspect a cocktail party?" I snorted. "Don't you have guys in dark glasses with suspiciously bulging jackets to handle this sort of thing?"

"Matter of fact, we don't," said Brian. "Apart from Samaranch, these IOCs are virtually unknown. A couple of bodyguards at the more public events, that's about the extent of their security requirements. Which also happens to suit our terrorism-free visitor-friendly image."

"Ambrose Buchanan isn't interested in disrupting the Evaluation Commission visit," I said.

"Yeah?" He couldn't stop himself smiling. "That's not what you suggested when you addressed the board yesterday morning."

Shit. Hoist on my own petard. By conspiring with Denis to inflate Ambrose's connection with the African IOC into a threat, I had hastened the MOB's endorsement of the Aboriginal Sports Institute. But I had also played straight into Brian Morrison's hands.

Building up Ambrose Buchanan as a threat to the bid, I now realized, had simply been a bit of professional game playing on Morrison's part. Create a problem — or the perception of a problem — then save the day by solving it. And choosing me for his stalking horse had been a way of massaging his relationship with Woeful and Denis.

But then Ambrose had gone and fulfilled his dire predictions by staging a demonstration on the Old Treasury steps. Which was a bone I had yet to pick with the bewhiskered Buchanan.

"Other duties as directed," Brian reminded me. "That's what it says in your contract."

"What do you suggest? Chaining him to a tree for the duration?"

"I'll leave the method to you." Brian tossed the dregs of his coffee into the sink. "You're a very inventive person, Murray."

Also an uncomfortable one. Every time I coughed, a sharp pain pierced my side. And I seemed to be coughing a fair bit that morning.

The white Fairlanes were gone when I went outside. According to the itinerary booklet, our VIPs had just been whisked down to the river for a water-borne inspection of the proposed Docklands Olympic Village. As I made my way down the steps, the temperature suddenly dropped five degrees and a squally shower blew across town, turning the sky into a miserable gray stew. With characteristic

Melbourne timing, the run of decent weather was ending in the first hour of the Evaluation Commission visit.

A tram was coming up Collins Street. I ran for it, clutching my side, and in less than fifteen minutes was standing in front of Phillipa Verstak, unbuttoning my shirt.

24

"PLAYING SQUASH." I sucked in my stomach and displayed my bruise. "Copped a whack from my opponent's racket."

Squash carried the right sort of social connotations, I thought. Business-class combat. The idea of telling Phillipa Verstak that I'd been bashed with a fence picket in West Heidelberg never entered my mind. Irrelevant to diagnosis. Inimical to prospects.

She wore a fawn linen jacket, the sleeves rolled once at the cuff. Scrubbed for action. Still no luck with the recalcitrant hair. "Anything else?" she said. "You look a bit wrung-out."

Perceptive, I thought. "I've just had some bad news. Friend of mine died last night."

"Oh," she said. Polite but distanced. Fair enough. She nodded in the direction of my heart. "I see you've started the patches. How are we doing so far?" Back to the Hippocratic we.

"Very little desire," I lied.

"Any side effects?"

"Been having these dreams," I said.

She nodded knowingly. "Nicotine stimulation at a time when the brain wouldn't normally be getting any. Not unless you smoke in your sleep."

I shook my head. "They're very explicit."

"Anyone I know?" She stuck a freezing cold stethoscope against my chest. "Cough. And again." Long cool fingers explored my tender regions. "Put your shirt back on."

"Anything broken?"

"If it was, you wouldn't be standing here dropping Freudian hints. But we'd better make sure you haven't damaged your pulmonary lining." Like it was my fault, or something. "Third floor, Suite B." She handed me an X-ray referral chit and told me to come straight back afterward.

As befitted one of the most lucrative branches of subsidized medicine, the pathology lab operated on the principle of maximum throughput in minimum time. A quick swipe of my Medicare card, a signature, a lead apron over the gonads, rapid irradiation with high-velocity electrons and I was out of there with my snapshot under my arm before you could say Wilhelm Konrad Roentgen, winner of the inaugural Nobel Prize for Physics, 1901.

Back in Bernie's anteroom, I waited for a break in the traffic. A business-bureaucrat with the sniffles. A woman in a bankteller uniform on early lunchbreak. Typical Bernie clientele. I absently flipped through the pile of magazines and found the most recent issue. *Newsweek*, a month or so old. It had a feature story on the fate of the Eastern bloc sports machines, post-perestroika.

In the six months since the fall of the Berlin Wall, the whole shebang had come unglued. Regimes seemingly as imperishable as concrete had evaporated like the morning dew, undone by the Home Shopping Channel and reruns of *The Beverly Hillbillies*. Everywhere, the shoe was on the other foot. In some cases, the fit was less than comfortable. Lech Walesa, hangdog candidate for the presidency of Poland, looked like he'd rather be back in prison. Gdansk for the memories.

Gone forever, too, were all those East German women shot-putters with their deep voices and baffled chromosomes. All those amenorrhoeal Romanian gymnasts and ox-shouldered Czech swimmers. For forty years, the East–West conflict had played itself as gladiatorial combat in the Olympic arena. Boycott and counter-boycott. Now it was all just sport, mere stopwatches and scoreboards, no longer Good v Evil.

But my mind was not on Manicheism. It was more concerned with deciding whether to use this opportunity to ask Phillipa out. Dinner perhaps? No, too obvious. And what if her professional ethics precluded her accepting a dinner invitation extended by a patient during a billable consultation? What if her flirtatiousness was no more than comfortable banter? And what if her excuse the other night at Mietta's had been just that, a polite rebuff?

My name was called and I handed Phillipa the big envelope containing the X ray. "Know anything about steroids?" I asked as she opened it. "This friend of mine, his nephew's a bit of a bodybuilder. He's become very aggressive lately."

"Not the sort of body building I've had any experience with, I'm afraid."

Her sort used spare parts. I could see her in a tin-roofed ward, fitting prosthetic limbs to children with stumps. Little kids who'd stepped on a landmine while running after a ball. And here was I, a grown man, come bleating to the doctor with my pathetic little bump. She held the transparency up to the window. She could see right through me.

"If you feel uncomfortable," she said, "take a couple of aspirin. And no squash for a while. But there's no real damage. You should be right for tomorrow night."

"The Olympic dinner?" Oh, that. Like I'd practically forgotten it. "I guess I'll see you there with your friend. Rodney, isn't it? Something to do with the Olympics."

"Rodney Elderton. Executive assistant to the chairman." Her tone was almost mocking.

"Hmm," I said, appreciatively. "Sounds important." Catty. But then the Nicabate instructions did warn of increased irritability.

"Try not to exert yourself too much, Murray," she said, opening the door.

The brief autumn squall had exhausted itself by the time I stepped back onto the street. I stood for a moment on the footpath, considering my options. It was not yet eleven, so there was no point in heading for the Stars. Buchanan would not be there yet. Red and Wendy would be arriving soon. I decided to check on Holly.

At the swank pharmacy in the arcade at the Hyatt, I bought a packet of Panadeine Forte and swallowed two of them dry, bringing on another jag of coughing. The shop assistant, terrified that I might crop-dust her display of Diorissimo, almost fell over her false eyelashes in her haste to fetch me a glass of water. When I'd regained my composure, I went upstairs to the health club.

To my immense relief, Holly was there. Hale and hearty as ever, she was just starting her eleven o'clock aerobics class. As I glimpsed her thrusting pelvis and heaving bosom, I felt my ears catch fire. Prurient images of nocturnal congress flashed before my mind's eye. Taking a deep breath, I pushed them away. It was just a dream, I reminded myself. The involuntary by-product of biochemical processes. Lest my thoughts were somehow visible on my face, I hurried into the locker room.

For half an hour, I lounged in the sauna, excusing myself from exercise on doctor's orders. Drenched in a miasma of heat, I pondered a number of things that had been lurking in the back of my mind since my appointment with Woeful.

There seemed something odd in the big man's reaction to the situation. The urgency of his need to know exactly what Denis said to me, extending to the use of a pretext to summon me to his office. That line about Marj Dogherty never forgiving him. The eager way he fastened onto my suggestion that Denis had gone there to comfort Steve Radeski in his time of emotional need. Even his lack of anger toward Radeski.

I thought, too, of Denis. And I remembered that the last name he spoke was not Woeful's but mine. *"It's up to you now, Murray,"* he'd said.

But what was up to me?

When I emerged, none the wiser, I found Holly on desk duty. She cocked her head sideways, inviting me into the comparative privacy of the boutique. "You really got me worked up last night," she said, sotto voce.

Christ, I thought. It wasn't all a dream, after all. Blood rushed to my face in the nanosecond it took to realize the thought was absurd. Holly didn't notice. She was busy with the news.

"You got me really worried," she went on. "So I rang a cab straight after you left, went home to Mum and Dad. Spent the night there. The police think it's a good idea if I stay there until they catch Steve. He didn't go home last night and they don't know where he is. And that old man, Denis, he's dead. Awful, isn't it? But you'll never guess what. He was Steve's uncle. That's how come he was there."

"You've talked to the police?" I said.

"I rang up that one who gave me his card," she said. Detective Senior Constable Casanova. "But don't worry, I didn't tell him about us going to The Climber. Not without talking to my lawyer first." Now she was the one cracking funny. "Anyway, I thought about what you said, how Steve might be out to settle a few old scores. So I told him how I remembered hearing Steve talking to his father one time, saying he was going to fix this guy if he ever got the chance, rip him limb from limb."

"What guy?"

"Cheech somebody."

"Cheech?" I wasn't sure I'd heard right. "As in Cheech and Chong?" She stared at me blankly, no idea what I was talking about. "Comedians," I explained. "Big in the early seventies."

Of course she hadn't heard of them. She would've been all of five years old at the time. "I don't think he's a comedian," she said. "More like some kind of weightlifting official. Maybe the one who got Steve kicked off the squad. Anyway, he said he'd look into it."

It sounded like a nickname. Another turbo-charged meatloaf who'd got into a contretemps with Radeski at the free-weight rack. Fallen out with him for monopolizing the shoulder press.

"You still want me to go with you to the Olympic dinner?" she said.

"Of course. If you want to." Turning up with Miss Gorgeous on my arm, I'd decided, would not do my image any harm. "Did I mention that my son Red is presenting the torch to the visiting IOC members. He's eleven now. My ex-wife will be there, too."

"In other words," she grinned mischievously, "you'll be too busy to jump me." She took a green and yellow windbreaker off the rack and held it in front of me, appraising the result. "Jeeze, you're a goose."

A goose was better than a lech. "I'm glad we've got that clear."

"The other thing I was going to ask," she said. "Those Aborigines, the ones you said are helping with the bid? Are they going to be there?"

I chuckled at the thought and shook my head. "Not their scene. How much are those Adidas water bottles?"

"Twelve dollars," she said, taking one down from the shelf.

"Bit expensive, aren't they?"

She went into sales mode. "They *are* non-slip. And you're paying for a prestige brand, don't forget."

"I'll take it," I said. Nothing worse than losing your grip.

25

IN THE PALACES of ancient India, the walls were tinted pink with the blood of slaves killed expressly for that purpose. A similar effect had been achieved in the lobby of the Hyatt Hotel although, at the insistence of the Building Workers Union, by a different means. The whole place was clad in marble the color of raw veal.

The large abstract paintings above the reception desk, on the other hand, looked like they were executed in egg custard and butterscotch sauce. It was past twelve-thirty and I guessed I was getting hungry. At least I wasn't thinking about a cigarette.

When Red and Wendy came up the escalator from the motor court, I sat watching from behind the floral display.

Wendy was a handsome woman and it wasn't difficult to appreciate why I'd married her in the first place. She had the makings of a fine husband. The life of a corporate high-flier clearly suited her. Long gone was the perpetually harassed air of a member of the Women's Industrial Research Collective. Wendy had come up in the world. So had her hair. Her wardrobe and personal grooming were exemplary. What with the understated power suit and the dark hose, she exuded all the unassuming authority of an SS *Obersturmbann-führer*.

Redmond, I was pleased to see, hadn't changed too much since his last visit. A little taller, perhaps, but I'd got used to that over the years. Just turned eleven, he'd shed his baby fat and his frame was reaching upward in the general direction of adolescence. That dubious destination remained, thankfully, some distance away. In the meantime he was still just a kid with his shoelace undone and his bomber jacket tied around his waist. While Wendy signed the register and frightened a room key out of the desk clerk, he cast a curious eye over his luxurious surroundings, doing his best to look blasé. Eventually, he spotted me.

He dropped his backpack beside Wendy and sloped over, smiling crookedly. This was partly because of the amount of stainless steel in his mouth and partly because these encounters were getting to be as difficult for him as for me. "Nice place you've got here," he said.

"It's modest," I said. "But it suits my needs." We embraced in a properly awkward way, all very manly, breaking the clinch even as it was formed. "Sorry I missed you on Parramatta Road," I said. "Ready for the big re-run?"

Red gave me the thumbs up and we ambled across in the general direction of his mother. "Murray," she said, punctiliously neutral.

"Wendy," I said, somewhat less effusively.

The family reunion complete, we headed upstairs to their room. In the lift, Wendy took the opportunity to outline her proposed arrangements for the next two days. Proposed as in brooking no argument. Taking into account quality time with the maternal grandparents, Red's social visits with his old friend Tarquin and preparations for the torch relay, there would be scant opportunity for father-son bonding. "You're probably very busy anyway," said Wendy. "God knows, winning the Olympic bid is the only hope this town's got."

For the sake of the child, I desisted from prising open the emergency telephone hatch and bludgeoning his mama insensible with the handpiece. Instead, I offered Red the Adidas water bottle. "Won it at the gym," I said. "Most Improved Father of an Olympic Torch Bearer. I thought you might like it." It wasn't much of a gift, I knew, but it's the thought that counts.

As thoughts went, this one didn't go very far. Red wrinkled his nose. "Adidas is for losers." Nothing personal, you understand. Just setting me straight, brand-consciousness wise. As we started down the hallway, I dumped the deficient object in a housemaid's laundry bin.

Their room was on the fifteenth floor, a suite with a wrap-around view that extended all the way to Antarctica. Clouds roiled and boiled and sprinted across the sky. Red went through the room like an infectious disease, testing the beds, counting the pillows, ferreting through the minibar and loading up his knapsack with the free toiletries. "Sealed for your protection," he called from the bathroom. Unlike his mother's mouth.

"I see the weather hasn't improved," she said. Like it was my fault. Like she hadn't lived in Melbourne for the first thirty years of her life. Like the climate should have got its act together, knowing she was about to arrive.

While Wendy was looking for something else to complain about, the porter knocked with the luggage. Dressed in a green monkey suit and built like a pretzel, he took approximately forever to insinuate one suitcase and an overnight bag from the hallway into the room. Then he took even longer to leave. "Don't just stand there," commanded Wendy. "Give him a tip."

"You want a tip?" I said. "Join the union. Begging demeans a man." I gave him a dollar a bag, more than fair and less than the recommended rate. Wendy's parents were picking Red up at two o'clock, which meant the boy and I had time for lunch together. I suggested McDonald's.

"Richard says no Maccas while I'm in training," announced Red.

McDonald's was Red's oldest vice, one I'd long given up trying to fight. Now it appeared that my competitor for the boy's affection had succeeded where all my lectures about the Amazonian rainforest had failed. "Don't be so cheap," said Wendy, off to a free feed with her Melbourne management.

For a special treat and the sake of convenience, I took Red

downstairs to the restaurant in the lobby, a small forest of potted palms. When the waiter pulled out the chairs and flapped the napkins, the kid took it all in his stride, quite the sophisticate. But then he lived higher on the hog in Sydney than had ever been the case with his old man in Melbourne.

The place was running a special bush-tucker promotion. Fillet of emu with quandong chutney. Wallaby sausages in a lilly-pilly coulis. Glacé of bush tomatoes. I opted for the braised hump of Nullarbor camel with a witchetty-grub cappuccino on the side. "Yuk," said Red and ordered a burger with fries.

So much for Richard's training regime, I gloated secretly. "It's a pity you can't stay until Saturday," I said. "We could go to the footy."

"If I start missing games, I'll lose my place on the team," said Red.

I knew the score. It was the same in the Labor Party. "Pretty strict for Under-12s," I said.

"Under-13s," he corrected me. "I'm playing above my age. And you've got to be strict if you want to go all the way to the top." He had it figured.

"Sounds like you really like this rugby thing," I said, fascinated by this hitherto unrevealed side of my son's personality. Red was once so easy-going, so laid-back, that he would have scoffed at the idea of such discipline. Apart from a passing passion for Batman merchandise or Star Wars figurines, he had never before displayed such commitment to anything. "What do you like about it?"

"Winning," he stated flatly. "What else is there?"

"Are you winning at the moment?"

"Killing 'em," he said, fiercely and without a shred of humor. "Absolutely murdering them." He threw out his chest, awaiting my approval.

"Oh," I said. "That's good."

It was the age, I supposed. That last year of primary school when a certain bravado was bound to emerge in a boy. Top of the heap in the schoolyard, yet secretly apprehensive of the imminent move to high school and instant demotion back to little-kid status. In sport, he had found a place to match himself against his peers, to find the potential of the present.

I empathized but I could not identify. Ruthlessly relegated to the bench by the match-hardened Sisters of the Good Shepherd, I had by Grade 4 reconciled myself to watching from the sidelines. A spectator rather than a participant, I had done little to encourage Red into an on-field role. Standing on the boundary line on a Saturday morning, screaming my tits off at the Under-7s, had never been part of my parenting experience.

Little Athletics. Rugby Union. Sailing. These were all part of Red's life without me, part of his growing-up, his inevitable declaration of independence. Part of his life with Richard, I thought darkly as I threw myself onto my fricassee of dromedary. Richard was the source of all this competitiveness, I was prepared to bet. A certain degree of competition was a good thing. Sport would be impossible without it. But I wasn't sure I liked the relish with which Red appeared to have embraced the concept. It smacked of the motivational lecture.

My first wife's second husband was reasonably okay, as far as I could tell. Red could probably have found a worse stepfather. Ambitious and slightly oily in that Sydney way, Richard was not actually a Liberal Party member to the best of my knowledge. He was, however, from a privileged background. Cranbrook School, father a judge, independent income. In that context, a tendency to nurture competitiveness had the whiff of ideology about it. If we were talking about a proper game, Australian football, I might have felt different. But rugby! Jesus.

I spent the rest of the meal big-noting myself, knowing I was doing it and not being able to stop. Talk about competitive. It was pathetic. Fortunately, Red was too busy to notice, preoccupied with trying to fit a triple-decker Hyatt burger into his mouth without getting the decorative toothpick up his nose.

By the time I'd finished my witchetty-grub cappuccino — a

frothy farrago of beige milk and wet sawdust — our conversation had flagged out to a series of long silences. I'm losing him, I thought. This is the way it will be, more and more, from now on.

As we rode back up to the room, the elevator doors opened at the gymnasium level. Holly was standing in the lift lobby, chatting with a customer. She beamed and waved cheerily, a cross between Margaux Hemingway and Jamie Lee Curtis. "My date for the big dinner tomorrow night," I whispered as the doors slid shut again.

Red's head turned and he perused me slyly. "You've got a date with *her*?"

"Sure," I shrugged modestly. "She's my personal trainer."

Red's eyebrows went up and down like a yo-yo and he gave a low whistle. Redmond T. Firefly. "Lookin' good," he said. "Dad."

26

THE STARS CAFE was open for business again but there was no sign of Ambrose Buchanan among its late-lunching clientele.

"Think we're running a secretarial service, do you?" said a woman in an apron behind the roast of the day. But her bark was worse than her bite and she pointed her electric knife through the front window, toward the hotel across the street.

The Royal was one of the last unreconstructed watering holes in Fitzroy, a reminder of the days when no member of the working class need be more than staggering distance from alcoholic oblivion. *Happy Hour 10 A.M.–12 P.M.* read the chalked sign at the door of the front bar. I stepped across the threshold and squinted into the gloom.

The atmosphere was not what you might call inviting. Tired paintwork, ratty carpet, the stale fumes of a million dead beers. About twenty drinkers, early starters. Koories, mainly, and a few paunchy Yugoslavs. Voices echoed off hard tile walls. A juke box thumped away in the murk at the back of the room. Merle Haggard, by the sound of it. The snick of balls came from a pool table on a step-up in the crook of the bar. Two men were playing: Ambrose Buchanan and Ernest Anderson. Ambrose had shaved his beard off, a definite improvement. Deadly's appearance, by contrast, had grown even more deadly. He'd shed the bandanna and his caramel-colored skull was as bare as the ball of a roll-on deodorant. The tight skin was covered with scars, a tonsure of cross-hatching. The sort of handiwork you do on yourself in a cell with a broken bottle during lockdown. He must have really looked like something when they finally got around to opening those doors. He glowed with a patina of unhealthy sweat and, in the wait between shots, his fingers knotted and unknotted themselves at his side.

I took a stool at the bar. Whatever the deficiencies of the decor, the pipes were clean and the beer was crisp. Buchanan was playing the low-numbered balls. He potted three in a row and dropped the 8-ball into the side pocket. A dark-skinned indigene of indeterminate age with a soft rubbery face and no teeth leaned against the wall muttering unintelligible encouragement. Deadly racked them again and broke. The impact was as loud and abrupt as a gunshot.

Buchanan played a couple of strokes then handed his stick to the spectator. Flashing the barman two fingers, he lowered himself onto the stool beside me. Up close, his skin was raw from shaving and his eyes were exhausted. He looked like he hadn't been to bed. Deadly, it appeared, took some keeping up with. He put his elbows on the bar and waited.

"Found Radeski yet?" I said. One possible reason why the police hadn't.

Buchanan shook his head. "Never been much of a black tracker, myself," he said. "But Deadly's been making inquiries." He nodded toward the payphone. "Currently awaiting developments."

"Then what?" I said. "Rough justice?"

Buchanan stared down into his beer. "Justice," he said softly. "That's Deadly's special subject. He's been studying it since he was nine years old. That's when they first put him in a home. Told him that's what little black bastards get for breaking school windows. Picked him up in a paddy wagon and handcuffed him to the seat, just to help him get the hang of things."

"Save the violins," I said. "Eraserhead over there isn't the only one with dibs on Steve Radeski. That old bloke, Denis Dogherty, was a friend of mine. He's dead now and I want to know why. If Deadly knows something, he should go to the cops and tell them. If he's worried about incriminating himself, tell him to take a legal-service solicitor with him."

"You tell him," said Buchanan wearily. "I'm sure you'll have more influence than me."

We contemplated the issue, sipping our beers. The brown man's burden. What I really needed was a cigarette. I thought about the idea, long and hard, using my entire body. Deadly went to the payphone and jabbed at the keypad. Waited for an answer, jaw grinding. Snapped a question. No joy. Repeated the procedure. When he picked up his cue again, my hand moved to my side, feeling the tenderness.

"Pretty close to Darcy, was he?" I said.

Buchanan snorted into his beer. "That's what you might call the irony of the situation."

Deadly and Darcy were proper cousins, he explained, but Darcy was born long after Deadly was taken away. What with one thing and another, Deadly being in and out of prison, the two of them never met. But Deadly heard about his young cousin, his closest living kin, the rising champion.

"He's real proud, eh? So when he gets out this time and hears that Darcy's here in Melbourne, he turns up, wanting to party. But Darcy's a bit freaked out, not sure if he wants to know. Maxie tells Deadly to piss off, not come around. Naturally enough, he's pretty cut up. Then this happens."

"In other words," I said, "Deadly's desire for revenge is some sort of attempt to make right his family obligations to Darcy."

Buchanan examined the inch of beer in the bottom of his glass. "You're not one of them anthropologists, are you?"

"Fuck you, too," I said. "Want another drink?"

I ordered again, three this time, and held one up to Deadly. The cops weren't having much success in finding Radeski. Maybe Deadly, his nose closer to the ground, would have better luck. "He'll get himself back in strife," I said, "if he does anything stupid."

"He's never been out of strife," said Buchanan. "More strife than Jacky-Jacky, that one."

Deadly laid his cue on the table, came over and downed his beer in a single contemptuous tilt of his head.

"Know anyone called Cheech?" I said.

Last night, for Ambrose's sake, he had tolerated me. But he'd said too much and he resented me for it. Now I was in his pub, asking fucking stupid questions. I could get stuffed.

"Word is, Steve Radeski is looking for someone called Cheech. Find this Cheech and you might find Radeski."

He didn't even look at me. Just wiped his mouth with the back of his forearm and went back to his game. But he had to be thinking about it.

"Cheech?" said Buchanan. "As in stoned hippy comedy duo?"

"Same name. Different bloke. Unless Radeski is looking for an Hispanic-American with a black moustache and a string of lousy movies."

"I thought he was a Mexican," said Buchanan.

I wasn't buying into that one. "This Sports Institute. Big wheels are already in motion."

Buchanan grinned. "So our little protest yesterday did the trick."

"That piss-poor effort? You've got to be joking."

He shrugged. Okay, so the demo hadn't been the most brilliant example of his work. "Not up to my usual standard, I admit. Some of the younger generation felt they should express their justified anger. I thought a demo was better than other options being discussed."

It was plausible, I supposed. "The MOB had already decided to back your proposal. Now they think you'll try to disrupt this IOC visit."

"Why would I do that?"

"Because you're a trouble-making agitator who's prepared to destroy the nation's hopes for a bit of cheap self-promotion."

"That's true."

Buchanan was smoking roll-your-owns. So was I. It must have

happened when I wasn't looking. "So I'm supposed to make sure you behave yourself while these VIPs are in town."

"Is that right?" The tips of his fingers tested the smoothness of his chin. "How do you intend to do that?"

"I was thinking of threatening to go to the cops about this Deadly–Radeski business unless you agree to cooperate."

Responding to some unseen signal, the barman put another round of drinks on the bar. My shout, apparently. "As they say in Arunta." Buchanan raised his glass in a toast. "Looks like you got me over a barrel."

I started telling him how I'd fleshed out his concept for the institute, how it might be structured, funded. Koories kept coming to the bar. Buchanan would introduce them and I'd buy another drink, bat the breeze. Every now and then, Deadly would hit the phone again, Buchanan never missing a move.

By five o'clock, I was slurring my words. My life was going to hell in a handbasket. Midweek afternoon, working hours, I was pissing on in a lowlife dump with men named Dikko and Toad. Colluding with a known criminal. Cigarettes were smoking themselves in my mouth. My son was turning into a rampant rugger bugger. I hadn't had sex with another person for months. The Righteous Brothers were on the jukebox. They'd lost that loving feeling. It was gone, gone, gone.

Time I was, too. I no longer had the body for this sort of thing. I walked, squinting into the low afternoon sun, past the flats, across Brunswick Street and through my own front door. The light on my answering machine was flashing, calls backed up since late morning. I took the phone off the hook, swallowed a handful of painkillers and went out like a light.

27

I WAS WOKEN three hours later by a knock on the door. Bang, bang. Thanks a lot. It was the tyro flatfoot from the Fitzroy cop shop, the one who'd taken my report on the stolen Charade. It was in relation to that matter, he said, that he was there. "You'd better come inside," I told him, standing in my suit pants and bare feet, smelling like a brewery. "Quick."

He sat at the kitchen table while I answered nature's call. More of a bellow, really. All that beer. "Turned up, has it?" I said, zipping my fly. "I was just about to send in the insurance claim." The form was sitting there on the table with the junk mail and threatening letters that had come in the afternoon post.

"You are aware, sir," he said, "that there are penalties for making a false insurance claim."

Hello. What was this? "You suggesting this is a put-up job? That I nicked my own car for insurance?"

He took out his notepad. "I understand you work for the water department."

"Not currently," I said. "I'm on secondment to the Olympic bid."

"Yeah?" He wrote it down. "What are our chances?"

"Pretty good," I said. "If our water holds out." He wrote that down, too. "What's my job got to do with my car?"

"Your vehicle has been identified as involved in the current spate of incidents involving fire hydrants. You wouldn't happen to know anything about it, would you, sir?"

"You're telling me some prick is using my car as a battering ram to knock over fire hydrants?" I said. Those pricks at the union. Probably their idea of psychological warfare. I'd give them warfare all right.

"We were hoping you might be able to assist us in this matter, sir." They were on to me, he was letting me know, big time. Now was the time to confess.

"I suggest you interview all members of the Miscellaneous Workers Union," I said. "The man you're looking for has a brown cardigan and a stutter. When you find him, tell him from me that if this little stunt affects my insurance claim, I will personally cut off his water supply."

The copper closed his pad and got to his feet. "If you do happen to remember anything, sir."

"That Aboriginal kid, the triathlete?"

He perked up immediately. "Yes?"

"I was just wondering if you've caught whoever did it? Shocking, something like that happening just around the corner."

"A random attack. Not much we can do to prevent that sort of thing, sir."

So much for the efficacy of the constabulary. Changing into track pants and a sweatshirt, I sloped down to the corner shop and bought a frozen lasagne, no cigarettes and a copy of the *Herald*.

Denis's death rated eight paragraphs on the inside front cover. He was described as "a government consultant and former union official," the circumstances of his death "probably a domestic dispute." Police were reported to be seeking a former member of the national weightlifting squad who they believed would be able to assist them with their inquiries.

In a separate item, a spokeskoori for the Aboriginal Legal Service, Graeme Talbot, expressed dissatisfaction at the lack of police progress in the Darcy Anderson case. He suggested that such foot-dragging presented a poor picture of Melbourne to the international community.

I put my Papa Giuseppe in the microwave, rang Ken Sproule on his mobile and learned that Radeski was still at large. That, he said, was all he knew.

"I wonder how the media will react when they learn that Gil Methven recommended not reporting Denis as missing?" I prompted. "If he'd been found earlier, he might still be alive."

"You wouldn't dare," said Ken.

True, but he got the idea. Ken was a man who didn't respect you unless you threatened him from time to time. He told me, strictly not for attribution, that a neighbor had seen Radeski move Denis's car off the street and into his garage late on Monday night. And that Radeski's own car, an early model Celica, had been found abandoned in Preston, not far from his house.

"Looks like he spotted them waiting for him and did a bunk."

Associates in the iron-pumping fraternity claimed not to have seen Radeski for several weeks. Described him as a loner. Nobody, particularly the bigger guys, knew anything about any steroids. Checks on planes, trains and ferries had drawn a blank, suggesting he was still in town somewhere. The closest thing to a lead was a report that two men had been looking for him at the nightclub where he worked shortly before he disappeared.

"Dark-skinned," said Ken. "Whatever that means. Nobody was paying much attention at the time considering he'd just been disturbed trying to rape one of the customers on the fire escape. Apparently the type of shit he's been using really puts lead in your pencil."

Maybe they should've been searching down at the stockyards, catch him humping a ewe. I kept that suggestion to myself.

"Speaking of which," continued Ken. "This ex-girlfriend of his, your little friend, reckons he might be gunning for somebody called Cheech. As in Cheech and Chong? Those dopey American comedians from back in the seventies?" Ken's range never ceased to amaze me. "I can never remember which was which."

"Cheech was the wetback," I said. "Chong was the chink."

"You'd know," said Ken. "Being the ethnic expert."

Which reminded me. "How about the father? Any joy there?"

"Totally ga-ga. A cerebral hemorrhage six months ago, compounded by early-onset Alzheimer's. Sonny boy is a regular visitor, every weekend, so the place is under surveillance, but the old bloke himself is a write-off. Half the time, according to the staff, he thinks he's on a ship. Keeps muttering in Polish. They got a translator in, but he accused her of being a member of the communist secret police."

Despite their lack of success, the coppers were optimistic that Radeski would soon draw attention to himself. "The way he's behaving, he's bound to clobber someone else sooner or later."

"Let's just hope it's a Liberal next time," I said. "Any progress on the Darcy Anderson case?"

"Operational confidentiality," he said.

"Come on, give."

"Interesting developments," he said.

But that was all I could get out of him. He promised he'd call again as soon as they collared Radeski but I had the feeling I'd exhausted my goodwill. The oven bell rang, so I hung up and demolished the lasagne in record time. While I was shoveling, I checked the phone book and found a Deloite in Pascoe Vale.

One of Holly's kid brothers answered the phone, bellowing her name over a background of television noise. "It's a man," he jeered.

"No it's not," I reassured her. "It's just me, Murray, calling to report still no sign of Steve. Had any other ideas?"

Not really, but she appreciated my calling to check on her welfare. "Was that your son in the lift today?" she said. "He's a good-looking kid."

"Takes after his father," I said. We let it go at that.

I popped a couple of Panadeine Forte — it wasn't a cigarette but at least it was a drug — and spent another hour on the phone, clearing the backlog off my answering machine. Detective Senior

Constable Sonderlund had rung, inviting me to attend the Fitzroy police station at nine the next morning to provide my written statement in relation to the Denis Dogherty matter.

Sonderlund was the one who'd called the previous day about my offer to identify the skinheads. First the Darcy Anderson case, now Denis. Either police resources were stretched or a crossover was happening in the investigations. Had they already made the connection, rendering Deadly's information redundant? Or was Sonderlund simply the homicide housekeeper, fielding the public and attending to the paperwork? I guessed I'd find out soon enough.

In the meantime, the news about my walk-in role in the discovery of Denis had been making rapid progress along the grapevine and various of my party cronies had thoughtfully taken the time to ring. Before I spoke to any of them, however, there was one person I felt deserved a call. I rang him at Parliament House, where he was piloting a raft of money bills down the legislative rapids.

"Poor Denis," said Agnelli. "He'll be a great loss to the faction. And to the party and Woeful. And to his family, too, I suppose."

The funeral was to be private, no flowers by request. The Labor Party had more than its fair share of Denis when he was alive, Marj Dogherty had complained. And she knew her husband's opinion of certain people only too well. The sight of them shedding crocodile tears over his coffin would be too much to tolerate. A proper wake was being organized for later in the week, details TBA.

After Agnelli, I made another half-dozen calls, passing on my version of the event and taking general soundings. Woeful had been out of the picture all day and there was already talk that he would soon decide to pack it in. The implications of a ministerial resignation were dire, given the fragility of the deals which cemented together the precarious architecture of the government. The factional balance hung on a knife edge and any attempt at a reshuffle would inevitably erupt into public brawling. Gil Methven, with characteristic sensitivity, had been heard doing mental arithmetic out loud in the corridors of Parliament House. The Premier, concerned for both the general stability of the government and the tenability of his own position, was a pillar of support to Woeful in his hour of bereavement.

My boundary-riding done, I turned on the television and caught the tail end of the late news. While I was at the Royal Hotel, doing my bit for race relations, the Evaluation Commission had been inspecting the Docklands, proposed site of the Athletes Village.

The footage showed them under umbrellas, boarding a luxury cruiser, the MV *Dream the Dream*, admiring the city skyline for the benefit of the viewers. Although this was the first visit to Australia by the African and Asian delegates, said the voice-over, it was a sentimental journey for the Polish delegate, bringing back memories of his time in Melbourne during the 1956 Games.

In a related report, the Olympic torch had reached Westfield Shoppingtown in Melbourne's northern suburbs. Shoppers had lined the mall to cheer on participating local schoolchildren. The torch was now on the final leg of its journey to be presented to the visiting representatives of the IOC tomorrow evening.

By now, it was nearly eleven o'clock, too late for a goodnight call to Red. Too late and too strange. The kid's bedroom was empty while he slept in a hotel only a few kilometers away. He might as well still be in Sydney. According to Wendy's schedule, we would next see each other at the rehearsal for the torch handover. It had come to this, I thought gloomily, that I should count myself lucky to get an appointment with my own son.

As I brushed my teeth, I surveyed my battered and Nicabated chest in the mirror. My little sachet of poison potion. So far, so good. A permanent headache, some crabbiness, a tendency for the concentration to wander, the odd instance of backsliding, a tender throat. Twenty-four hours since my last cigarette, not counting one for breakfast and three grayhounds in the pub.

To stay patched overnight or not, that was the question. To chance waking in a nicotine-starved state, a pushover for the first fag that came along. Or to wrestle with the sandman, drenched with chemical stimulants. To sleep, perchance to dream.

I'll have a dream, I told myself, and hit the hay.

But the vision that visited me that night was no succubus with a stethoscope or smoke-wreathed nymph. It was a leprechaun with rope-veined fingers and fading breath. *"It's up to you, now, Murray,"* Denis kept repeating. *"You promised. You promised."*

28

"HARD NIGHT, Mr. Whelan?"

On the face of it, Detective Senior Constable Carol Sonderlund was a netball dyke with a bad haircut and a personality like a clenched fist. On the other hand, maybe I was just having a bad morning.

"I'm giving up smoking."

Barely through the door of the cop shop, I was already pleading mitigation. Sonderlund pretended to be sympathetic but she wasn't fooling me. In her line of work, the customers usually had worse things to worry about.

"We'll get this over and done with, then, shall we?"

She opened the security door and ushered me into an empty office with a computer on a bare desk.

My dreams had been complex and troubling and not at all erotic. Twice or three times I had woken in a cold sweat, pursued by a hulking green figure in a torn shirt, Denis's dying words echoing in my ears. On top of which, I'd arisen to find myself out of milk and muesli and was forced to stagger, bleary-eyed, to the shop for my breakfast necessities. By the time I read the papers, picked up Hugo from the dry-cleaners and made myself presentable, it was just on nine, time for my appointment.

"Rounded up Steve Radeski yet?" I asked. Bad choice of words. Didn't mean to sound critical.

"We will," said the detective. "Believe you me."

She took the cover off the keyboard.

"What about Darcy Anderson? The skinheads still your main suspects?"

"We usually ask the questions," said Sonderlund, thin-lipped.

Despite the NO SMOKING sign, cigarette burns pitted the floor and the air smelled of stale smoke. The walls were bare but for a Police Credit Union calendar and a loudly ticking clock. Welcome to the home of the third degree. "Fire away," I said.

"Tuesday night," she said. "West Heidelberg."

Detective Sonderlund was a pretty good touch-typist and my statement took less than fifteen minutes to dictate, print out and sign. I'd had plenty of time to rehearse it and in the interest of brevity and consistency I didn't add any new revelations. Once all the paperwork was in order, I was thanked for my assistance and shown the door.

Which left me pretty well at a loose end. According to the schedule, the Evaluation Commission was currently inspecting the proposed equestrian facility at Werribee. A cow paddock, fifty kilometers away. Well out of Buchanan's reach, even if he wanted to make a nuisance of himself. Which, I believed for a certain fact, he did not. With Radeski still at large, Ambrose had his hands full riding shotgun on Deadly.

And Deadly, presumably, was attempting to cherchez le Cheech. Fishing in the same water as the cops. I wondered who would land Radeski first.

Just because I was being paid to do nothing, there was no reason to get myself into a lather. My ribs weren't too uncomfortable, the day had dawned fine and mild and the rehearsal for Red's torch presentation was still two hours away. I caught a tram into the city and went into one of the little arcades running off Collins Street.

A wise man approaches the tasks of government, according to

Lao Tzu, as he would the cooking of a very small fish. Sardines on toast, in this particular instance, prepared by a woman named Magda Lipsky.

Unlike the Italians and Greeks, Melbourne's Polish community was neither large nor conspicuous. Poles formed no visible subculture and colonized no suburbs. Polish Jews, to be certain, could be found in the borscht belt extending from St. Kilda back into the hinterland of Caulfield and Balaclava. But that was a different matter, modern European history being what it was. Apart from a minor influx of refugees after the declaration of martial law in 1981, most of the city's Poles were aging postwar immigrants, models of assimilation whose children had vanished without a trace into the wider community.

In my four years at Ethnic Affairs, only once had a Polish issue come to my administrative attention. Two old codgers turned up one day, referred by their local MP. Men with a dream.

During World War II, Piotr Lipsky and Jerzy Melnyk were members of the Free Polish forces fighting in the North African desert. After the war, they refused repatriation and opted to settle in Australia. Both had done modestly well in business, Jerry in sheet metal and Peter in real estate. Restless in retirement, they had decided it was time to reaffirm their roots.

Not only was the famous author Joseph Conrad born a Pole, they explained, but he had actually visited Melbourne in the 1880s as the captain of a trading ship. Would not a statue of the author of *Heart of Darkness*, prominently located, preferably with a marine outlook, be an ideal way to celebrate the historic links between Poland and Australia? Funds were not an issue but an appropriate site needed to be found and official sanction obtained.

Statues were for the birds as far as Angelo Agnelli was concerned. But Peter and Jerry were likeable and persistent old bastards and for two years I conspired with them to get their monument afloat. We sometimes met at the Do Duck Inn, a small coffee shop in Howey Place owned by Peter Lipsky and run by his daughter Magda.

The Arts Ministry showed some initial interest, especially when somebody there realized that it was Conrad who had written the first draft of *Apocalypse Now*. But by the time the Harbor Trust found a site in the carpark of the new container terminal, cultural priorities had shifted. Couldn't we do something in postmodern pre-contextual dance, Arts asked? When Jerry died at seventy-seven of a coronary occlusion, Peter's enthusiasm for the project waned. Eventually the whole thing ground to a halt and he returned to getting under Magda's feet at the Do Duck Inn.

It was one of those narrow old-fashioned places, once common but now rarely seen, where ladies enjoying a day's shopping in the city could rest their tired feet beneath a bowl of tomato soup and an asparagus roll. In a world gone mad for radicchio focaccia and sushi negri, it was a bastion of buttered crumpets and apple crumble. I found Peter in the tiny kitchen, slicing ham for the lunch-order sandwiches.

At that time of the morning, there were few customers and Peter took off his apron and joined me, leaving Magda to get on with it. A pinched, avaricious woman of my own age, she seemed to regard my friendship with her father as a ploy to cheat her of her inheritance. But she made the best sardines on toast in town.

Peter Lipsky was always a spare man, but I was shocked at how much weight he'd lost since I'd last seen him. His black turtleneck sweater and gray permanent-press slacks hung loose off his rake-like frame and the strut was gone from his cavalry-officer tread. "The Big C," he said, answering my unasked question. "Lungs. Let's not talk about it."

We talked ancient history instead, sitting in a chintz-cushioned booth beneath a poster of Jemima Puddleduck.

"Rudy Radeski? Now there's a name I haven't heard in yonks." After five decades of speaking English, Peter Lipsky's idiom was perfect but he retained a distinct accent. Deliberately, I suspected. Part of his hand-kissing continental-gentleman persona. "Not pestering you about a statue, is he? These New Australians can be such a nuisance."

"You should know," I said. "But I'm not with Ethnic Affairs any more. I'm working for the Olympic bid."

"So what are our chances?"

"Very good, apparently," I said. Magda put a plate of sardines in front of me. Comfort food. Wedges of lemon. Little points of toast on the side. "Best in town," I told her. "What's your secret?"

She tapped the side of her nose. Classified information. "Horseradish," Peter whispered when she was back in the kitchen. "It cuts the oil. I remember 1956. Biggest thing ever happened to this city."

"You were saying — Rudy Radeski."

"The defector? Yes, whatever happened to him?"

"That's what I was hoping you might be able to tell me. Background for something I'm working on. Former Olympians, that sort of thing." Less than frank but entirely necessary unless I wanted to spend the rest of the day in the Do Duck Inn. Peter Lipsky was a born talker. In his current condition, I could see, it was also a form of therapy. One that simultaneously exhausted him and sustained his vitality. "How do you mean, defector?"

"One of those who stayed behind after the Games. Quite a lot did, you know. Some Czechs, Romanians, even a Russian. Mostly Hungarians, of course."

The reason for this was too well known for him to bother explaining. The 1956 Olympics opened only days after Russian tanks poured into Hungary to smash the liberalizing regime of Imre Nagy. When the Hungarians and Russians met in the final of the water polo, the match quickly degenerated into an all-out brawl. Blood in the water, screamed the commentators, and the crowd would have lynched the Russians if they hadn't been rushed from the building.

"Almost the entire Hungarian contingent refused to return home," said Peter. "Most of them went straight to America where they had been offered jobs and money. Only two Poles stayed, even though the situation in Poland, too, was pretty grim. A girl from the track-and-field team. Anna, I think her name was. Stayed to marry a Polish boy in Adelaide. And Rudy Radeski, of course. Don't tell me he's trying to sell his story again. All this fresh interest in the Olympics gave him the idea, I imagine. You want something else? Magda! Bring some apple pie and ice cream."

"No ice cream," I said, patting my stomach. "I'm trying to lose weight. How do you mean, sell his story?"

"I should be so lucky," said Peter, skin and bone. "His dramatic defection. How The Communists Stole My Medal. You haven't heard this?"

"Not yet," I said. "He was a weightlifter, that's all I know."

Magda brought the pie. It was nothing to write home about, not a patch on her mashed Santa Marias. She put a plate in front of me and a large glass of green slime in front of her father. "Extract of wheat grass," he explained. "It's supposed to regenerate the cells. Tastes like frog shit. Tell you the truth, I don't know what's worse." Magda stood, arms crossed, until he'd taken a mouthful.

"Very boring," he said. "Weightlifting. Circus strongmen. Grunt, lift. Grunt, lift. Not very interesting at all. I preferred the fencing. We won a medal there. Poland, that is. But I did go to the weightlifting, I admit. In those days I was still hungry for the sound of my mother tongue."

As soon as Magda's back was turned, he tipped the slimy liquid into a potted plant. It had very green, very shiny leaves.

"Radeski got through to the final but he withdrew before the deciding lift. I forget who won in the end. Nothing more was seen of him until after the Games. Suddenly he reappeared, waving a bandaged arm, telling the most dramatic story. He said the communists broke his wrist to stop him making a big public defection at the medal ceremony. He said some teammate had informed on him, so the commissar made sure he wouldn't be able to compete. He claimed they made a prisoner of him on the Soviet ship, the one they used to transport the Russian and Polish and Czech teams, and he escaped just in time, right as it was about to sail away."

"Claimed?" I said. Actually, the pie wasn't too bad. "You weren't convinced?"

Peter turned a ring on his long, thin, nicotine-stained index finger. "I believed that the communists were capable of such a thing. So did some of the émigré groups. They wanted to make a hero of Radeski. He wanted to sell his story to the newspapers, just like the Hungarians did with the Americans. He even thought the Australian government would give him a job."

A self-made man, Peter took a dim view of those he suspected of chasing a free ride.

"But it was all too fantastic. Even if they wanted to, the communists would not have dared do such a thing. They were too far from home and everybody was watching them. There was a lot of fraternization. The Russian athletes even used to go over to the American section of the Athletes Village to see Frankie Laine singing. The commissars couldn't stop it, even if they'd wanted to. In the end, they just went along with it."

"You mean there were easier ways to defect than jumping off a ship?"

"These were the Friendly Games, remember. It was made very clear that there were to be no political demonstrations or nationalist outbursts, and émigré groups were warned not to make trouble. But it was well known that nobody from the communist bloc would be forced to go home against their will. They just had to wait until the Closing Ceremony. The only person who defected during the Games wasn't an athlete at all. She was a stewardess on the Russian ship. Some local communists took her to the zoo. She said she wanted to go to the toilet, then slipped away. That's how easy it was. She went to Myer's and declared to the lady behind the counter in the millinery department that she wanted political asylum."

Poor woman must have been on tenterhooks. You can stand in Myer's for hours before the staff even notice you. "What about the broken wrist?"

"Very convenient. Maybe he knew he wasn't going to win the medal, after all. Better to be a hero of the war against communism than a has-been strongman coaching high school students in Lodz.

Maybe he hurt himself by accident, ruined his medal chances, invented the story to console himself."

"But at the time," I said. "The height of the Cold War. The whole anti-communist atmosphere. Why didn't he get more publicity?" Why hadn't I heard this story before? It should have been a sensation, on par with the blood in the water-polo pool.

"You were just a child," he said. "You don't remember how proud everybody was about the Olympic Games. It was bigger than Ben Hur. The greatest thing that had ever happened to this town. Nobody wanted to think anything bad had taken place, even if the communists were responsible for it. It would have left a sour taste in people's mouths. The newspapers knew that."

It was certainly true that the Melbourne Games belonged to that golden era when the Olympics were unsullied by politics or violence. Back before Mexico City with its machine-gunned student protesters and Black Power salutes. Before the Munich massacre and the era of boycotts. An era for which the current IOC must yearn. Apart from the money, of course. There was no money in it, back then.

"So what happened to Rudy Radeski after that?"

Peter shrugged his shoulders, sharp triangles inside his turtleneck sweater. "Last I heard, he married an Australian girl. This is more than thirty years ago. More apple pie?"

"I've had about as much as I can digest for the moment," I said. It was past eleven, time I was elsewhere. Peter Lipsky's story was fascinating but was it relevant? And relevant to what? Was my curiosity about Rudy Radeski no more than a blind groping into the unknown?

You bet it was.

Murder is never a private act. The death of Denis Dogherty was already having political repercussions, still subtle but potentially significant. More to the point, the man had reached out in his final lucid moment and exacted a promise from me. A promise which, so far, I had kept. But which I might not be able to keep indefinitely. Not unless I understood what it meant.

If there were clues here, they were successfully eluding me. Too many missing pieces. Too much history. The women could probably fill the gaps, the Boag sisters, Beth McKenzie and Marj Dogherty. And Carmel, she'd know a thing or two. But they had no reason to speak to me. Nor I to presume to interrogate them. Even if I knew what to ask. Which I didn't. Any answers would have to come from Woeful. At the right time, I would ask the right questions. In the meantime, I had an appointment.

"See you later, Peter," I said.

"Only if you're quick."

29

APART FROM A MINOR MISHAP on the outskirts of Wangaratta when a member of the support team was inadvertently sprayed with hot asphalt during an animated discussion with a municipal road-repair crew, the 2000 kilometers of the *Dream the Dream* Torch Relay had been unmarred by accident or incident.

Hundreds of children had proudly carried the hopes of the nation and the logos of the sponsors through town and country, shopping precinct and rural municipality. Tens of thousands of names had been added to the petition to award the 1996 Olympics to Melbourne. Acres of newsprint and hours of television had been devoted to the spectacle, raising national awareness of Melbourne's ambitions.

Now, the peripatetic flame was nearing its date with destiny. Soon would come the final leg, its ceremonial passage down Collins Street from the Old Treasury, its progress into the Hyatt Hotel and its formal enthrustment into the waiting hands of the visiting representatives of Olympism's highest body. By my boy, Redmond Evatt Whelan.

I found him in the hotel motor court with a half-dozen of his fellow relayists, a collection of bony little knees in flame-motif T-shirts and running shoes. They were hunkered down in the lee of a logo-bedecked minibus, sheltering from the wind while they awaited further instructions from the relevant authorities. Red advanced to meet me with a self-deprecating grin, flexing his muscles and showing off.

"Lookin' good," I told him. He looked like an albino flamingo. This rugby thing couldn't possibly last. "What's happening?"

"Hangin' loose," he drawled. "Freezin' our butts off."

"How were Roger and Iris?" The maternal grandparents.

"Same as usual." The toe of his running shoe probed a crack in the artificial cobblestones. Wendy's parents were an ordeal to be endured, Liberal voters from Camberwell who insisted that Red visit whenever he was in town, then spent the entire time fretting about the furniture.

The motor court was a hive of activity. Taxis came and went, air crews and group tours arrived and departed, MOB logistics people buzzed about, going into huddles with the hotel doormen. Wendy materialized at my elbow. "About time," she said. "I've rescheduled. When the rehearsal's over, you can have him until four."

"Great," I said. An improvement of two hours on the prior arrangement. Now all I had to do was figure out how to entertain him on a Thursday afternoon on zero notice. Being short on practice and all. Red kept anxiously swiveling his head back toward the other kids, afraid of missing some vital directive. The boys were hoppo-bumping each other, acting the goat, while the girls maintained an air of superior indifference.

As Wendy vanished, an official with a walkie-talkie appeared and called the runners to attention.

I hung at the fringes with the other adults, listening as orders were issued. The minibus would distribute the runners to their allocated places along the last section of the route, from the Old Treasury to the Hyatt. Red and a girl called Amber would await the arrival of the baton at the hotel before proceeding upstairs to the ballroom. In the interest of gender equity, the torch would be carried up the escalator by a runnerette. Lest I cramp Red's style with my presence, I headed upstairs to await his arrival there.

Preparations were in full swing. Workmen swarmed about the ballroom foyer, erecting an exhibition of Olympic paraphernalia. The place looked like a sports store clearance sale. Badminton racquets, javelins, baseball bats, boxing gloves, fencing foils, bows and arrows, ski stocks and judo suits were being hung on every surface in sight. A rowing scull was suspended from the ceiling, volleyball nets draped the walls, and store dummies dressed in historical costumes stood in glass cases on either side of the ballroom doors.

Inside, roadies were setting up a sound system on a temporary stage. Technicians wearing headphone mikes fine-tuned the focus on Olympic rings thrown against the walls by a bank of projectors. Members of Brian Morrison's innumerable staff moved around the tables, checking place cards against seating plans and conferring with the banquet staff.

Morrison himself was standing on the stage, hands on hips, casting a proprietary eye over the proceedings. He spotted me lurking in the doorway, beckoned me over. He was not a happy man.

"Your mate Buchanan rang the hotel early this morning, asked for Pascal Abdoulaye. Some idiot put the call through. Buchanan told Abdoulaye he'd like to catch up, discuss issues of mutual concern." He puffed his cheeks and slowly exhaled. "Abdoulaye says sure thing, brother. I'll see you at the official dinner. Then he asks Hugh Knowles to make sure Buchanan gets a ticket." He shook his head glumly and radiated disappointment in my direction. "Just the sort of thing you're supposed to stop happening, Murray."

"Gee, mate, I'm sorry," I said. "Ambrose must have gnawed through his bonds."

He thrust an invitation card into my hand. It was made out to Ambrose Buchanan and Guest. "I'm putting him on your table. And I'll hold you personally responsible if there's any trouble. Knowles will be announcing the Aboriginal Institute of Sport initiative during his speech and the last thing we want is heckling from the only blackfeller in the room."

"The institute was Ambrose's idea in the first place," I said. "He's hardly likely to object to it."

"Yeah, well," admitted Brian grudgingly. "You never know."

At that point, we were joined by an immaculately besuited man carrying a clipboard. He had a buttonhole rose, a sly twinkle in his eyes and manners that had been buffed to a mirror sheen. Brian introduced him as the MOB Director of Protocol. He was looking for volunteers, he explained, to act the part of the dignitaries who would formally accept the torch. "Come on, Murray," ordered Brian. "It's about time you started earning your pay."

Along with the other conscripts, I was seated at the high table and briefed on my role. "You three are the members of the IOC," the protocol man told us. "When you hear your names announced, step to the front of the stage." He handed each of us a name tag. A roadie named Gus was Pascal Abdoulaye, Brian was Kim U-ee and I was Stanislas Dziczkowszczak. "As the most senior member of the delegation, the gentleman from Poland will accept the torch."

The head honcho relay official appeared at the doorway and signaled that the arrival of the torch was imminent. Seconds later, Red appeared, holding aloft a rolled cardboard tube. Framed by the doorway, he paused for maximum effect. "Ladies and gentlemen," announced the protocol chief over the PA. "Please welcome Redmond Whelan, representing the aspirations of the young people of Australia that Melbourne play host to the Games of the Twenty-sixth Olympiad, the Centennial Games of the Modern Era."

Red looked tiny, dwarfed by the pharaonic scale of the hotel. He'd got the gig by dint of finagling, but my heart swelled with pride anyway. "Applause, applause," said the protocol director. "Rhubarb, rhubarb."

The house lights dropped away and Red began his circuit of the empty room, tracked by a spotlight. His face was a mask of such intense concentration that it was hard not to laugh. It was the same expression he'd used as one of Santa's elves at the kindergarten Christmas pageant. Moving at a slow lope, he twice orbited the dance floor. Finally, reaching the steps leading up to the stage, he again paused and held the torch aloft.

"And to accept the torch on behalf of the International Olympic

Committee," intoned the voice over the PA. "Please welcome the Chairman of the IOC Evaluation Commission." This was my cue. As Red mounted the stage, I readied myself to step forward.

The protocol director spoke slowly, at pains to pronounce the difficult name correctly. "Mr. Stanis-las Zitch-kovs-chuck." He peered closely at his clipboard and said it again, enunciating every syllable. "Zheech-kovs-chuck." The ch was a soft buzz.

I stepped into the circle of light and Red thrust the rolled cardboard into my hand. "Cop this," he whispered. We turned to face the darkened room, shoulder to shoulder. "Shake hands," instructed the voice through the PA. "And please don't hold the torch in your armpit, sir. Photo. Snap, snap." Red wheeled briskly and left the stage. "Now hand it to the African gentleman."

The light widened to include Gus the roadie. "And what do I do with it?" he said. Smoke it if he had the chance, by the look of him.

"Hand it to the Korean," sighed the protocol director.

Gus passed the torch to Brian. A tracksuited relay official then reached up from the side of the stage, took the object and followed Red through the door into the kitchen. Where the real thing, presumably, would be doused in a Waterford crystal tureen of turtle soup.

The ultimate destination of the torch was not my problem. My energies were otherwise engaged. I was warming up for a shot at the world record in jumping to conclusions.

30

WHILE RED CHANGED BACK into his civilian clothes, I sat on the edge of the bed with the phone in my lap and picked the salad out of his room-service lunch. Waste not, want not. Ambrose Buchanan wasn't at the Stars, so I left a message that his invitation was waiting at the Hyatt reception desk. Not exactly personal delivery, but the best I could do. Short of an exploratory probe into darkest Fitzroy, scouring the known haunts of Deadly Anderson, there was no guessing where Ambrose might be.

Then the kid and I stood together at the window and looked out over the vast amorphous sprawl that is Melbourne. Through the windows of nearby skyscrapers we could see empty offices, fruit of the busted building boom. Below us flowed the Yarra, green-flanked and segmented by bridges. And Jolimont railway yards, one of the finest collections of scrap metal still in public hands anywhere in the world. On the far horizon sat the faint smudge of the Dandenong Ranges. The bay extended vastly, gunmetal gray and dotted with ships idling for a berth. We played spot the familiar landmark and Red pointed out the brick-red bowl of the Melbourne Cricket Ground, light towers poised around its rim.

"They look like giant fly-swatters," he said.

They did, too. "I've got an idea," I said. "Let's go to the Gallery of Sport."

We could just make it out, stuck to the rear wall of the MCG Members' Stand. A shrine to sporting history. A collection of artefacts, records, rolls of honor, statistics and team lists. "It's like a museum." I realized my mistake. "But good."

And only a few minutes away. If he didn't like it, I said, we could always take in a movie. Fair enough, he agreed. I left Buchanan's invitation at the front desk and let the doorman hail us a cab.

Five minutes later we were standing beside the walls of the venerable old stadium. Through an open gateway we could just glimpse the green expanse of the playing arena, the city's most sacred site, holier than any cathedral. A row of identical white Fairlanes was drawn up at the entrance to the Gallery of Sport, each with the customized number plates of the Melbourne Olympic Bid.

As we paid our admission, an entourage of navy-blue blazers with flame motifs on their breast pockets came down the stairs from the upper level. At its center were the three gods of the Evaluation Commission. Asia, Africa and Europe. "See that man." I nudged Red and discreetly pointed. "He's the one you'll be handing the torch to."

At close range, Dziczkowszczak looked to be in his mid-seventies. He was chatting with his hosts, the relaxed elder statesman of sport. But I thought I could detect a definite wariness behind his apparent ease. Wariness and weariness. Occupational hazards for a member of the International Olympic Committee, no doubt. Another day, another city, another pestering army of sycophants.

An apparatchik, I thought. But that was an obvious guess. Nobody got to be the most senior office-bearer in one of the old Iron Curtain sports machines by bucking the system. He descended the stairs with care, gripping the banister with bony arthritic fingers. Like the system he represented, his best days were behind him. "Gee, he's old," said Red, a little too loudly.

"Shuddup." I clapped a hand over his mouth. "You'll fuck up our chances."

In 1956, Dziczkowszczak would have been almost forty. No

spring chicken by athletic standards. I wondered what his sport had been. Something for the longer in tooth. Horse-riding? Yachting? Shooting? We waited in respectful silence while the official party passed, then went upstairs.

The entire top floor of the museum was dedicated to the Games of the XVI Olympiad, Melbourne 1956. All the usual stuff — the sacred objects and blown-up photos, continuous-loop videos and push-button commentaries. Betty Cuthbert hurtling open-mouthed down the track. Murray Rose and Dawn Fraser blitzing the pool. Vladimir Kuts on his last lap of the stadium, the cheering crowd on its feet. Ron Clarke lighting the cauldron. Red picked up on that one, so I told him the story. How Clarke stumbled in the final stretch of a big race, I couldn't remember exactly which, and how his rival John Landy paused to help him up before continuing.

"Yeah, yeah," said the kid, rolling his eyes. The lives of the saints. "So winning isn't everything, right?"

"Except in politics," I said.

The exhibit was deserted but for a lone attendant. His boredom was palpable, a groundsman relegated to indoor work for the off-season. A man who knew where to place the screens and when to roll the wicket and who harbored serious doubts about the durability of some of the newer ryegrass-fescue blends. Keith, according to his name tag. "I see you've just had the IOC in here, Keith," I observed, chatty. "They said on TV that the Polish bloke was here in '56."

"Oh, yes indeed," said Keith, stirring to life. "We've even got a picture of him from back then. Part of a special display on Poland's participation. Did the same for South Korea. Do it for all of them, we do. Not that he was here in '56, the Korean fellow. Actually, there were only seven Koreans here, as against more than a hundred in the Polish team. Which is not to say that Korea didn't do well, considering. Won a silver in boxing. Bantamweight. Song Soon Chung, I believe."

Keith believed right. A captioned photograph of the man was right there behind glass, along with the names of all other participating Koreans. More Parks than an urban design manual. "Beaten by a German, Wolfgang Behrendt. The Germans fielded a combined team in those days, East and West together. Came eighth in the medal tally. Just behind Britain. Germany, that is. Poland was eighteenth. Bad luck for the African chap, of course. His country didn't exist back then."

I had misjudged Keith's vocation. He was, in fact, a torpid encyclopedia. A Friend of the Gallery of Sport, lying in wait for an unsuspecting visitor to whom he could demonstrate his boa-constrictor grasp on the minutiae of Melbourne '56. Quite possibly, he was just what I was looking for. If only I could get him to shut the fuck up. "Not too many African teams at all in those days. South Africa, of course. This was back before the boycotts. They were still in the Commonwealth Games at that stage as well."

"The Polish IOC member," I said, talking right over him. He didn't seem to mind. "What sport did he play?"

"One gold, four silver, four bronze," he recited, though I hadn't asked, and marched me to the relevant array of photographs. Fencers in white, visors under their arms. Women gymnasts poised on the Roman rings. Shooters holding armfuls of flowers. A formal group portrait, entire delegation, names listed. "Third from the right, bottom row. Deputy chef-de-mission. Originally a cyclist, apparently. Never made it to an Olympics as a competitor. The war and all that, probably. Although you'd be surprised how few of these IOC actually competed at an Olympic Games. Some, on the other hand, did very well. The Dutchman, Geesink, beat the Japanese at judo in Tokyo '64. We had him in here a few weeks ago. And the Guatemalan."

"Deputy chef-de-mission?" One figure among a hundred, Dziczkowszczak's face was no bigger than a speck of confetti, a meter away behind a sheet of glass. No clues there. "That's like assistant team manager, right?"

"Exactly," said Keith. "As I was saying . . ."

"Rudy Radeski?" I found the name in the caption, looked in vain for the face. "The weightlifter, right? Wasn't there some controversy there?"

Keith sensed a piss-take. "Fair go, mate. There were 3,342 competitors from sixty-seven nations. You can't expect me to know about every last one of them."

"Hey, Dad," called Red, fingers jabbing a touch-screen display. "Guess what city holds the record for the largest crowd at an Olympic opening ceremony?"

"Los Angeles?"

"Wrong," he whooped. "Loser."

"It was Melbourne, wasn't it, son?" said Keith. The two of them ganging up on me. What sort of an idiot was I?

The sort who'd probably gleaned as much useful information as any Friend of the Gallery of Sport could provide. The question I now wanted answered was beyond Keith, beyond even the library in the basement. It related to the exact function of the deputy chef-de-mission of the Polish team. Was Dziczkowszczak's role, I wondered, exclusively sporting? One of the team managers, it was reasonable to assume, was responsible for political matters. Somebody must have had the job of keeping the boys and girls on the straight and narrow. Of seeing to it that they did nothing to embarrass the socialist motherland.

"How did he like it?" I said. "The display?"

"Tickled pink," said Keith.

Red had pushed every available button and his interest was waning fast. I thanked Comprehensive Keith for his assistance and took the kid down to the next level, a sideshow alley of hands-on interactive opportunities to test our physical skills. A basketball hoop, a long-jump pit, a rowing machine, a golf tee. This time I pulled no punches. Despite my sore rib, I beat the little bastard every time I could. "Not fair," he bleated.

"Sore loser," I said. As we left, we passed the open gate into the stadium and couldn't resist a quick look inside. Red ran ahead, down the tunnel beneath the Members' Stand, all the way to the fence. The vast green of the playing surface spread out before us, framed by the curved lip of the grandstands, silent and empty, lidded with a perfect ellipse of sky.

The last time we had both been there, so had forty thousand other people. Melbourne versus Essendon, three years before, on one of Red's term-holiday visits. A lousy, scrapping game of football. Not much in it for anyone, let alone a little kid dragged along by his sometime father as an exercise in intermittent parenting. We threw in the towel at three-quarter time. The rain had set in and Melbourne was so far ahead it didn't matter. It was more aversion therapy than cultural education and I feared it had done nothing to endear the game to the boy.

"You remember?" I said.

"We had pies," said Red. "It was good."

The lure of the majestic oval was too much to resist. Peeling off my suit jacket, I vaulted the low fence and crossed the boundary line. Red was right behind me. An unspoken dare passed between us and we sprinted for the center, expecting at any second a challenging shout from one of the custodians of the temple. When none came, we slowed to a jog and turned for the white posts. "And it's the Whelans into attack," I yelled. "Heading into an open goal."

Shoulders forward. One bounce, two bounces. I feinted to avoid an invisible opponent and passed an imaginary ball to Red. He marked it on his chest, played on and ran for the sticks. Twenty yards from the goal mouth, he steadied and took a ping. A huge kick for a kid of his size, a high torpedo punt that sent him reeling backward from the effort. Up, up, it arched, spiraling overhead. Straight through the high-diddle-diddle. The crowd she roared.

Suddenly, he had the ball again, tucked under his arm this time, rugby style. Head down, he charged me. "Wrong game." I sprinted for the back pocket. "Kick it. Kick it."

He pulled up sharp and snapped me a pass. It came high and I had to jump, plucking it double-handed from the air above my head. I fired it back, too short, and Red ran to meet it, swerving to follow the bounce, scooping it one-handed off the ground in a tight circle. He drew back and took his time, tugging at his socks. His run-up was long and again the kick was tremendous. "Woof," he exhaled as his foot swept through the empty air, the sound of boot on leather.

In the distant past, when he was much smaller, Red and I occasionally bandied a thin plastic ball around the backyard, constantly breaking off play to retrieve its dented shell from beneath the shrubbery or off the roof. This new, invisible model was infinitely better. Especially when used on hallowed turf with the inaudible murmur of a capacity crowd in our ears. Every grunt and shout echoed back from the circling stands, every kick unerringly found its target, every mark was a screamer.

Red reveled in the pretense, running all the way to the Punt Road end of the oval, a 150-meter dash that scored him an uncontested goal and left me coughing my lungs out at center half-forward. Fortunately, before I could pull a hamstring or die, a groundsman appeared and told us to piss off.

As I put on my jacket and wiped the flecks of grass from my shoes, I gazed back across the arena and tried to imagine what it must have looked like in 1956, the flags of sixty-seven nations fluttering above the grandstands. Tried to imagine, too, the climate of the times. Russian tanks in the rubble-strewn streets of Budapest. Witch-hunts and blacklists. Petrov and the ALP Split. Fascist hyenas and fellow travelers. Blood in the water.

I thought about Rudy Radeski and his broken wrist and events alleged to have taken place in the Olympic city some thirty-four years before. Wondered, too, if they might have any bearing on the intentions of a certain psychotic young man currently eluding capture by the Victorian police force. And what role, if any, Denis Dogherty might have in such a scenario. Or the current Minister for Sport, for that matter.

31

WE HEADED BACK into the city on foot, going leaps and bounds through ankle-deep drifts of fallen leaves. At Captain Cook's tiny stone cottage in the Fitzroy Gardens, we stopped to wonder aloud that a continent as big as Australia had been discovered by a man the size of a midget.

At the Hyatt Hotel, I put my arm around Red's shoulder and reminded him not to drop the torch when he came through the ball-room door. Then I handed him back to his mother.

"You're late," she said.

"It's not his fault." Red flew to my defense. "The game went into extra time." A rugby expression, I took it.

"Time-on, mate," I said. "That's what we call it in proper football."

But Wendy was right. There were things to be done. I was beginning to have a theory. On the way downstairs, I stopped at the City Club.

"That name, Cheech," I said to Holly. "Do you think it could've been Zeech? Think hard."

She could see that I was agitated, jiggling up and down beside the pec-deck like a man with a urinary tract infection. "Excuse me, madam," she said to the petite Japanese tourist trapped inside the padded cage. "Sumimasen." She bowed slightly, then grabbed my elbow and dragged me over to the glute isolator. "Can't you see I'm working?" she hissed.

"Sorry," I whispered. "But could Cheech be Zeech?"

"Like I told the police, I really can't remember. I'd already decided to give Steve the flick and I wasn't much interested in listening to him bicker with his father. It only stuck in my mind because he said he'd rip the guy limb from limb if he ever got the chance."

"And what did Steve's father say?"

"He said he'd believe it when he saw it. Something like that."

"Did Rudy Radeski ever talk about the 1956 Olympics?"

"Steve told me not to ask him. Said it was still a sore point, that he was cheated out of winning a medal. Said not to get him started or he'd never shut up. Why? What's going on? It's Steve. He's killed someone else, hasn't he?"

"No, no," I said quickly. "Not that I know of." Not yet. "Pick you up at seven, okay? Your parents' place. Better give me the address."

"Make it my flat," she said. "That's where I keep my party dress." She swiveled her hips and made with the cha-cha-cha. "Seven-thirty, right?"

It had just gone five. I went up to Parliament House and found Ken Sproule in the Police Minister's office, feet on the desk, conspiring on the telephone. He put his hand over the mouthpiece and shook his head. Nothing to report. Steve Radeski was still at liberty. I backed out, leaving Ken to his dirty work, and went upstairs to the public gallery of the Legislative Assembly.

With only a few sitting days remaining in the autumn session, a considerable backlog of legislation still to be cleared and a majority no bigger than a bee's dick, the party whips had been cracking. Bereaved or not, Woeful McKenzie was in his usual place, propped between the Minister for Agriculture, a town planner by trade, and the Minister for Education, poor woman.

Although he had been prevailed upon to buck up and stand to his post, it was clear that Woeful was feeling the weight of a considerable burden. The big, bluff man of the previous week appeared inwardly drained, a diminished version of his former self. Oblivious to the Treasurer's plaintive ramblings, he stared absently between his feet, his sad caterpillar gaze fixed on the oak-leaf pattern of the carpet.

When the going gets tough, some politicians turn brittle and bite the head off anything that moves. By the look of it, Woeful was going the other way, spinning a cocoon of silent introspection, sharing his burden with the pixies. His eye was definitely not on the ball.

I mentally marshaled my evidence. The newspapers in Steve Radeski's room. The obsessive training for no apparent purpose. The threatening talk overheard by Holly. The pronunciation of a name. It didn't amount to much. Chances were that I was wrong. But if I was right, only halfway right, the stakes were too high to risk hesitation. The clock was ticking. Time to do a Denis. Dash onto the oval and have a word in the fullback's ear.

I got out one of my business cards and wrote on the back. Block capitals, headline style. OLYMPICS MINISTER'S NEPHEW IN IOC REVENGE PLOT. It seemed just too bizarre. I hoped to Christ it was. I added a question mark, scant extenuation, and asked the sergeant-at-arms to hand the folded card to the Honorable Member for Melbourne Docklands.

The fuse lit, I stood in the empty hallway outside the door of the chamber and waited for the explosion. I needed a cigarette like a cigarette had never been needed before. A wave of nausea rose in my throat. Panic. What if I was wrong?

When Woeful emerged, it was with a look of such utter defeat that I knew immediately I wasn't. Not entirely, anyway. "So they've got him, at last," he said, wearily.

"Not yet," I said.

He jerked upright, chins quivering. "So what's this crap?" But the cat was out of the bag. The question now was how to skin it.

"Somewhere a little less public," I suggested. "Let's go outside."

We went through the side door into the rose garden and walked together beneath a sky the color of aluminum, the gravel path crunching at every step. "Who else knows?" said Woeful.

"Nobody who heard it from me."

"You worked this out yourself?" The idea made him look even more depressed.

"A stab in the dark," I said. "But it's bound to come out eventually. And when it does you'd better be ready."

He squinted at me warily. "Who are you working for, pal?"

A good question. I looked back the way we'd come, toward the seat of government. "Us?" I shrugged. We true believers, clinging by our fingernails.

You've got to hand it to Woeful. When push came to shove, he was every inch a minister. "Tell me what I should do," he said.

"I'd like to know what I'm buying into," I told him. "If I'm buying into it."

We stopped at a rose bush, the last of the late blooms. I could hear Woeful breathing in the silence between us. "It's a long story," he said.

I had the time. And when it came right down to it, Woeful didn't need all that much persuading. He seemed relieved.

"Talk about the dead weight of history," he said. And so he did.

This is the story he told me, hands thrust deep in his pockets, the pathway of the Parliament House gardens crunching portentously underfoot.

Woeful and Denis were children of the Depression, beasts of burden by birth, fighters by temperament. Never actual members of the Communist Party, but not ill-disposed toward its militants who ran the union. Who in turn appreciated the occasional gesture of support from a local sporting identity. And, when the Communist Party turned on a bit of fraternal hospitality for the socialist athletes in town for the Olympic Games, Woeful and Denis were happy to help make up the numbers.

Their girlfriends, too. The Olympics were just about the most exciting thing that had ever happened and Beth and Marjorie had no intention of being left out of the festivities. For two weeks, there was sport by day, music and beer in bohemian St. Kilda flats by night. That was how they came to be aboard the *Gruzia*, the Soviet liner moored at Appleton Dock, home base and hospital for the socialist bloc teams.

It was two days after the Closing Ceremony, after the athletes had created a new Olympic tradition by breaking loose from their national teams and mingling freely across the arena in one exuberant, youthful mass. Even Irene was there, a raving Catholic like her mother, caught up in the mood of the moment, prepared to risk her immortal soul for one last taste of Olympic glamor.

The ship was scheduled to sail the next morning and the hosts were relaxed, all the more since the police had cleared the anti-communist demonstrators from the wharf at sunset. As well as Russians there were Czechs and Poles and Bulgarians. The boisterous Australian comrades crowded into the staterooms, the vodka flowed freely and many toasts were drunk to the undying friendship of the sport-loving peoples of the world.

Too many toasts for Denis, never much of a drinker anyway. Head swimming, he found his way through the throng and out onto the open deck. Summer had arrived, but the breeze was cool and the sea air went straight to his stomach. In the darkness between two lifeboats, tossing his pickled cucumbers into the water below, he felt a tugging at his sleeve. "Please, friend," whispered an urgent voice. "You help. You help."

It was pretty clear what kind of help was wanted. Others among the Australians might, perhaps, have been less responsive to such a plea. Others might have seen the man in hospital pyjamas with the bandaged wrist as an enemy of socialism and a traitor to his homeland, might have drawn attention to his overtures. But he had, by luck, chosen the right person to ask. Denis Dogherty was ever a friend of the underdog.

"When Denis sidled up to me and wanted to know what I'd done with my hat and coat, I thought it must have been time to go," said Woeful. "I didn't know what he was talking about."

But Irene did, and it was on her arm that Rudy Radeski was smuggled down the gangplank when the party finally ended and the Australians were poured ashore. On Irene's arm, in Woeful's coat and hat, at the center of an apparently well-tanked party of friends. Reliable friends of reliable friends, wharf laborers and proletarians.

"You ended up brothers-in-law," I said, cutting to the chase. It was a good story but not the one I wanted to hear. The history that interested me right then was much more recent. "And now his son Steve is out for revenge against the man who did his father wrong."

"Rudy's a prick. The way he treated Irene, I used to wish we'd left him on that fucking ship. He saw sport as a way out of Poland. And he played his cards well enough until he got here. Except he couldn't keep his mouth shut, started telegraphing his punches. Let it be known that he intended to defect. Decided he was going to be world-famous. But it all blew up in his face. And since Rudy would never dream of blaming himself, he passed his grievance down to the boy."

"Did you know this Stansislas Dziczkowszczak was the one who broke his wrist?'

"No idea. Not until Stevie rang me at home last weekend. Said he was going to make the bastard pay."

The tendency to telegraph punches seemed to run in the Radeski family. "Did he say how?"

"He didn't say. But he was quite het up about it. Enough to get me worried."

"But you didn't inform the MOB or the police of the threat."

"Denis reckoned he could hose Stevie down. He was closer to the boy than I was." Woeful faltered at that thought and put a hand to his face.

Denis's discretion was more than family loyalty. It was not the possibility of violence that was the problem. Protecting Dziczkowszczak from Steve Radeski would be a relatively simple matter. Just employ a few men with bulging armpits and tell them to be on the lookout for a demented dipstick with a body like a bag of potatoes. The real problem lay with Steve's motive. That's what needed to be kept under wraps.

If word ever got out that a serving member of the IOC had deliberately injured an athlete at an Olympic Games, the ensuing scandal would blast Melbourne's bid right out of the water. The IOC closet was probably standing-room only with skeletons. All those dukes and generals and third-world potentates certainly weren't going to thank us for bringing to light the misdeeds of one of their members.

But there was also a more immediate political matter, one much closer to home. To inform the police about Stevie would put Woeful in the hands of Gil Methven. Apart from the humiliation this would entail, there would be a price to pay for the Police Minister's discretion. Sooner or later, sooner probably, Methven would want his pound of flesh. When Denis went to see Steve Radeski, to talk him out of acting on his threat, it was to protect Woeful from the possibility of political blackmail.

"So Denis went out to West Heidelberg on Monday night?"

"When he didn't show up on Tuesday, I thought he must've taken Stevie somewhere. You know, convinced him to leave town while the Polish IOC was here. Gone along to keep an eye on him or something. Never occurred to me that Stevie would do anything like what he did."

"Anyone else know why he went out there?"

Woeful shook his chins. "We were playing this one close to the chest. With Denis dead, I decided to keep it that way. Telling anyone wouldn't change the fact of what happened. And Marj would never forgive me for letting him go out there alone."

"Because Steve's been violent before?"

He bristled. "Who told you that?"

I let it go. We were back where we started. "For what it's worth," I said. "I think you've done the right thing, keeping it to yourself."

It wasn't like Woeful hadn't been pondering the issue. "Yeah, but what happens when the police get hold of Stevie?"

"At the rate they're going, that could be weeks," I said. "With luck, Dziczkowszczak will be long gone. Anyway, Steve'll have zero credibility. A homicide suspect out of his tree on veterinary steroids. You can plausibly deny knowledge of any threat he might have made. If he wants to make an issue of it, we'll get Brian Morrison on the case, massage the media. In the meantime, sit pat. Don't lose your nerve."

He was still holding my business card. I took it back, tore it into small pieces and scattered them around the base of a rose bush. "That's what Denis would want, don't you think?"

Woeful didn't look too convinced. But as I walked him back into the House, I flattered myself that I had braced up our back line at least a little. That I had, in part, acquitted my promise to Denis.

32

MY DINNER SUIT hadn't seen service for nearly eighteen months, not since I'd escorted Angelo Agnelli to the Our Lady of Lebanon dinner-dance. Removing the mothballs and leftover pistachio baklava from the pockets, I discovered to my surprise that it fitted like a glove. All that work on the Stairmaster was finally beginning to pay off. And what man does not feel debonair in a tux?

"Whelan," I told the mirror. "Murray Whelan."

At seven-fifteen, I took a cab to Holly's flat. While the driver waited out front, I walked around the side and knocked on the door. The peephole flickered cyclopically. Suddenly, rough hands seized me from behind and threw me to the ground. My arms were wrenched up violently behind my back, a shoe bore down on my lumbar declivity and a cold metallic object which I registered instinctively as a gun was jammed into my ear. "Police," barked a frenzied chorus of voices. "Freeze."

It sounded like good advice. I did as I was told.

The door to Holly's flat flew open. "Wrong one," hissed a female voice. "This guy's the new boyfriend."

"Dinner suit," insisted the foot connected to my kidneys. "He's wearing a fucking dinner suit."

Who were these guys, the Sartorial Standards Squad? Since

when was possession of formal wear grounds for police brutality? The Victorian wallopers had a reputation for excessive zeal, but this was ridiculous. It wasn't like I was wearing a pink shirt or a velvet bowtie.

"Go. Go," urged the woman. Grunting something unintelligible, the foot and gun obeyed. A hand grabbed me by the cummerbund, hauled me upright and propelled me into the flat. The door slammed behind me.

"Sorry about that, sir," said Detective Senior Constable Carol Sonderlund. "They thought you were Steve Radeski. We believe he's in the vicinity."

Apparently, I had stumbled into some kind of stake-out. As I stood there, indignantly brushing down my lapels, Holly wandered out of the bedroom, busy attaching an earring. "That you, Murray?"

Her hair was up and she was wearing a shrink-wrap, strapless, red vinyl dress that clung to her tighter than a shipwreck survivor. The full front yard, hem up around the nature strip, no visible means of support.

"Wow," I said. A man could get arrested just for being in the same city. Sonderlund scowled at me like she was keen to lay the charges.

Holly finished fiddling with her ear and straightened up, offering herself for scrutiny. "It's not too . . . you know?"

Definitely. But somehow she carried it off. "Apart from the risk of pneumonia," I said, "you look fantastic."

"You, too," she reciprocated. "That style's coming back into fashion."

The flat was a disaster area. Dirty dishes and discarded food containers were strewn everywhere. The fresh, girlie bouquet had been replaced by a rank, zoological fug. The bottles of Midori and Galliano, now empty, lay discarded on the floor along with an exhausted blister pack labeled *Animal Use Only*.

"Found it like this when I arrived to get changed," explained Holly, wrinkling her nose. "Bastard ate everything in the place. Shed hairs in the bed. Pissed in the sink. Lucky for him he wasn't here when I turned up, eh? Ready in a minute, okay? We're not late, are we?" She darted into the bathroom.

While Holly was doing whatever it is that women do in the bathroom, I prised an update out of Detective Sonderlund. Steve Radeski, the police now believed, broke into the flat through a side window early on Wednesday morning, soon after Holly left for her parents' place. He'd probably been holed up there ever since. According to an upstairs resident, a man in a dinner suit quit the place shortly before Holly returned. Acting on the assumption that Radeski, still in his bouncer's uniform, was out refreshing his supplies of food and drugs, the coppers had placed the joint under close surveillance.

Holly emerged, lusciously lipsticked, hot to trot. "Make yourself at home," she told Sonderlund. "Sorry I haven't got any k.d. lang CDs. And if Steve does turn up, kick him in the nuts for me, will you?"

"No Lana Cantrell?" said the detective as we went out the door. "Dusty Springfield?"

The taxi was still waiting, engine running, twenty dollars on the meter already. As Holly climbed aboard, she peered quizzically at the cabbie. "Did you write *The Seven Keys to Eternal Youth*?" she asked.

"I am a Sikh, madam," he said. "We all look like this."

Leaving the constabulary lurking in ambush, we headed past the proliferating pasticceria of Lygon Street, bound for the Hyatt. For a woman whose domestic space had been violated by a psychopath and commandeered by the Keystone Cops, Holly was extraordinarily chipper. "There'll be, like, sporting personalities and that?"

"Sure," I said. She wouldn't have any trouble finding somebody not to talk to.

Barricades had been erected across the motor court of the Hyatt and a small army of *Dream the Dream* Youth Relay officials swarmed about, clad in identical artificial-fiber flame-motif tracksuits. According to the head honcho, Red was currently posing for press photographs and I should await his arrival in the ballroom with the rest of the guests.

The vast, pink-tinged lobby was a sea of dinner suits and silk bodices as the blue-ribbon crowd sailed across the marble floor and up the dual-carriageway escalator to the ballroom. Checking at the front desk, I was told that Mr. Buchanan had not yet picked up his invitation. I wondered if he'd got my message. If he hadn't, I decided, there was nothing I could do about it.

Ambrose Buchanan, of course, was not the only one whose presence interested me. Was there, I wondered, a Doctor Phillipa in the house? Only one way to find out. We went upstairs and threw ourselves into the thick of it.

The Olympic bandwagon was gathering speed and everybody, it seemed, had jumped aboard. Society wives and advertising gurus. Radio motor-mouths and former Lords Mayor. Property developers, of course. Brewery CEOs and Merton Hall old girls and Liberal Party bagmen. One-time Davis Cup seeds and third-generation scions of retail fortunes. Poultry heiresses and former swimming greats. Half the Cabinet. People I should have been gladhanding. Some I was keen to avoid. Clutching flutes of Domaine Chandon Vintage Brut, they percolated through the display of sporting memorabilia, bubbling with confidence at Melbourne's Olympic prospects. The thing was in the bag.

The fox on my arm was an ornament to my masculinity. But she was only costume jewelry. While I scouted for the sight of Phillipa, Holly was busy playing Spotto the Celebrity. "Hey," she whispered. "Isn't that whatsisname?"

No, it wasn't. It was Angelo Agnelli. "I can see why you've been so hard to find, Murray," he said, casting a knowing Latin eye over my companion.

"I'm his personal trainer," said Holly, right on the program.

"Then I hope you have more success than me," sighed the Minister for Water Supply, allowing himself to be sucked back into the swirling current.

Brian Morrison gravitated our way, caught between working the room and inspecting the merchandise. "Aren't you going to introduce us?"

"This is Ms. Deloite," I said. "From the Australian Kickboxing Federation."

Brian chuckled nervously. "Any sign of Buchanan?" he muttered out of the corner of his mouth.

Before I could answer, an electric ripple of excitement ran through the room and the crowd parted like the Red Sea. One by one, the members of the Evaluation Commission appeared at the top of the escalator and advanced toward the ballroom doors, objects of undisguised curiosity.

First came Stansislas Dziczkowszczak, escorted by Mr. and Mrs. Hugh Knowles. The chairman's bird-like wife was so petite that the tall Pole had to stoop to hold her arm. Next came Kim U-ee, flanked by Woeful and Beth McKenzie. Finally there appeared Pascal Abdoulaye, locked in animated conversation with a figure in faded denims.

Brian Morrison stiffened. "Holy shit!" he muttered.

But Brian didn't know the half of it. Trotting alongside Ambrose Buchanan was Deadly Anderson. He was wearing a ruffled apricot shirt and a spangled green tuxedo, boob tattoos peeking from the cuffs. The bandanna was back. Thank Christ, or they would've had to clear the exits with a crowbar. As it was, Deadly looked like the emcee at a Bandidos bingo night.

Brian started hyperventilating. "Do something," he ordered.

Abdoulaye and Ambrose were sharing a joke, laughing as they made their way toward the high table. Then, shaking hands, they broke off contact. As the Senegalese took his place with the other dignitaries, Ambrose turned and scanned the room.

"Something like this?" I waved, catching Buchanan's eye. Brian put a couple of steps of distance between us.

"It's those guys," said Holly brightly. "Your clients."

As Ambrose and Deadly came my way, heads turned to follow their progress. Buchanan had seen this sort of gig a thousand times before and regarded it with faintly amused indifference. Deadly strutted, both relishing the discomfort he was clearly causing some of the snootier elements in the crowd and also a little intimidated by the unfamiliar surroundings.

"He's cool," Buchanan reassured me. "He's had some sleep and calmed down a bit. Just about given up on Radeski." He was definitely a lot calmer than last time I'd seen him, punching numbers into the payphone at the Royal Hotel. "How about the cops?"

I shrugged. "Hopeful of an early arrest."

"They're with the band," I heard Brian tell somebody. Pass it on.

"Aren't you going to introduce us?" said Holly.

I did the honors all round. "I see you got your entree card, then," said Brian, somewhat redundantly.

"Deadly's my date," Ambrose told him. "I asked Miss Advancement League but she's washing her hair tonight."

"Nice outfit," I said to Deadly. "Brotherhood of St. Laurence?"

He copped it sweet, entirely focused on Holly. She looked like about ten million dollars. "Seen youse the other night," he mumbled, bashful all of a sudden.

"Saw you, too," she said, coy itself. Now here was a girl who really knew how to pick them.

"Brian Morrison?" said Ambrose, dredging his memory. "Not the Brian Morrison who called the cops on Reggie Plunkett?"

Waiters erupted through the kitchen doors, laden with plates.

"You'll like this," blurted Brian, nervously herding us toward one of the tables, well away from the top brass. "It's bush tucker. Shovel-roasted breast of emu for the ladies. Paperbark-wrapped loin of kangaroo for the men."

Wendy was there to meet us. In keeping with her SS theme, she was wearing a silk pyjama-suit the color of bruised avocados. She'd probably bruised them herself. "Pleased to meet you," she told Holly unctuously. Me, she fixed with a look of dick-shriveling contempt.

"Neil," said a voice, and I nearly did.

It was Wendy's escort, introducing himself. He stared at Holly's tits like they were scoops of vanilla ice-cream. "Regional Director, Privatization." I bet you are, I thought.

Phillipa Verstak materialized at my elbow. "Hello, Murray," she smirked. "I see you found yourself a date." She was decked out in a natty little gold-frogged bolero jacket. Ole!

"My niece," I said, tongue stuck firmly in cheek. "And this must be Rodney. Executive assistant to the chairman."

"We sort of met the other day," he nodded. My star turn before the MOB management team, I assumed. He eyed Deadly charily.

"My squash partner," I said. "Rod."

We found our seats and sat down. Boy, girl. I had Holly to my left and Phillipa to my right. Holly was already deep in conversation with Deadly. "Aerobics isn't a sport," she was telling him. "It's an activity."

"I work out a bit meself," he said. Their heads were almost touching. Some kind of weird chemistry was definitely brewing. Beauty and the Beast stuff.

Brian Morrison's better half, Sandra, waved at me across the floral centerpiece. Her husband was watching Ambrose Buchanan like a hawk. Ambrose was seated beside Wendy. Judging by the way she was squirming in her seat, he was running her to ground on Aboriginal representation in the higher reaches of Telecom management. At the head table, Pascal Abdoulaye was engaged in the customary pre-prandial bonhomie with Woeful and the other high-ups.

As I turned to Phillipa, the first course arrived. Fillet of Barramundi in a Macadamia Crust. All prospect of conversation was immediately lost in the gnash and clatter of a thousand knives and forks. "Fish?" said Deadly. "Where's the chips?"

Between bites, I stole a closer look at this Rodney joker. Call me biased, but I couldn't see the attraction. Neither, it seemed, did Phillipa. Compared with the animal heat now emanating from the general direction of Holly and Deadly, their relationship struck me as a very low-kilowatt affair. They showed more interest in their nut-encrusted fish than they did in each other.

Phillipa saw me looking and leaned over. "Rodney's an old friend," she said. "We go back a long way."

Back before Cambodia. Before she realized that she wasn't all that keen. Or I hoped that's what she meant. "That's nice," I said, letting her know that I knew.

The wine was a sauvignon blanc. It had a big herby nose and plenty of zest to the finish. Head tilted back, savoring the aftertaste, I noticed that the ballroom ceiling was mirrored. You could see everything, upside down. The white circles of the tables. The chrome domes of the trucking magnates. The ant-farm teeming of the black-clad waiters.

I'd never done banquet work myself, strictly bar, but as the descendant of three generations of hotelkeepers I always took a semi-professional interest in the organizational side of such matters.

Harry Hyatt ran a tight ship. Commis-waiters clearing. The service door flapping on its hinges. Captains at their stations. My plate was whisked away and I tracked its inverted progress across the room. Piled onto a tray, it disappeared through the service door where a stout, ram-headed supervisor stood sentry. He bounced on his toes, scoping the scene, engine ticking over.

Steve Radeski.

I felt a hand on my sleeve. "How long now?" said Phillipa.

"Eh?"

"How long since your last cigarette?"

"Thirty-seven hours and fifty-two minutes," I said. "Approximately."

Radeski's attention was fixed on the stage, raking the head table. His eyes, manic raisins in his doughy cheeks, alighted on Stanislas Dziczkowszczak.

Phillipa reached for her purse. "I'd better find another partner in crime, then."

This quitting business sucked. My criminal confederate, Deadly, shifted his concentration from Holly for a moment. Just long enough to see what I was seeing. Holly followed his stare. "Steve?" she exclaimed. "What's he doing here?"

"Distinguished guests," boomed the public-address system. "Ladies and gentlemen."

Deadly was out of his seat, rocketing headlong across the room, elbows flying.

"Please welcome, representing the young people of Australia, our *Dream the Dream* torchbearer, Redmond Whelan . . ."

"Murray!" shrieked Wendy. "Where do you think you're going?"

33

THE LIGHTS DIMMED. The ballroom doors swung open. A small figure in white appeared, a guttering flare in his outstretched hand. Suddenly, the entire crowd was on its feet, applauding wildly, craning for a view.

"And to accept the torch on behalf of the International Olympic Committee . . ."

As Stansislas Dziczkowszczak stepped forward, the concentrated hormones of a hundred rampant jumbucks surged though Steve Radeski's bloodstream. This was the moment he had waited for, trained for, longed for. These arsehole officials would soon know better than to fuck with the Radeski family. He lowered his head and charged.

Deadly Anderson, swerving to avoid the husband of the MOB Director of Facilities Planning, collided with him. Head-on, with all the force of a runaway patrol car. Completely unexpected, the impact of the collision threw the would-be assassin sideways, back through the swinging doors.

Apart from Holly and me, who had bolted after Deadly, nobody else seemed to have noticed. With the house lights down and the room echoing with applause, all eyes were focused on the torch and its bearer. Looking upward to the ceiling, I tracked the bobbing ball of light that was my son's progress around the dance floor.

For about three seconds.

Then the kitchen doors flew back open. Radeski's hands were wrapped around Deadly's throat, throttling him. The Koori's legs were off the ground, writhing and twitching. Holly flew forward and threw herself at Radeski in a mad melee of punches and kicks.

Heads were beginning to turn. Red's big moment was about to be upstaged. The success of the torch relay, the Olympic Gala, possibly even the entire bid was in jeopardy. Denis Dogherty's killer was on a berserk rampage. Somebody had to do something, and soon. Somebody did. Me.

I played the man. Grabbing Radeski's ponytail, I dragged the flailing cluster-fuck of bodies back into the kitchen.

We burst into a bedlam of steam and stainless steel, a forest of freaked-out faces in tall white hats. Radeski's feet flew from beneath him and his oily hair slipped from my grasp. As he hit the tiles, he flung Deadly aside as if he were a rag doll.

Shimmering like a green tree python in his iridescent tux, Deadly ricocheted off a brace of tray-laden commis-waiters and collided with a vat of bubbling brown liquid. It toppled over and a steaming mud-colored wave cascaded across the floor.

Radeski staggered upright and turned toward the door, apparently still fixated on his mission to dismember Dziczkowszczak. Holly blocked his path. "Hey, babe," yelped the berko bully-boy, bewildered by the sudden turn of events. "Where you been?"

Holly went into a kung-fu stance. The Bunny Confronts the Wart-hog. The Vixen Transfixes the Mullet.

Up to my trouser-cuffs in a melange of marsupial morsels, I grabbed a giant stirring paddle and smashed Radeski over the head. The wooden spoon snapped in half, making no impression whatsoever on Muscle Man's armor-plated skull.

Deadly slithered around on the floor, attempting to find his footing on the gravy-soaked tiles. An imperious presence in a towering toque barged through the astonished cluster of onlooking sous-chefs. "My wallaby jus!" he roared, beetroot-faced with rage. "What are you doink in my wallaby jus!"

Two security men burst in from the ballroom. Beyond them, through the flip-flop of the swinging door, I caught sight of Red just as he handed the torch to Dziczkowszczak. He turned, took the plaudits of the crowd and jogged toward us.

"You pissed in my sink," screamed Holly. "You killed that old man, you mongrel." She kicked out, aiming for her former flame's face. A red, high-heel shoe detached itself from her foot, flew through the air and struck the chef de cuisine in the mouth.

Swiveling on their toes in the spilt sauce like a pair of twist aficionados, the two protective services personnel stared first at the green Aborigine, then at the scarlet virago, then at the bloated bodybuilder.

"Nobody move!" they shouted, reaching for their underarm bulges.

Word was finally reaching the deep-fried recesses of Radeski's brain that his plan had come unstuck. His insane yellow eyes darted about, desperately searching for a way out.

The door swung on its hinges and Red burst into the kitchen, adrenaline pumping. "Hey, Dad," he beamed. "Did you see me, huh? Did you see me?"

I was standing there with my bowtie on sideways and the stump of a stirring paddle in my hand, ankle-deep in potaroo ragout, facing off a maniacal meatloaf with a skin problem. "Yeah," I said. "You were great."

Radeski saw his chance. He grabbed Red, effortlessly tucking him under his arm. "Back off," he bellowed. "Or I'll fucken snap the little fucker's neck." His words resonated with a tremulous bleat, as if amplified through a wa-wa pedal.

A tracksuited relay official burst through the door. The torch-disposal specialist. He was attempting to switch off the gas-flow valve at the base of the flaming object. The two security men drew their walkie-talkies and started waving them around in a commanding manner. Deadly hauled himself upright. "Leave the kid alone, you prick," he yelled, and lunged forward.

Radeski swatted him off with a forearm jolt and began backing away, bearing Red off into the deeper recesses of the hellish kitchen. "Put me down, you piece of shit," cursed the boy, flailing and squirming, vainly attempting to writhe free. "Dad! Dad!"

I stood there, frozen with horror.

"Hey, kid," hollered Holly. Wresting the torch from its astonished custodian, she darted forward and thrust the still-burning baton into Red's hand. He waved it like a sparkler, slapping it ineffectually against Radeski's tree-trunk thighs. Then he jabbed it up over his shoulder, blindly stabbing in the direction of his demented kidnapper's face.

With an audible whoosh, Psycho Steve's hair caught fire.

Emitting an animal cry, he dropped Red and began furiously slapping at the flames. Talk about a bad hair day. Trailing smoke like a blazing oilfield on legs, he turned and ran.

I hoisted Red off the floor. "You okay?"

Apart from a bit of gravy on his knees, the lad seemed none the worse for wear. "Did you see me? Did you see me?"

"That's MOB property," the tracksuited official reminded us, prising the torch from Red's grip. "It's not a toy, you know."

Herr Meisterchef clapped his hands. "To verk, to verk," he commanded. "Begin plating ze emu."

Toques bobbed. Crockery clattered. Steam rose. A mop slopped across my shoes. Waiters swarmed like extras in an Errol Flynn movie. The head pirate, Deadly, took off after Radeski. "Where's my shoe?" demanded Holly. The security men jabbered into their walkie-talkies. Hustling Red back into the ballroom, I ran slap-bang into Wendy. "Sweetie," she cried, clutching the mortified warrior prince to her loins. "Mummy was so proud."

Hugh Knowles was at the podium. "The important contribution of our indigenous people to the sporting achievements of the entire world . . . ," he was saying.

Woeful McKenzie glanced down from the high table and I caught his eye. "Steve," I mouthed, index finger inscribing a corkscrew in the air beside my earhole. Woeful's eyes widened in alarm.

"Guess what just happened?" said Red to Wendy.

Moral coward, I turned tail and ran back into the kitchen.

Holly came at me, triumphantly brandishing a vermilion Salvatore Ferragamo slingback. Beyond a freight train of warming cabinets, the crash of shattering glassware indicated the direction of Steve Radeski's retreat. Holly and I joined the stampede, thundering down a carton-lined corridor, tracking the telltale vapor of freshly incinerated coiffure, led onward by the verdant shimmer of Deadly's diabolical duds. Doors loomed, the concrete changed to carpet and we were suddenly in the ballroom foyer. It was deserted.

Almost.

Radeski, still batting at his spluttering scalp, was dodging and weaving through the exhibition of Olympic memorabilia. He was heading for the escalator. For a man of his size, he was moving remarkably fast. Deadly, twenty steps behind, was moving even faster.

A crack appeared in the ballroom portals and a security man sidled from the hushed interior, his cufflink pressed to the side of his head. Spotting Radeski rocketing toward him, he wrestled a gun from his jacket and leveled it.

"Freeze," he ordered. Another fucking movie buff.

He might as well have been talking to a herd of elephants. Radeski's momentum was unstoppable. He careered headlong into Dirty Harry, sending him backward into a massed arrangement of native orchids. The security man's gun skittered across the floor. With an agility born of a million knee-bends, Radeski scooped it up and waved it wildly in the air, still headed for the escalator.

Pulling up sharp, Deadly Anderson wrenched something from the array of sporting accoutrements attached to the wall. It was the aluminum javelin with which Glynis Nunn won her heptathlon gold medal in Los Angeles. Bracing his legs, he tested its heft. He opened his stance a little and marked his target. Then, in one single, fluid movement, he drew his arm back and pitched the missile forward with all his might.

The long shaft flashed through the air in a high wobbling arc and embedded itself in Radeski's thigh.

Radeski didn't know what hit him. He staggered forward a step, twisted around and wrenched the spear from his perforated flesh. Gushing blood, he teetered at the top of the escalator. Then, his mouth gaping in a silent scream, he pitched headlong between the moving rubber banisters and vanished from sight.

Deadly stood rooted to the spot with astonishment.

As did we all. "Wow," said Holly. The spell broke. She rushed to Deadly's side, squeezed his spear arm in both hands and pressed her cheek against his shoulder in abject admiration. "Wow."

The three of us hurried toward the escalator, arriving at the same time as the florally rearranged security man.

It was the up-escalator. Like a harpooned whale, beached by the waves of an incoming tide, Radeski's unconscious body advanced to meet us. Carried upward on the relentless machinery of the metal steps, his twitching carcass was dumped bleeding at our feet. As we stood there, stunned, staring down, Woeful McKenzie shoved me aside.

"Stevie," cried the minister, falling stricken to his knees. "My son."

"WE HAVE SEEN DEMONSTRATED here tonight the profound senti-
ments which sport engenders in the heart of our city." Hugh Knowles
paused meaningfully, looked up from his speech notes and fixed the
Evaluation Commission with his most sincere expression.

Navigating the maze of tables at an apologetic half-crouch, I
crept across the ballroom. "Psst," I whispered into Phillipa's ear.

"Not yet," she whispered back. "But I will be if this speech goes
on for much longer."

"Medical emergency." I tugged at her sleeve.

"Thank God for small mercies," she murmured, allowing herself to be drawn out of her seat.

Wendy looked daggers at me across the table. Sabers. Foils.
Epees. Small-bore pistols. Double-trap 12-gauge shotguns. Red was
perched beside her, oblivious, wolfing down a plate of handmade,
chocolate-coated Kakadu plum pralines. Brian Morrison also gave
me a dirty look. Ambrose Buchanan had slipped into Woeful
McKenzie's vacant seat at the high table. A knowing smile creased
his lips as Pascal Abdoulaye whispered, tête-à-tête, into his ear.

"Bring your napkin," I told Phillipa.

While I was in the ballroom getting expert assistance, the security bloke must have got onto his cufflink and signaled red alert. The

woodwork had come alive. Men with shoulders the shape of bricks were swarming all over the scene like a rampant dose of whispering psoriasis.

Phillipa and I arrived in time to see four of them extract Radeski from the escalator mechanism and roll him onto a tablecloth. He lay there, inanimate, all color drained from his velcro-textured face except for the zebra stripes of cinders where he'd smeared himself with cremated ponytail. His zit-infested forehead was split open and bright arterial blood was gushing from the slash in the seat of his trousers.

"What happened?" said Phillipa.

"Payback." I indicated the red-tipped javelin lying on the carpet. Sorry business.

Before I could say more, she was hunkered down, stuffing her serviette into the hemorrhaging hole in Radeski's thigh. "Tourniquet!" she said, tugging at my cummerbund.

There was no sign of Holly, Deadly or Woeful. The only civilians in sight were the hotel manager and a diminutive Hispanic cleaner. The morning-suited manager was reinstating the deranged orchids with the composed imperturbability of a senior instructor at the Neville Chamberlain School of Ikebana. Manuel was at the top of the escalator, wringing his mop into a bucket of pink-tinged water.

As soon as Phillipa got the bleeding staunched, four of the security detail grabbed the corners of the tablecloth. They hoisted Radeski off the floor and ran into an open service elevator. Phillipa trotted beside Radeski's sling and I went along for the ride, down two floors, out the elevator and onto the apron of the loading bay.

As we arrived, a *Dream the Dream* Torch Relay transit van backed into the dock and the rear doors flew open. Radeski was bundled inside and the vehicle zoomed away, orderlies and all. "Clear, clear," the remaining security man shouted into his personal communication device.

"What was that all about?" said Phillipa.

A fat guy in kitchen whites was sitting Buddha-like on a milk crate, smoking a cigarette. "You again?" he grunted.

I snatched the cigarette from his mouth and took a long, deep drag. Then Phillipa took it out of my hand and did the same. "Hey," said the slob on the milk crate. "Gimme me smoke back."

Reaching into my shirt, I tore the Nicabate patch off my tit and slapped it onto his forehead. "Try one of mine," I said. "You'll live longer."

I conferred briefly in an undertone with the security guy and he gave me leave to step down into the lane. Phillipa jumped down beside me and we walked slowly toward Collins Street, security trailing a discreet distance behind. As we passed the cigarette back and forth between us, I told her as much as I could about what had just happened. It was as clear as mud, but it covered the ground.

We reached the fairy-lit trees of Collins Street and had turned toward the hotel entrance when a loud shriek suddenly rent the air. There was something oddly familiar about it. A butter-yellow Daihatsu Charade was heading down the street from the direction of the Old Treasury, its brakes emitting a characteristic telltale whine. The car's radiator grill was severely dented. Accelerating suddenly, it mounted the curb and rocketed toward us.

I pushed Phillipa into the doorway of the Louis Vuitton boutique and pressed myself against her. The screeching yellow rattle-trap streaked past, continued down the footpath another twenty meters and slammed into a fire hydrant, shearing it off at ground level. As it came to rest, water surging from beneath its chassis, the driver's door flew open. A man in a brown cardigan clambered out and fled down the street.

My body was still pressed against Phillipa. In relief at our narrow escape, I kissed her softly on the mouth. She didn't resist.

"Ah, shit," I said, when we broke for air. "I'm sorry." In the glow of the street-light, her frogging was streaked with Steve Radeski's blood.

"I suppose I'd better get it off," she said. "Give it a good soaking."

As we stepped back onto the footpath, the force of the water welling up beneath the Charade tilted the small sedan onto its side. A great foaming geyser exploded upward. A torrent of cold water fell out of the sky, drenching us to the skin.

"You think this hotel has any rooms?" I said.

"Nice try," said Phillipa. "Let's find out."

35

TWO DAYS LATER, the Evaluation Commission gathered up its notes and left town. Three months later, Melbourne learned that it had failed in its bid to host the 1996 Olympic Games, crossing the finishing line well behind Atlanta, Athens and Toronto.

It was a humiliating rebuff, considering the millions of dollars the city had spent whipping itself into a frenzy of anticipation. There is, after all, nothing more demoralizing than coming fourth in an arse-licking competition.

As far as Brian Morrison was concerned, the responsibility fell squarely on my shoulders. "If you'd done your job properly," he complained bitterly when he rang Water Supply to arrange for the disposal of the *Dream the Dream* luxury launch, "we wouldn't have lost black Africa." Given that it was a secret ballot and he was in no position to know how Botswana and Burkina Faso voted, I thought the accusation a tad unfair.

Especially knowing what Ambrose Buchanan told us when Brian confronted him after the gala dinner and demanded to know what he'd talked about with Pascal Abdoulaye.

"Family matters," he said. "As they say in Olympic circles. Pascal was telling me about his sons. All seven of them have just won scholarships to Georgia Tech. He's a very proud man, considering that one of them is still in primary school. He said he's planning on being there for their graduation in six years' time."

With the loss of the bid, Buchanan's idea for an Aboriginal Sports Institute hit something of a brick wall. He plans to take up the issue a bit later, after he's finished his current work with the Black Deaths in Custody Royal Commission.

Under the circumstances, no charges were laid against Deadly Anderson. In fact, I haven't seen Deadly since that night, standing there in the ballroom foyer with a satisfied look on his face, Holly Deloite nestled into him, the sole of his foot resting on the side of his knee.

I asked Holly about him when I saw her the next Monday at the City Club. "He's a wild man," she said, smiling enigmatically as she handed me my complimentary fluffy towel.

Deadly's out there somewhere, a model of successful assimilation, blending inconspicuously with the general petty-criminal population. Selling pigeon steroids to high-flying ruckmen, probably, and frightening the hell out of the hairdressing fraternity.

Radeski was dead by then. He expired shortly after arriving at St. Vincent's Hospital. Cause of death was a combination of shock, blood loss and an adverse reaction to the drugs administered during emergency treatment. Apparently, they did not combine well with the concentrated cocktail of veterinary products already flowing through his bloodstream. His natural father was at his side when he passed away, holding the perforated power-lifter's limp hand and confiding into his comatose ear the long-concealed circumstances of his conception.

According to the Health Minister's adviser, who was told by the Hospital Employees Federation assistant secretary, who heard it from the St. Vincent's workplace delegate, who was living with the charge nurse from intensive care, who overheard it while changing Radeski's IV-drip, it was a piteous tale. Not, perhaps, particularly extraordinary but made both tragic and ironic by the events which flowed from it.

It was the story of a family secret. Of how Steve's mother, Irene, had always been keen on her older sister's boyfriend. How even after the young footballer and Beth Boag were married, Irene had continued to carry a torch for Woeful McKenzie. And how eventually she had appealed to him for help when her own husband, the disgruntled Rudy Radeski, began to slap her around. How that succor had become guilt-ridden adultery.

Irene had long been praying for a child but all that God had sent her were miscarriages. So when her shameful intimacy with her brother-in-law resulted in pregnancy she took it as a sign that she should dedicate herself to making good her marriage. Unaware of the infant's true paternity, Rudy Radeski duly mended his ways and stopped beating his wife. And when, in young Stevie's seventh year, Irene went to meet her maker while changing a light bulb, Rudy insisted on raising the child himself. By then, there was no question of telling him the truth.

Beth McKenzie, too, remained oblivious to her spouse's brief episode of infidelity. The revelation that he had been romancing her little sister would hardly have gone down well with the mother of two young girls. Daughters upon whom Woeful doted and could not bear the thought of losing. "But Stevie," he told the recumbent form in the hospital bed, his voice choked with fatherly grief. "You were my only son."

I still don't know if Woeful has got around to confessing the situation to his wife. What with one thing and another, I haven't really had the opportunity to discuss the matter with him. In the immediate short-term, I was tied up dealing with the security people.

Despite Brian Morrison's assurances to the contrary, there were quite a few of them in the ballroom that night, maintaining a discreet but heavily tooled eyeball on our distinguished Olympic guests. Dziczkowszczak in particular, whose name had rung a bell with the old cold warriors who continue to haunt the higher reaches of our national intelligence apparatus. All things considered, it was deemed advisable to keep the entire incident well under wraps as in '56.

The hush-hush boys were certainly faster off the mark than the Victoria Police homicide squad, who spent the entire evening fruitlessly staking out Holly's hacienda. Steve, of course, had no intention of returning there. He planned to go down in a blaze of glory.

Familiar with the backstairs byways of the Hyatt from his time at the Typhoon nightclub, he had slipped unnoticed through a side door behind the motor court concierge's desk. For three hours, he'd remained hidden in the room-service storage hold, mentally rehearsing his next move and working out with two magnums of Veuve Cliquot he found stashed beneath a pile of linen tablecloths. Only when he felt sure that the Olympic gala was in full swing had he risked taking the fire stairs up to the banquet kitchen, where he passed unremarked through the bustle involved in plating six hundred edible portions of the nation's coat-of-arms.

Not that I can be too disparaging about the boys and girls in blue. They did, at least, catch Darcy Anderson's killers. Or so it would appear, pending outcome of the trial. We read the story in the next morning's complimentary newspaper, Phillipa and I, over a tray of room-service croissants and a presumptuous young filter-tip cigarette.

In a combined Victorian–Tasmanian operation, all four members of a Launceston-based gang of white supremacists were arrested and charged with the manslaughter of Darcy Anderson. The officer in charge stated that a large quantity of literature had been seized, most of it foreign in origin. Lacking hometown opportunities for the expression of racial pride, the skinheads had traveled to the mainland to conduct what they described as a "training exercise" in expectation of the imminent outbreak of a global race war.

According to Ken Sproule, the coppers had a watertight case based on a confession from one of the skins and the testimony of a steward on the *Princess of Tasmania* who overheard the crop-top hoons discussing their mission during a feed of spring rolls in the after-deck cafeteria.

As to the Daihatsu, I'm still dickering with Auto & General. The vehicle was a write-off, of course, but they seem to think that my being there when it was recovered smacks of complicity in its original disappearance. Insurance company logic. They may pay up eventually, but I'm not holding my breath. And, since my MOB consultancy fee was exactly ten dollars more than the price I was asking for the car, I figure I ended up slightly better than break-even for the week.

So, too, did the staff of the Water Supply maintenance department. Rather than cop the political flak engendered by all those ruptured water mains, Angelo caved in to the Missos and granted them their pay raise.

Another nail in the coffin of fiscal rectitude and the straw that broke the Premier's back. Shortly after the Evaluation Commission left town, he announced his resignation. The resulting Cabinet reshuffle also disposed of Woeful McKenzie. The big feller is spending a lot more time with Beth and the girls these days and can sometimes be seen sitting beside Denis Dogherty's grave in the St. Kilda cemetery.

Angelo Agnelli got the Transport portfolio and he took me with him. It's a step upward and in the wrong direction. Compared with the good old Missos, the Transport Workers Federation is the Mongol fucking hordes. Our new Premier is a woman, which should not be misconstrued as an expression of commitment to gender equity. It just means the boys are losing their grip.

Wendy and Red returned to Sydney as scheduled and I'll need to eat a lot of crow before I see the kid again. We do talk on the phone, though. He rang last Saturday after the Swans beat Fitzroy. "Nyah, nyah," he said. "We beatcha." But at least he's stopped playing rugby. After he told Wendy what he did to Steve Radeski in the kitchen, she decided that all this sport was making him too aggressive.

Meanwhile, Phillipa and I are thinking of opening a mattress-testing laboratory. And applying for a productivity bonus. I find I have lots of stamina these days, even though I don't go to the gym so often. The sex is great, but the part we both like best is the cigarette we share afterward.